About the author

David Kirkland has worked in the building trade all his life, starting with his father and being joined by his brother, then finally working alone as a sole trader.

He has also trained in Reiki, reaching Level 3 (Master), and various martial arts.

He believes that this planet and humanity are fantastic, and that we are finally starting to evolve and to see the planet for what it is: home.

EARTH BUILDER

DAVID KIRKLAND

EARTH BUILDER

Vanguard Press

A CIP catalogue record for this title is
available from the British Library.

ISBN 978 1 80016 342 3

*Vanguard Press is an imprint of
Pegasus Elliot MacKenzie Publishers Ltd.*
www.pegasuspublishers.com

First Published in 2022

Vanguard Press
Sheraton House Castle Park
Cambridge England

Printed & Bound in Great Britain

Dedication

To my parents, Cliff and Hazel, to Tony, and to Peaches and Poppy. May you all be in a better place.

Acknowledgements

To Martyn Bramhall, for telling me to 'go for it' when I wasn't sure, and the encouragement of Gemma Fisk, and to my sister, Angela.

Thank you.

1

The van won't start — iffy starter motor. Is today the day it finally packs up? It misses again, but I keep trying. It fires and I hold it on until the engine reluctantly coughs into life. Then follows the radio, demister, lights, and off I go. I'm so relieved that it's started, I can get to work, earn a day's pay, and hopefully keep one step in front. The feeling of desperation is constant and gets me down. I feel like I'm drowning and every time I come up for air somebody throws a spanner at my head.

Still, I have plenty to be grateful for, a beautiful girlfriend, five adorable toy poodles, and my own transport, however temperamental. I'm glad Deborah's asleep and doesn't have to witness my daily start fiasco; I will get a new starter, just as soon as I get in front with the money.

Breakfast is eaten behind the wheel. The traffic hold — up each morning just about gives me time to eat what I packed. All by the time I reach the traffic island at the end of the viaduct.

Here the game is to jump ahead of the queue, cutting across a lane of traffic to reach the motorway entry.

It was quite fun. I even began to think that I was developing a special sense for detecting who would cut me up, then I realised that they all were, and it lost its appeal.

For a while I started to drive alongside, matching their speed, watching the slow, dawning panic on their faces. Now I prefer to give them a gap, let them through safely, at least that way I am controlling the situation, guiding them through.

Even as I get to work, I want sleep. Another grey, cold, and wet morning. I just want to be warm and dry, preferably tucked up in bed, and at fifty-six, the work is starting to become draining. Hard work even. Of course, there's a dogged pride that I can still do the hard graft, but there's a dawning realisation that I am beginning to whinge about it.

Still, it's an easy day today. Just need to brick up some holes in the gable end. The owners are building a timber extension, I need to make good a few areas before the footings go down. At least mixing the gobo will get me warmed up a bit. I hope the ladder is long enough; it must be close to its limit where I'm working.

It rained last night, heavily, the ground is thick with mud and broken masonry. I stand the ladders on an old, short batting, take the bucket of gobo up, hook it on the ladders, and fetch a couple of bricks up. I reach out, perhaps too far. The ladder slips and I have a moment of panic, the realisation that I am going to fall as I feel the coarse brick under my fingers slide away and the ground rushes up towards me.

2

I can feel movement, but everything feels far off and disconnected. I'm confused. I see glowing shapes, not quite solid. I'm dreaming or hallucinating, and it all feels odd, wrong. I am suddenly more aware of my body. I can feel my eyes are closed, but I am seeing these figures. I decide to open my eyes.

Everything is blurred, red. I can make out a man bent over me, but I can't make out what he's doing. He's not very happy.

I'm in an ambulance, I work out that much, there's medical things, and the man is shouting to the driver. I feel odd, as I'm fading out, and I hear him shout, "Losing him!"

Suddenly I feel calm, peaceful even. I try to ask the man what's wrong, but nothing seems to be working. I can clearly see now — a screen stops showing jagged lines and shows a straight line. The man has a pad in each hand.

Bang. I'm back, and oh my, it hurts so badly now, all over. I'm fully aware; I feel a mounting pressure behind my eyes. It stings so I close them, and there's the glowing figures again, more now and they are crowding around me, pushing each other to get closer. I see more details, and boy, I wish that I didn't. They are ugly, more are appearing, and I feel weaker. Still more appear as my awareness fades out to black again, against my will. I become aware of some light, bright, but not so that it hurts the eyes. They come closer. There are voices in my head, faint as if at a great distance. They are talking, I think about me.

"This one?" a vaguely human voice said from the group of figures.

"Perhaps," replied another.

"Will it survive?" said the first.

"Even we can't see that far," the second figure said with a hopeless resignation.

The lights are incredibly beautiful. I stare at them, and then try to greet them. "Hello, are you angels?"

"Listen, I can almost hear it…" the brightest light seems to say, the voice distant and ethereal.

"Hello?" I say again.

"It's trying. Perhaps?" the second light replies, and the voice sounds interested, questioning, but not unfriendly.

"It is the last chance."

"We shall influence as much as possible," says the second light, more positive now, as though a decision has been made.

I can feel my head hurting, deep down inside, at first at a distance but becoming more focused, concentrated as my awareness grows. I feel muffled, like I'm inside a sack. I can't fully make things out. I open my eyes, and this fact strikes me as odd. I thought that they were open. Things look blurred but are coming into focus. Bingo, I'm in a room with some sort of machinery and I'm wired to it. I hear somebody come in but can't move my head properly. A woman's face appears, concerned, a smile, speaking, but it's like she has cotton wool in her mouth even as the sound begins to focus. She goes out of my view, but I can sense her moving around me, then more people arrive. I'm still not focussed fully, my head is held rigid, but for some reason I still don't feel panicked.

I try to move my mouth, my face then my head. OK, don't do that; a wave of pain washes over me. I try to feel the rest of my body, I start to wish I hadn't. My breathing is wrong, I'm struggling to get a breath, and it hurts, in fact all over is hurting. My head is really hurting now, around my forehead especially. It's all muffled, confusion hits me and at the same moment unconsciousness takes me back again.

The next few days are various tests on my faculties. At least I can hear now, the thick bandages plus a foam head restraint, so that I couldn't move my head and jiggle my brain, was simply over my ears. That's one box ticked on the road to recovery, anyway. Otherwise, it's a few broken ribs, so sneezing isn't an option, strained ankle, some highly colourful bruising covering pretty much everywhere. On the whole pretty damned lucky, I think.

The only real problem seems to be inside my head. I mean really deep inside; something feels different. Whenever I start to doze off, I see the glowing translucent figures. I can't make them out fully but do see something. Still, I'm off for a brain scan tomorrow, hopefully it will reveal what's happening inside my head. Of course, my friends and family all hilariously tell me that they won't find anything there, especially brains, to see if they can find one at all.

I'm not finding it funny. I have heard that those scans are claustrophobic and highly unpleasant.

My girlfriend, Deborah, visits me each day; she isn't fond of driving, so I know it's a big thing for her. I have personal accident insurance, so at least the bills are covered; in actual fact, I'm better off than when I'm working, so that's good. I had begun to worry over how the mortgage company would manage without my monthly contributions.

I had a bit of a weird experience this morning. I was having the bandages removed, as the doctor had to check on the stitches in my forehead. Along with some pretty impressive bruises, there are a few minor cuts, so some blood had dried onto the bandage, and it pulled when he lifted it. I winced and I closed my eyes. Immediately I saw the luminescent figures of several different colours. They seemed to be clinging to the nurses, the young doctor had two crowding over him. They were filthy, dull rotting greens and browns, but they had a faint glow and a pulsing appearance. Another appeared, headed for me but before I could react, it appeared to be repulsed, and instead latched onto the doctor. The flinching and jumping around I did merely convince all in the room that I am a big wuss and scared of a tiny bit of blood. As he calmed me with witty, soothing words, I decided the best thing to do was keep my mouth shut. I hadn't made a good impression and he clearly wasn't aware of a four-foot pulsating grey, green slug stuck to him. Anyway, as soon as my eyes were open again it had gone.

Once I am alone again, in my very own posh little self-contained room, I start to think about it, and the more I think, the odder it seems. How could I see the doctors and nurses when I had closed my eyes?

I reach up, and wow, can I feel that. My entire body hurts at the movement, but my ribs, they really hit the higher notes on the pain register. I wince on and push the bandages off my head the best I can.

It's not long before a nurse comes in to do another blood test, and the blood nurse isn't nearly as friendly as the rest of the staff, in fact she seems almost vindictive. I probably have said something to annoy her. Deborah says it is a thing that happens often.

So, as she enters, I close my eyes and wait.

Big mistake…

Instead of the slimy slugs I'm expecting to see, I see a seven-foot-high lizard, almost a dragon, not clinging to her gut, but merging with her as the last thing had done. I start to flinch but am instantly told to calm down by the nurse. "It's only a drop of blood."

As she leaves, I quickly close my eyes again. There it is again, walking awkwardly in the same space as her. It starts to turn as if sensing I can see it, so I open my eyes and give a stupid smile, but the nurse turns to look at me, sees my daft face and walks out.

I am worried now. I make it, wincing and whingeing into the bathroom, and looking into the mirror, I lift the bandages on my head.

Bang in the middle of my forehead is a dint, a sort of elongated triangle, a brick must have hit me corner first, punching a hole into my forehead. Apart from the multicoloured bruising around, it does look remarkably like another eye. Great, I get a third eye, and someone gives me a shiner. I hold onto the sink with both hands, feeling groggy now after the exertion of standing up after laying down for so long. I close my eyes… and I take a good look at myself.

Bloody hell! That's not supposed to happen. I open my eyes, slowly close them again, and yes, I can actually see a little clearer with them shut.

My knees feel weak and I feel sick. Slowly I slide down the sink onto the floor, reach the toilet and throw up into it without ceremony.

Somehow, I work my way back into bed. After the initial shock, my mind is now racing with ideas, most involve magician's tricks, covering the eyes and being able to read, wow amaze your friends, and other utterly ridiculous thoughts, but it keeps me amused. I need glasses now, just for reading, but can foresee problems getting off the peg pairs to fit, and the nickname 'six eyes' will no doubt enter the builders' vocabulary on site.

Only one thing to do! Go to the fountain of all knowledge, Deborah. No, that's going to take a bit more explaining than I can handle, so I get my phone and Internet it.

This leads me down many strange and varied sites, some plain daft, some possible, but after what I'm seeing, they all seem increasingly believable. I fall asleep with the phone in my hand and wake up to a porter prepping me.

Brain scans, now there's an experience.

Loaded into a missile body while somebody plays one hundred favourite jack hammer noises at full volume.

Afterwards, Deborah said we could spend a bit of time together, as I normally have to spend most of my time at work. She decided that she would push me to my appointments in the hospital.

She wheels me through the long halls but I'm heavy and Deborah is an elegant, slight build and she is struggling to push me, and besides that, her pushing me, it just feels wrong.

"Deborah, we're both tired. Let's just stop for a second here." I tap her hand with mine. We stop and I close my eyes to rest. After only a few moments there's a rush of the spooks, as I now call them, all colours. Dozens of them rush past, avoiding me, a few cling to Deborah, but soon let go to follow the others, they veer off into a ward. I'm frightened by so many of them, acting so urgently, and open my eyes in a panic.

"What's wrong?" Deborah asks with tender concern. I just mutter about needing a toilet quickly and direct her the way the spooks went. I realise now that Deborah often has two or three of the damn things fastened to her, but glancing back at her now, I see they are gone. I notice she seems stronger again.

A nurse rushes past distracting us both, then more nurses. Each carrying lots of things, they seem excited. Deborah moves us forwards, closer to the room they're bustling into. But when I look into the room it is so full of the ugly glowing pulsating masses that I can barely make out the nurses and people. I can sense almost a frenzy now as they are writhing over each other, piling up, getting brighter and more solid looking, the different dirty stagnant colours mixing, slightly out of focus but awful. I stand up, holding the door frame for support.

"Careful, love!" Deborah remarks as she watches me with growing worry, clearly unable to see what I see.

Suddenly, beside me, is the biggest, most defined spook I have seen so far. It's clearly over six feet, brighter than the others, and horrifying to look at. Far more like a huge lizard, but no tail. Walking upright, it faces me, fully and slowly it scans me top to bottom and back again. I am terrified, none have paid any attention to me before, but this one is. It's a pale green colour. The spooks you can see through them to varying degrees but this thing is solid, orange eyes look back at me through reptile slits. Its face is somewhere between lizard and human, but scaled, these spread all over its muscular body. It slowly reaches out to touch me, slender fingers, I expected claws but am surprised by its rather elegant hands. It has a soft white glow covering its body. I freeze in terror, but just in front of me its hand stops, it is trying to reach me but can't. Its head cocks to one side as if in surprise, it withdraws its hand and examines it, as if confused. It turns away and walks into the room parting the spooks as if they are afraid.

The clearing it creates allows me to see nurses working frantically on somebody. I can't see the person but see the head spook calmly walk over and place a hand right inside the head of the person. It raises its head in what appears triumph, and the spooks go frantic, pushing and clambering over themselves to get as close as they can to the body. Then abruptly it stops.

They begin to disappear; some attach themselves to the nurses and doctor, but almost in a lazy manner. The boss turns to leave, it is brighter now, but on approaching me, it suddenly grabs out catching a small red spook. It smashes it into me, but something is repulsing it. Before I can even flinch, it's grinding it into my face, my back is against the door frame so I have nowhere to go. All I can see is the red spook writhing, apparently in pain, held at about six inches from my face. I'm totally frozen. It appears to be getting closer but starts melting like a warm, dirty jelly over the boss spook's hand. It drips to the floor and oozes off. The boss spook looks, as its hand reaches out for me, much closer this time. It tries pushing, I can actually feel a pressure against me, then it withdraws its hand, examines its hand again, then walks away, and then it's gone.

Deborah is talking to me. I wasn't aware before, but she is going frantic, asking me what's wrong, and do I need a doctor. She's panicking trying to get my attention, the spooks on her seem to be enjoying it, more start to join in. I move suddenly, hurting my ankle doing so, but get between her and the spooks. I love her so much and want to protect her. I reach out for the nearest spook on her back. To my surprise, I feel its texture cool, jelly, not fully set, slimy but not actually wet to touch. It writhes as if in pain, wriggling frantically then just begins to liquefy and melts. I look stupidly at my hands, I actually feel bad about killing it, but the rest get the message and leave Deborah alone. I fall over, my ankle just gives way, my knees are shaking, and my legs are like jelly. I put my head in my hands. "What's wrong what's wrong?" is all I can hear Deborah saying.

I turn my face to her. "Debs, you know I love you, but trust me, you really don't want to know."

"What happened?" asks Deborah, but I can't bring myself to answer.

I start looking on the Internet on my phone to see if I can find out just what is happening. I find out that ninety-nine per cent is drivel, people peddling 'facts' that are mere opinions and their imaginings. Then there's the tiny amount of information that's backed by provable documented facts. Then there's the fact that every culture on the planet tells stories that are identical, and then there's the one per cent, of course only half of this one per cent is relevant to me, but the other half a per cent is truly terrifying.

Of course, there's nothing to suggest why it is that I'm suddenly seeing the beasties.

Also, if I take it that half of one per cent is relevant and real, then digging the odd gem out of the mountains of utter drivel is going to take some doing. I start to get quite obsessed with this process, finding snippets here and there, but nothing I can find suggests why I can now see them. Why I don't have my very own resident spook, why the boss spook couldn't touch me, just what happened to the smaller spook, and the one that I touched. All these questions I am trying to find answers to, but most importantly how I get them off Deborah?

3

Result day! The scan apparently found my brain cell.

There's always been an old, long-standing joke in our family that we only have one brain cell between us, and we keep that in a jar for emergency use only. So, reading through the humorous texts and emails cheered me up before I went to see the scan man. I have to call him this because I can neither spell nor pronounce his name.

I'm greeted by a wonderful, slim, energetic if short man of Indian origin, who still speaks with a heavy accent. After greeting me with the doctors', 'And how are we today' style questions, he gets down to my results. At least I think so as I have frankly no idea what he's talking about. But he does mention something that starts alarm bells ringing in my head.

"Now that you have a lovely third eye…" His voice drifts into my awareness.

Third eye, a third eye — distant memories stir.

One thing I am realising is that I feel normal. But my brain is slower than before. I put this aside and listen, as something he is saying has caught my attention. Apparently, most of my brain is normal, undamaged, but the impact of the brick has smashed the calcification that grows over the pineal gland, and it has been cleared away. Also, I have what amounts to a hole in my forehead, which I must admit does resemble a closed eye. A perfect shot bang centre between the eyes and centrally between my hairline and brow. I'm thinking about this and have lost track of what he is saying, so I ask what he knows about the third eye.

From what I understand, in many Eastern beliefs, the third eye refers to the 'ajna' or brow chakra, often called the inner eye, and is a concept referring to an invisible eye, that provides perception beyond ordinary vision. Except that mine is very visible, some friends are now referring to me as a *triclops.*

The doctor goes on to explain all about my injuries, then it's bombshell time. It is said to be directly connected to the pineal gland, but most people in the West have a calcium deposit that grows over, encasing the pineal gland. "Now that yours is clear, do not be surprised if you begin to sense things that you can't normally see."

I am still worried that if I should tell people what I'm seeing that I will be in the padded cell with a massive drugs stack to keep me quiet. Also, most people would not welcome comments like, "Hello, did you know that there's a five-foot spectral reptilian slug clinging to your back?" It's just not what people want to hear.

The soothsayer of scans gives me his card; he's looking at me in a way that suggests he knows I'm not telling him everything, but I'm not ready yet. But this man does seem to be, let's say, more open to the unscientific, probably due to the understanding of an Eastern religion. He may be able to tell me more, but my time is up. As I stand up, I quickly close my eyes and scan him. To my surprise, there's no spooks. This man I need to talk to, and soon.

4

In the films you watch, the hero knows what to do, what to say to the right people, and all is explained. Is it just me, or does everybody see themselves in their mind's eye as the hero, the one who is right and others wrong? At this point I'm starting to think that the painkillers for the hole in my crust are quite a bit stronger than I'm being told, my thinking is more as if I'm trying to run underwater, lots of thrashing about, but no actual progress.

I am outside the small Indian doctor's office, and to be honest I'm struggling to make sense in my mind. Also, my sides hurt, so does my back, ankle, and my head feels mushy on the inside, and hurts on the outside. I am now trying to manage with a walking stick. I do want to know why the painkillers mash up my thinking but don't seem to stop anything else from hurting. I'm also getting utterly pissed with the constant taking of my blood every day.

I'm about to go to the doctor's door but he walks out, telling somebody that he will be back in an hour. I try to step forwards to meet him, twist my ankle, and with the most totally embarrassing display of incoordination seen to mankind, fall headlong waving my arms and stick wildly as I go. I'm just glad that Debs wasn't there to be embarrassed as well. And I hurt myself, but as a plus the doctor rushes over to assist. I knew he was a good bloke. He gets me into a chair, I have landed on my ribs and my breath is coming in rasps and wheezes. Now I have his attention I tell him I need his help.

"I'm sorry, but I'm not that kind of doctor, I diagnose not repair."

"I need to know about my third eye, it's open, I mean fully open, and I need to know what to do."

He looks at me and he slowly shakes his head.

"No wonder you are acting so bloody odd."

I'm about to tell him that this is quite normal for me, but I think better of it.

"Are you seeing visions, anything odd?"

"Oh boy, yes, but not visions."

"Oh, dear me."

He suggests we go into his office where it's more private. His pretty, petite receptionist helps me into the office. I try to pretend I'm OK and can manage, but secretly I'm so glad of the help.

"Now... tell me what you can see?"

So, I tell him everything, even the patient dying, and the incident with the boss spook, and how I only see it when I close my eyes.

To my relief he seems to take it seriously and doesn't either laugh or phone the men in white coats. Instead, he sits down and thinks for a moment.

"The reason that you don't see them when your eyes are open is that your brain is working on a normal level and is filtering as it should, but when you close your eyes, the information is no longer travelling down the optic nerve to reach your brain, so the input is getting to your brain by a different route, and you are picking things up on a different wavelength, or frequency."

I sit back in astonishment. "Oh."

"It's like you are a radio tuned into a frequency, a set station, when you close your eyes, then you move onto the next station on a different frequency."

He is quite relieved when I tell him that he doesn't have any hangers-on himself.

"I do not know for certain, but when I was growing up in India, I heard stories, from the older members of the village, who talked about such things. I only thought that they were stories.

"I do believe that they are feeding off us, but why we aren't palatable, I don't know, but it has to do with energies. It seems that they are drawn to illness, so I would guess that they feed off the lower energies, but looking at the state of you I would have thought that you would be a veritable feast for them."

He explains that he eats an organic vegetarian diet, meditates daily, and does yoga, otherwise is just ordinary. But why not you?"

"Well, I'm not good at meditation, I tried but my mind just runs away with itself, I used to do meditation when I was doing reiki but haven't done either really for years."

"Ahh, what level did you reach?"

"Level three, in two styles."

"Oh, a master."

I don't refer to myself as a master, it always sounds too pretentious, too much ego for me.

"I am not totally sure, but when you do certain things, like yoga, reiki and suchlike, you raise your body's natural frequency. I think that is the reason we are not so tasty to them, but beware, there are many things that lower the frequency of your body, illness, pain, bad diet, alcohol and smoking, all lower the frequency leaving the body open to attack. Drugs especially, even the medical drugs given to you here, so beware."

I think of whatever is being given to me that is killing my brain, and decide I'm stopping it now.

He has to go. I thank him, and he advises me to meditate, exercise and do some reiki on myself.

He calls for a porter to take me back, rather than risk further injuries to myself. A chair arrives and a friendly porter takes me back, whistling happily and cracking jokes with me, even helping me to get back onto my bed.

5

Deborah is sitting in the chair beside my bed. We are talking, or rather, she is talking. My mind is drifting. You see, as a man, if I am asked a question, then I will do my best to answer it, which is good! But, if asked a lot of unrelated questions, or lots of random topics discussed in quick succession, my mind will try to answer question one. Once I have done this my mind will either move on to question two, providing it remembers what it was, or drift off, settle down or merely switch off. I don't know if this is a man thing, or just me. Deborah's mind is moving between topics like quicksilver and mine is moving, if at all, in more of a tectonic speed.

So it is while my mind is drifting away, I just start to feel a nasty change, I can sense it growing. Deborah is quiet, I think that she is picking up on it also.

When she does talk to me, her tone has become sharp and icy.

"Just how long are you going to sit here? It's not nice for me you know, having to visit you every day, just having to watch you lying here useless."

She keeps on, digging more and more at me. It feels as if she is doing all she can to hurt me. But she just goes on, saying really hurtful things. She is accusing me of ignoring her, of being unfaithful. I am getting more upset and hurt, but as she goes on, I begin to sense the words, a mere moment before she speaks them. It's indistinct at first, but I sort of tune into it, becoming clearer, until I can hear a voice in my head. It's an ugly, mithering cruel voice, whining and manipulating. It becomes so clear to me that I hear it fully now.

"And when you go out, you can see the young men looking at you, young attractive men, they are rich, successful, they would spend more time with you. They don't need to work all day, every day just to get by. He thinks that his work is more important than you are." I hear it and I see Deborah opening her mouth to speak.

"Don't be so daft, I love you, of course men look at you, you're beautiful, and very sexy!"

She still has her mouth open, but no words come out, well for a moment anyway.

"H-how do you know what I'm thinking?"

She is angry now, starting to raise her voice, shouting, saying things to hurt me, I feel like weeping. She is telling me that she has had enough, she's so bored. I'm about to answer, to think more clearly. I close my eyes to try to concentrate my thoughts on what to say to her.

What I see shocks me, the room is full, and I mean actually to the ceiling, with the spooks. They are slithering over each other, pulsating, and there's almost frenzy as they push to get closer.

Deborah's barrage has struck deeply into me, and in front of me I can see the hideous faces of the spooks, pushing closer, only inches from my face now. But worse than this, Deborah is smothered with the things. She's shouting at me now, that I can't even stay awake when she talks to me. But I can hear the words being fed to her, clearly in a hissing insipid voice, pushing, persuading and vile. I hear them before she speaks them to me.

Coming into focus, I start to make out a leader, lost amongst the other spooks until now, a faint white glow starts to come from his body, growing brighter. It's holding her head in its hands, its long claws sunk deep into Deborah's face. It's the one feeding the words and the feelings to her, as it does it feeds off her emotions. Even as it speaks the words to her, I can see its body rhythmically pulsating, as it sucks the energy out of Deborah's body. The more negative the thoughts she has, the more it can feed off her emotions. And right now, they are feasting, the disgusting creatures hanging off every part of her body.

I can hear the boss spook telling her to finish with me, here and now, forever. She's about to say it herself, so I leap up, lunging at the boss spook, but my sudden move frightens her. She thinks I'm lunging at her, going to hit her, she cowers away, and with the fear even more spooks swarm over her, rushing to feed of this new emotion.

Deborah's face looks drawn, exhausted, the boss spook looks into my eyes, it draws all of its energy into taking the last of Deborah's energy, she drops forwards to her knees, and weeps.

The boss looks at me with triumph, seeing Deborah this way is hurting me so much,

"What have they done to you?"

I feel my energy starting to be drawn away, and I realise that whatever was protecting me before has gone. They start crowding over me, I feel disgusted to see them slithering and pulsing over me, this just excites them and draws more. As they feed off me, it feels like my very soul is being sucked out and a feeling of despair sweeps over me.

I can barely make Deborah out. She's so covered in spooks; I try to get to her to protect her but it's so hard to move and feels so useless. I just feel like giving up and dying there. The top spook stands over her, then it looks at me, gloating. It's going to destroy her mind and health, I can make out its thoughts in my mind, then do the same to me.

It raises a fist to her head, pressing down on her, raises it again to strike into her face. I can see her face racked with pain, I feel unable to move, but I shout, "No, Deborah, I love you!"

I think of the love I have for her. It rises up in me, growing suddenly like a dam bursting its waters. I will protect her, with the last breath in my body and the last ounce of my soul. I push forwards and there's a change in the room, a sudden panic amongst the spooks, they begin to slither away from me. I feel my love for her, my one and only, my soulmate, it fills me, and I will not allow this to continue.

I lurch, grab the reptile top spook by its raised arm, I can sense its purpose and I suddenly feel its arm break. I let my love for Deborah fill me, it gives me strength and the spook writhes in my hands. I think of the love I feel for the people I know, and I grow stronger. I think of the beauty there is in the world. I put my hands on the spook's head, remembering the reiki, how to use its protection, I put it on me and then send loving energy to Deborah. I ask for the loving energy to flow through me and the spook goes frantic, squirming and shaking to get free. Throughout the room there's panic, climbing over themselves to get away, they start to rip each other apart in an attempt to escape, some even then stop to feed off the dying ones but then themselves begin to melt, or get pulled apart themselves. I send loving energy and forgiveness to the boss spook, it shakes a moment, turns bright white and in a flash of energy disintegrates.

I send loving energy into the room, and it clears, I sense a bright white loving light fill the room, I put protection into the room, and then all the love I possess into Deborah.

The room clears, goes back to normal. I pick her up, gently lay her on the bed and send her all the loving energy I can. As she slowly starts to come round, I put on my most cheerful voice that she fell asleep and has had a bad dream. I gently kiss her lips, she kisses me back and quietly says, "I do love you."

6

We walk outside, well, Deborah walks. I sort of hobble out onto a grassy area, where we sit against a large old tree. I look up into its spreading branches. It's cold out, lovely blue skies, a bright day, it feels good to be out. I close my eyes, there's a slight shift of vision and I can see the aura surrounding the tree, it shimmers slowly into focus. Is it just me or is the whole world going doolally?

Deborah turns to me and says, "I saw things, just for a moment, I don't know what, is that what you can see?"

I take a breath and tell her slowly, "The spooks, I call them, oh boy do I get to see them. You don't have any on you now, they don't like to be near to me, it seems."

"Seems? Can't you be a bit more positive?" she asks crossly.

"Well, actually, you have hit the nail on the head, you see the spooks, they feed on the negative energies, the lower frequency emotions, such as fear, hate, disease. As they do this, they draw you down, so that it gives them even more food."

"So, are you saying that we should all go round skipping and doing the fluffy bunny routine?"

My mind goes onto Deborah dressed as a bunny girl. I for one wouldn't be complaining, especially the 'skipping around' bit. But this probably isn't the time to mention it to her. Come on though, I am a builder, I don't just sit around drinking tea!

"No, it's not about being artificial, you raise your frequency through positive thought, exercise, a healthy diet, and meditation, it all helps."

"How come you are suddenly the guru, a big expert on such things, eh, YouTube?"

"Well, sort of. I did look some things up, but not just that, when that thing had me, as soon as I thought about how much I love you, it couldn't touch me, so I know it works.

"Look, that's the best that I can do, I know that it helps. Also you know the reiki, well that seems to help as well. Do you remember the protection, how we were shown how to put protection on ourselves, well that works."

We had done the level one reiki together years ago, I loved it.

"Put your protection on every morning; it keeps them off your back."

7

After Debs went home, the nurse came for yet another blood test.

Do you ever get the feeling that something isn't quite right, but you just can't put your finger on it. Well that's what I'm getting now. So, in my friendliest voice I joke, "If you take any more, I will have none left, you must have taken a full transplant by now. Is that what's happening, stocks are so low I have to give every few hours?"

The nurse doesn't even acknowledge me, stabs me hard, takes the blood, and goes.

Mardy cow!

Moments later, another nurse walks in, smiling, friendly, as you would normally expect.

"Have I said something to upset her?"

"Who's that?"

"The nurse who comes to take my blood all the time."

"Why would they want your blood? Anyway it's no one off this ward."

This does nothing to reassure me. I'm feeling even more concerned, so I decide to go for a walk as it always helps me to think.

Now I have the worst sense of direction of anyone that I know. Deborah says that it's because I'm dyslexic. I tell her that I simply get lost a lot. So when I set off I simply walk, I know that I will get lost. I don't worry, I will simply ask directions back, no problem.

I would like to say that some inner sense guides me, but it doesn't, I'm simply not paying attention to where I'm going. I step into a ward, I don't know why, open the door, and I go in, no particular reason. I have to sit down, my ankle is giving me what for. I see a chair and sit down. I get out my phone and start fiddling with it. Down the corridor, a door opens and out walks a family, the mother weeping, supported by her husband, behind a boy of about five follows holding onto a teenage lad of about fourteen.

I feel bad watching them walk past, as if I'm intruding, even though I don't think that they even notice me. I keep watching the door, it's just facing me, that's all. I'm rubbing my ankle when I see a man in an expensive suit hurrying down the corridor, it's only grey, but it has such a good cut to it that it stands out. I watch him walk enthusiastically into the same room that the family just left. I assumed that he must be a consultant, but he rubbed his hands together in a way that suggested he was expecting a treat, and as the door closed, I heard him cheerfully calling out something about his little angel being ready for him.

I take out my phone and casually start to film the door. Sure enough, about fifteen minutes later, he emerges looking very smug and satisfied with himself, he turns round as he leaves calling sweetly into the room. "Sleep tight," then adds. "You sweet little bitch, it's been such a pleasure."

He swaggers off, leaving the door open. I close my eyes. To my horror I see not spooks, as I expected, but a large deep grey reptile of about seven feet high, but it is in the same space as him as if they are not just connected but melded together. It's similar looking to the green boss spooks I have seen, and believe me they are ugly, but he is really frightening, he has an air of hatred about him.

I want to know what's happening, no one is about so I walk to the door, and casually as I can, walk in. Inside is a medical bed, surrounded by a lot of medical machines, you know, dials, screens with lines on, the heartbeat line is not very strong, I can see that. But more to the point, are the spooks filling the room, and the four boss spooks standing at the head of the bed, reaching down.

I tune into my reiki, taking a few moments to put on my protection, applying the symbols and letting the energy grow. I ignore the utter panic now filling the room and walk over to the bed.

On it is a girl of about nine or ten, it's hard to tell. Her face is covered by an oxygen mask, she has no hair, her dark-ringed eyes are sunken, the skin pulled tight over her bones. I begin to send the energy to her, asking first for her to accept it, if it is right for her greater and higher good to do so. I hold my hands about six inches above her body, and concentrate. I can feel the energy flowing through my hands, it tingles and has the feeling of when you hold two magnets of the same pole to each other, and it sort of pushes away. I keep going, I use every symbol, and every ounce of energy that I can. I go over her entire body like this, never touching her, just pushing all the energy I can into her frail body.

Finally, I can feel no more resistance, so gently sweep down her aura and ask for her to be healed and helped as much as possible. I put into her aura all the protection I can, give thanks, and I'm done, so switch off the energy. I have no idea how long I have been there. I sense I'm finished and look up.

One of my pet grumbles is when people say that they are powerful healers, especially with reiki, it becomes an ego problem then. You see, you do not heal, you are taught how to allow the energy to flow through you, you become its conduit, your purpose is to guide it with your intention. It's like focusing the beam caused by a magnifying glass, get it just right and the concentrated energy can set paper alight. But if you wrap the lens in paper, it doesn't cause the paper to burn. So it is with reiki; the energy flows through you and doesn't come from you.

I notice a movement behind a chair. My eyes are still closed from concentrating hard. One of the boss spooks is hiding there, not hiding from me, but from the energy that's now coming from the girl. It's using the

43

chair as a shield as if to protect it from the heat of a fire. I walk over, now I have turned the energy off, my body acts to shield it, it looks less frightening than the others. About five foot, I would guess, much smaller, and it has much finer features, in fact not that much different to human, apart from the fine light green scales. It is definitely female, and looks quite young to me, the truth is apply a bit of make-up and she could be a young woman, and certainly not an unattractive one.

I try not to be threatening, I concentrate hard, remembering how the boss spooks spoke into my mind.

"You're shouting."

"I am? Oh, sorry, I'm new to this, how's this?"

"Better, you can see me?"

"Only when I close my eyes."

She cocks her head to one side, studying me.

"How do you know how to talk to me?"

"Ah, well, one of the boss spooks got his hands into my head and I remembered how it felt."

"Boss spooks?"

I feel a bit embarrassed by this. "No offence to you, it's just a name I made up."

She cocks her head again, studying me, "You survived that?"

"Not completely unscathed, but more or less."

She looks over at the young girl on the bed. "You were going to kill her?" I ask.

"What, don't be stupid, I don't kill."

"Looks like it to me." I can remember how it felt with the boss spook getting into me.

"No, no, I feed off the energy released during death, but I don't kill. We aren't like you, who farm animals then slaughter them for food, we can feed off you humans again and again, so killing you would be stupid. I take the energy, but it's released whether we are here to feed or not."

"What about the one who left just before I came in?"

A look of disgust passes over her face.

"The controllers, they walk in both worlds. I hate them, they control both of us with fear, they feed off the pain and terror they inflict onto children of both our races, killing them after abusing them, feeding off the blood, and the energy. They rule over us."

"Nice."

"They appear to you as humans so that they can get into positions of power, that way they can keep you in permanent slavery to the system that they created. This keeps you all in permanent low energy for us to feed off."

"Well, that explains politics and bureaucracy."

"This is hurting me, I'm stuck here because of the energy, will you help me? Please."

"What can I do?"

"Shield me with your body, just to the door, but don't touch me."

So, I do. Outside she thanks me, and just disappears.

"Did that really just happen?" I ask myself, but a small voice interrupts me.

"Mister, can I have some water please?"

I turn to see the young girl trying to sit up.

"One moment, I'll fetch a nurse."

I find the nurses' bay. "The little girl has asked me to get her some water."

I get a sort of a scowl, so I continue. "In the room there, the door's open and she saw me passing," I smile my most innocent smile. "Is it OK, or do you have to do it?"

The nurse slowly gets up, walks down and is suddenly back at full speed. I slide away as smoothly as my ankle allows, but can hear excited voices.

What an odd day it turned out to be. Suppose I had best start to find my way back.

8

The next day I casually meander to the ward where the little girl is, to be greeted with a ward with balloons of film characters and a much warmer atmosphere. I make my way to the door and do my best not to be noticed. Inside there is a family in utter happy disbelief — I feel all emotional I must admit. I catch sight of the little girl sat up, talking and looking a much better colour. I'm about to leave before I get all weepy and look daft, but she sees me and shouts me over. I try to disappear, but the mother comes over and almost drags me in.

"That's the mister, I said that he was real, didn't I. Tell them how you made me better, you chased off the nasties didn't you?"

I scan the floor searching for a hole large enough to swallow me up. Not finding one, I go for telling the truth, but in very small, edited sections. But then I see the look on the little girl's face, so wanting someone to believe her, I think 'sod it'.

"Yes, that's right, I thought that they were hurting you, so I chased them away."

"See, I told you it's true."

"Liza is here now, but I can't see her as clear now."

"Who is Liza?" asks her mother.

"Oh, she is one of the lizard people. They were frightening, but she was nice to me, she held my hand and she talked to me, she didn't have a name so I called her Liza."

I close my eyes, and sure enough, there she is, by the bed, looking over the girl and smiling.

I give a little startled jump when I see her, and she has to stop a laugh.

"Hello, I'm surprised to see you here."

"I just wanted to see how she is; she looks well, I am glad. Tell her I'm glad she feels better."

"She said hello, and is glad you are feeling better."

"Will I see her again?"

"Possibly, but let's hope that it's not for a very long time."

"Will I see you again soon?"

"I certainly think that's possible."

I stay a little longer. I pretend that I can do magic by covering my eyes and telling the family what they are holding, how many fingers, that sort of thing. When I leave, the parents come to me at the door.

"Look," the father starts, "I don't know what went off here, she hasn't been well, and I'm not sure that filling her mind with tales of nasties, spooks, and lizards is such a good idea—" He's about to go on, but the mother heads him off.

"I don't know how, but I think that you have helped our little girl. All I know is that we were given a day for her to live, now she has a life to live, and we are grateful.

But she insists that it was you who did this. Well truth now. Did You?"

I begin to mumble, not sure what to say, then I think, "Oh sod it, it's not like I will ever see the family again."

I look them squarely in their faces, stand up tall and say, "It was me, I used reiki on her, anyone can learn it, there's no age, religion, culture or any other restrictions. In fact, I suggest that you all learn it yourselves, to make sure that she never gets as ill again."

I give them the name of my teacher, turn to leave, but the father stops me again, this time I see a tear in his eye. "Thank you, for giving us back our little girl." I shake his hand and I'm leaving when the young lizard moves over to me. We walk out together.

"The controller is furious with you. She was his play thing; he was ready to feed off her blood."

"I thought that you only took the energy."

"We do, but the controllers have a physical body in this dimension, so need physical sustenance, and you took it away from him."

"Do you know, I suddenly feel really well, I think that I'm going to go home…"

"Good idea."

"Anyway, it's mad here, I need a rest."

"By the way, do you have a name?"

"Not that you could say, why?"

"I will call you Liza, is that oOK?"

She shrugs. "OK, if it helps you."

And she's gone again. I begin the trek to my room, time for me to go, I think.

Back in my room, I begin to go through what I have learned through my Internet searching. I only have my phone, and though it's not brilliant, it gets some results. How true they are, that's a different matter. But here goes, as I understand. Each atom is made mainly of empty space, and the parts that aren't empty are made up of energy. These clump together to form cells, therefore, the cells are made of energy. So anything that is made of atoms, that is everything, is basically made of energy. So everything is atoms, but packed together closely and into different shaped things. These atoms vibrate — they have a frequency. So a stack of atoms bunched together into a chair shape, will vibrate and have a chair frequency, so whatever we see is a group of atoms vibrating at the frequency of the object that we see.

Therefore, a person is a complex cluster of vibrations, vibrating at a person frequency. Food has its own frequency, depending on what it is, the higher its frequency the better it is for you, for example, food freshly picked has a better, higher frequency than stale, old or preserved food.

Also, our diseases, illnesses and ailments all have a specific frequency, as do our emotions, and when our emotional frequency matches an illness, the two match up and bingo, you have that illness. The lower the emotion, the worse the illness. When was the last time you saw a depressed person who was a picture of good health?

But onto bigger things, the Earth has its own frequency. Well, it's made up of atoms, a lot of atoms, therefore it vibrates at its very own Earth frequency, as do all the other planets, stars and universe. This has now been studied and recorded by NASA. And what's really, really, exciting, is that it is actually increasing in frequency. The whole solar system is.

This means that the solar system, and especially important to us, Earth is increasing, that means that as occupants of Earth, we must increase our own frequency in order to keep up. If we are left behind—

I think about how we live our lives, people glued to their mobiles, young people on childish video games, pretending, instead of actually doing it for real, or watching violence, even from a young age. Then there's the food, utter lifeless, zero frequency food that doesn't feed you and yet makes you crave more. Food that doesn't rot, or digest.

I look out of the window, down at a family below; the children are fat, unhealthy and unfit, as in unfit for purpose. The whole lot of them are in awful fleece jogging bottoms, although the only time they jog is to get to more fast-food outlets. They are grubby, tattoos on any part of bare skin, which they proudly display to all, wobbling fat, dimpled, and spotty. I feel utterly depressed at the sight of them.

As I look on, I begin to get changed, I close my eyes and watch the parents walk on, spooks clinging to them, almost completely covering them. My point of view is like Watching two, six-foot piles of slugs moving in unison. They are the muddy grey, brown ones, the lowest caste of spooks, they actually match the family well. I note that the children are free of the hangers-on, so perhaps what Liza was saying is true about them not feeding on the children.

Slowly I pack my few belongings together, and get dressed into my scruffy work gear. I am midway between putting on clean underpants, when I blink, and for a moment I see the room crowded with very large reptiles. I turn let out a cry of horror, twist my ankle and fall, all while trying to get my other leg into my pants.

A large, green, scaled and ferocious face appears over the bed, and turns to one side. "This…" It pauses for effect. "This can help… us?"

9

They stand, watching me getting dressed, limping about. It's not a big room, and they are almost filling it. Finally, I have on a T-shirt, and work trousers, so I turn to them. They haven't moved in any aggressive way, in fact look rather embarrassed at being there at all.

"Are you sure he can hear us?"

"I doubt that it could understand us anyway."

"Hello again…"

I recognise that voice in my head.

"Liza?"

"It can speak!"

Liza is pushed forwards. "Yes, and understand, perhaps it's best if I speak to it."

"It?" I shot her a look, but I don't think that it had the slightest effect on her.

"We have come to tell you that the controller is coming to kill you. He has been monitoring your red juice."

"Red juice? My blood? What about my blood?"

"You have begun to produce a chemical in your head, it's increasing exponentially, it happened as a result of your accident. It is normally only produced during your birth, and your death, but you didn't die, you were returned, and the gland that produces it, the pineal gland, is increasing production, that's why you can now see us, and more unusually, can hear us also.

"The controller knows that this could possibly happen, but has no way of knowing whether you can or not, so anyway, he has decided to kill you. He is on his way now, along with his assistant."

"Miss bloody whiplash."

"Yes, they will inject you, then they can pretend to cut you up to find out why and they can have your brain."

"To find out why it's producing the chemical."

"Oh no, not at all, it will get them stoned on the chemical."

I have my boots on now and I think it's time to be off.

"Why are you helping me?"

"Your accident, the chemical, they are causing you to awaken, to evolve, your frequency is increasing, quite rapidly, actually. Many of us are also increasing in frequency, but the controllers fear that we will evolve past their ability to control us. The means of controlling us is by violence, extreme violence, far worse than they use on your people.

"The energy that you used against us in the room with the girl, it didn't kill me, my frequency is far higher than normal for us, but it really hurt. We here represent the awakening amongst our type, you are the same, I fear that we must work together for both our types' sake.

I have spent my life hidden away from the controllers, but there are few places left for me now. I will explain more as soon as I can, but now we must go."

"We?"

She looks down at her feet, I sense what I can only think of as unhappiness about her, whether reptile lizards do happiness I have no idea.

"You are the only place that is left for me to hide"

"Oh," my mind is no longer keeping up. "Well, I suppose that we had better make good our escape then, come on."

She looks relieved.

"You don't mind?"

"No, I always wanted my very own invisible friend when I was young, but didn't have the imagination."

I bundle my few belongings into a plastic bag, and walk out the door, about ten paces down the corridor I turn around. "I not sure, but do you think that the controller may notice you all following me, and think it looks a little odd?"

There's a bit of muttering and they disappear. There's just me, I'm trying to work out the way to the exit when Liza appears beside me, though my eyes are open I hear her shout, "Run!"

10

I see a sign for the stairs, head for that, through the doors, down a couple of flights then slow down to a normal walk. We continue to the main exit onto the street, staying close to the building so that I can't be seen from the windows above, head round to the back of the building then strike out down a tree-lined street, hoping that if I am being looked for, I will get some cover from them. There's the local shopping centre in sight, I head for the closest charity shop and pick up a pair of aviator-style sunglasses for a pound, and I feel a bit silly. I know as a disguise it's pretty naff, but now I can walk with my eyes closed so I can see any spooks around. Of course I see lots of spooks, but all going about their normal business of feeding off us, but doing it in a very casual manner. I notice Liza's face looking on the lower castes with an undisguised grimace.

"Snob."

"What?"

"Oh, never mind, do you see any sign of us being followed?"

"Nothing unusual. Why do you all move around like this, all crowding over each other, and carrying things, walking?"

I realise that walking is totally new to Liza; she can just pop into her reality, her dimension, and pop up where she wants to be. I know of a nearby park, I head for this, find a large tree, sit with my back against it and try looking relaxed. I figure that the boss spooks will be picking up on stressful emotions, so keeping calm will help hide us.

Liza stretches out on the grass; I look at her properly for the first time. She is about five foot six or seven, some of the lizards have very reptilian faces, all teeth scales, fangs rows of knobbly scaly protrusions, and an overall terrifying appearance. But she is most definitely female, slim in an athletic way, her face is very human like, small nose, her mouth looks normal, well to us anyway, except if she opens it wide when you see rather sharp teeth. Her skin is smooth, the scales so fine as to appear smooth, with a silky appearance, from the tip of her nose a light yellow colour goes up between her eyes and spreads out at her forehead and over her head. Her eyes look almost human, but looking closer the pupil is a black slit, with a deep golden orange to either side, then white. Her eyes may be slightly larger than humans, I'm trying to decide but she sees me looking at her. She puts her head on one side and looks questioningly at me.

"Sorry, you have seen loads of us, but you are new to me. I don't mean to offend, but you look far more like us than do many of your kind, I mean some look bloody frightening to me, but you are pleasant. And you seem to show more emotion."

Liza has been stretching out, enjoying the warmth of the sun, in much the same way as a lizard would, basking on a rock.

"I am quite close in my make-up to all of your kind, do you want me to tell you about it?"

I take a long look around, there's no sign of spooks, or humans, acting abnormally.

"Sounds good to me."

She gets up, sits down with her back against the tree and sighs a little, she is acting a little sad, but I'm not even sure if she has emotions. "I am considered a freak. I am too human, I have feelings, affection, anger and look like a human hybrid. I have a much higher frequency, so I can stay close to your dimension, where most can only visit for short times to feed, but must return immediately after.

"A long time ago, the helixitors came to this planet, with the intention of colonising, they did this all across the universe, and when a suitable planet was found, they would build a suitable race to inhabit it. For for convenience they would use many dimensions, that way they can have many experiments simultaneously on the go."

She stretches out her arm, looks at it thoughtfully. It is pretty much human, pale green admittedly, but in design it's the same. "They had long ago found that basic bipedal frames are the cheapest working model, but will design to suit the environment."

I am surprised with this.

"You mean that us humans look human because it's a cheap design to manufacture."

"Yes, thin skin, few limbs, economy build, but make them breed fast enough to overcome the shortfalls."

"Nice."

"So with a collection of parts they get the basic frame together, then add the helixes into their cells from many existing races, to suit the needs, and off they go, travel into space at near the speed of light, a couple of days away and thousands of years passes here."

"You can do that?" I ask, amazed.

She looks at me as if she is about to recommend what type of therapy would suit me best.

"No." She looks a bit cross with me. "I am not an alien, you know, this is my planet!"

I look at her for a moment, the realisation slowly slides into my mind, just because something is unfamiliar, to me anyway, doesn't mean that it doesn't belong.

"Sorry, I'm new to this and a bit slow to catch on."

She looks at me a moment, to see if I am serious, realises that I am, and visibly relaxes again. "OK." she remembers where she was in the explanation.

"If they like the results, they allow the race to thrive, for whatever reason they were designed for, if not they're erased. We were a sort of joint project, you had a reason and we feed on you. No idea what the reasons are though. We are sort of related, though, you see they did use parts of our brains that came from a common source."

"The reptile brain?" I try hard not to look at her. "It's thought to be the oldest part to our brain."

"Originally the experiments involved only reptiles, you call them dinosaurs, and awesomely successful as a genre, awesomely dull, all very well being successful, but their rate of evolution was beyond tedium. They never bothered with intellect, all instinct, fear, sex and food, after that, nothing. So when the next experiment got started, and then continuously got eaten, the good old terrible lizard had to go. Well, once a number of brain stems had been saved to help the newer species on their way, and here we are."

She looks at me, trying to decide if they made a huge error of judgement.

"Of course there's been a lot of manipulation of existing creatures, advancing one here, removing the relevant parts and adding to other things to create something closer to what they need."

"What do they need from us?"

She looks thoughtful and tense.

"I don't know. All I can tell you is that you were a multi-culture project, there was about eight or ten different groups involved in your creation, all adding bits that they wanted to see developing."

She relaxes and smiles a little, cheekily.

"Anyway, you finally got upright after a long time, but I do believe that your purpose is emotions, not physical. We are a lot older as a race than yours, and we have had a straight run through, yours is on its sixth incarnation.

"I think that initially we were to feed on lower emotions, to see what happens. If you can be easily controlled, will you become intelligent, or progress, who knows?"

"Well, certainly not me."

"I was told that originally we both shared the same dimension, and we happily fed off you, until that is, you developed cunning and became carnivorous, things got messy. One of us had to go, we got our own dimension and the ability to travel between them."

"You say that we are based on different species?"

"Yes, most added a bit to you."

"Is that why when an embryo first develops it has gills?"

"Yes then fur, and a tail, and is basically a reptile first."

"No wonder I get so confused."

I can't say that I understand much of this. "Why don't the children have spooks on them?"

"Their energy is wrong for us, until they start to change into adults; it is just the wrong type of energy."

"I see," I said, not seeing at all. "But you said that the controllers can?"

She goes quiet, looking sadly at the floor.

"They feed off the fear, but worse than that, physically they get sexual pleasure from the child's energy, and the things that they do causes terror in the children. This releases a hormone into the children's blood, it's this that they must devour in order to maintain their physical body in this dimension. Not just your human children, but our children also."

"How can you feed on energy alone?"

"Well, firstly it makes sense to, you see, you rear a cow, it takes a couple of years, say, you slaughter it and it's gone, eaten. We feed on you time after time, year in year out, so we thrive."

"Hmm, I see."

"But if you get an atom, it is made of fields of energy, these have frequencies, these join together and become things. So as a group, say a tree-shaped group of atoms, must therefore vibrate at a tree frequency, so it appears to be a tree. But emotions are also energy, so for us it's no different to take in emotion energy as for you to take in the fruit from a tree, it's all energy, it just comes in different shapes."

I can vaguely see where she is coming from, but it's making my brain hurt thinking about it.

I rub the sides of my head, trying to take it all in.

"To speed up the process of developing you, the creators altered the breeding cycle from one season a year to about twelve. At first there were many experiments taking place on you, but most overlapped to find the best reptile forms, that's us, and the most useable humans. It's a very fine balance, the first lot had strength for work, but no Intelligence, these were aimed to be a slave race, to mine for gold mainly. But were an utter failure, not sufficient intelligence to carry out the simplest of tasks, so the next lot would have needed strength and intelligence, not a good combination, not in a slave race. So instead, they also made them docile. Again, an utter flop."

She grins at me, she really has a cheeky grin. "They just had no get up and go in them, so getting them to work was impossible. So testosterone was added, yes the male ego, the competitive edge, the need to mate, and all the rest of lunacy that makes a male."

Oh great, I'm talking to a feminist lizard.

"Meanwhile, we also had to deal with beings with their own agendas, which is why we vary so much in size and shape. I am a very close hybrid to you humans, this was to find out if the reptilian race could develop emotions, feelings and especially intuition."

"How do the controllers fit in?"

"That bunch of creeps are another race completely, but as both our races developed, they began to develop unwanted independent tendencies, so they had to be herded into the necessary direction. Such as living together in cities, to concentrate the negative energy, the controllers do the herding, setting a thousand ways of holding you back, causing unhappiness, misery, addictions. The controllers also feed off the energy created by large crowds, but not sporting event type crowds, but riots and anger, protesting, that's why so many peaceful protests break down into open violence. We were developed to feed off specific energies, some different types of disease. All a disease is, is a cell at a different frequency, so each disease has its own, as you say, spook. Some feed on depression, controllers fear and anger, and so on."

"What about you? What type of energy do you feed on?"

A pained expression crosses her face. "When somebody dies, they release a large amount of energy. It's the energy that holds the mind and body together, well, I feed on the release of that, I can't help it. It's simply what I am, I don't get pleasure from it, and I do try to soothe the person, to make it smoother for them."

She got quite emotional about this point.

"OK, I'm not judging you, only wanting to know, that's all."

"You don't hate me for that, do you?"

I am surprised that she is showing genuine emotion about this, and that it should matter, hating her or not. It's just not very reptilian.

She moves closer to me and rests her head on my shoulder.

"I'm just a freak. I don't like what I have to do to feed, but I have no choice, what can I do?"

I put my hand on her shoulder. "Well, it's not like you go round killing, is it, so don't worry. Lots of people eat meat, it doesn't make them bad people, it's just how it is, survival."

Her skin is surprisingly warm, for some reason I had expected it to be cooler.

"You know an awful lot about our distant history, have you read up about it or something"

She looks at me like I'm an utter imbecile. "Don't be silly, they told me."

"What like in a dream or something?"

I get a look to show that I have just convinced her I'm an imbecile.

"No, I told you, I spoke to them."

"The beings that actually created us, humanity, you talked to them?"

"Yes."

"So you spoke to god?"

"God? You are experiments, not divine." She sighs. "It's them who asked me to join up with you."

I got a look that I thought was reserved only for Debs when explaining things to me.

"Most see you as a waste of resources, but I got a message to meet one of the top elders, after I had first met you. He told me that I should work with you."

"Oh." I decide not to say I see, because I clearly don't.

"OK, let me explain. Because I'm of a higher frequency than most, I can travel further than the next dimension, that's also why I can spend time in this particular dimension, close to yours, without it tiring me."

"Ah, at last something I can understand."

"It's to do with the universal increase in the frequency, this planet's energy is evolving, and I mean fast, now! And as a result, the energy begins to raise in all the things on the planet, even humans."

"Even us?" I ask this entirely through sarcasm, but it's not noticed.

"Even you humans! Well, no, that's not entirely true, not all humans, you see there is a choice, move on, or get left behind."

"If you keep in tune with the planet, you advance, evolve, the higher your energy the more evolved you get, the closer to the planet's energy you get, the more is available to you."

She faces me. "That's why we have to work together."

"We do?"

"Yes, to stop the controllers."

I think of the huge terrifying reptile and feel that stopping one of them alone may not be an easy task.

"Doing what?"

"Well, if you evolve, even a few of you, then they will lose control, they can't evolve, you see, so a controller without control is nothing."

"What are they going to do?"

"Are doing! Food without vitality, obesity, addictions, drugs, alcohol, lack of physical energy, it's all to slow your frequency, even getting you to live in crowded environments. Then there's the next war coming, it's designed to reduce your population by about eight in ten people. And us by the same, so we both will be easier to control and so feed off us. But it's not just that, for them it's all about fear, they need it, not just as a food source, it's an addiction!"

"Whoa there, back up a notch. War?"

"It's been planned for a while now, but yes, they feel that they now have the technology to reduce the population sufficiently to make humanity live in sufficient fear, to live forever in their grip."

My head is going to explode, and I feel as though I'm going to vomit.

"What's been done to prevent it, somebody must be able to stop this."

"Something is being done, I was created differently, and you have been made different, I think that we are supposed to work together, together we form a bridge between the dimensions."

Whereas I think that this sounds very poetic, I really don't think that somebody, somewhere has made a very good choice.

"So hang on, there's about seven billion of us, reduced by eighty per cent—"

"Or more."

"Thanks, that's over six billion people. And I assume there's roughly the same of you. That's twelve billion lives."

"Ten times more."

"Pardon?"

"Ten times more of us than you. That makes sixty-six billion. Are you all right, you seem to be regurgitating your food?"

"Sorry." I try to stand but my legs are weak.

I look at her. "Liza."

"Yes."

"I think we need a bigger boat."

"What?"

"Never mind, against how many controllers?"

"Well, somewhere between a quarter of a million and a million, but that's only approximate."

She sounds like she is avoiding telling me something.

"What is it?"

"Well, they have an army as well, the blackguards," she adds quickly. "But they can only come into your realm for a few seconds!"

"Oh, that's OK then."

"Is it? Oh good."

I try to stand, but my legs are suddenly shaky from fear, so I sit down again, she watches me, uncertain of what to make of me.

"You still don't get sarcasm, do you?" I take a deep breath. "And approximately, pray tell, how many, and what come to think of it, what are, the blackguards?"

She sits facing me, looking seriously at me.

"They sort of, are the controllers." She shrugs. "Well thugs, I suppose, they do the heavy violence and spread fear amongst us, there's a million or so, you would probably think of them as demons. You are doing that regurgitation thing again. Are you sure that you are all right?"

Everything feels unreal, I take a look around, everything appears normal, people in the distance going about their own business, everything appears in ultra-sharp focus. It's like every leaf, every tree has suddenly been projected in ultra-high definition, I suppose my body is reacting in a survival mode, looking for a danger hiding somewhere close. A couple walk close by, holding hands, I can't help but wonder if they would be as happy if they was talking to an invisible reptile, who is talking me into facing a demon army? Oddly though seeing the couple helps me to decide, I watch them walk into the distance.

When I get my breath again, I stand shaking. "Great, so the pair of us are facing an inter-dimensional army of two million demons?"

"Approximately, two million, it might be less!"

She stands by me, looking afraid, but hopeful that knocking the figures down a little may yet convince me it will be OK.

"Well, that makes all the difference; they won't stand a chance against us, will they?"

She brightens up at this, looking a little more hopeful at me.

"Oh good, so you will help us?"

"You still aren't getting the sarcasm thing, are you?"

"What?" She looks small, afraid and vulnerable, I have no idea what I could possibly do against so many. I can't even do my tax returns, never mind face an army alone, but I have a sneaking feeling that even if I tried to get away from this, it will come after me.

"Oh, never mind. How is it there's so many of you?"

"No enemies, we feed on energy, so there's no waste, no filler. So we don't need to feed often."

I think of the reptiles here on Earth and I don't think that they need to eat too often either.

"You seem to know a lot about what's going on."

"The controllers in our dimension tell us to make us afraid, to control us and feed off our fear."

"If there's so many of you, why not just stand up to the controllers?"

She looks sad at this.

"The majority of us are the lower caste." She gives a slight sneer. "You call the spooks, not great thinkers, only instinct to survive, and those of us who are more advanced, well, our brains are basically reptilian, food, fear and mating, all for oneself, no team players."

"They tell us to do as they want, and live, anyone stepping out of line is shown to be killed horrifically by the blackguards, and their families."

She shudders. "That's what happened to my family." She looks away. "But our frequency, it's beginning to increase also, many, especially in the higher castes are developing, like you are, so the controllers fear losing control over us also. So if you all die, we also will starve down to controllable numbers. We have known this for a long time, but only when you broke through, were we able to tell you."

"Can't you speak to the people in charge of us, to tell them what's happening, like they did to Debs and me?"

"No, that was simply a guide to an emotion, we have tried it, tried to warn you, but someone hearing voices in their head about demonic armies and evil controllers generally went mad or became religious or both."

"Hmm, I see what you mean, which reminds me, how is it that I understand you, I would imagine that your language is very different to mine?"

"It's complex, but when I think something that I wish to speak, it forms in my brain in the same way as if I am about to say it, like you, but it's projected by my mind in waves, like sound waves but so much higher, and you pick it up in your brain as if you have heard it, only your brain picks up the intention of each word and feels it rather than hears it, so you translate the patterns of intention as you would words, does that make sense?"

"No, but then I'm a builder, so it wouldn't. What does your language sound like? What's your name sound like?"

"You really want to know?"

"Yes, why not?"

"OK, here goes…"

There follows a series of clicks, snarls and high-pitched screams, birds fly panicking from trees, a little old lady walking her dog finds it suddenly going frantic, barking and snarling before attempting to run away. Squirrels are running away in blind panic.

"Oh, I see, head speaking it is then."

"You insisted." She grins.

"Why, if the creators created us as an experiment do they allow the controllers to kill us all off, surely, that messes up the original experiment?"

"Well, as we don't know what the original experiment was, and each race wanted to run their own agenda, who can tell what is the creator's work."

"Surely having a race of super hybrids bump us off isn't in their agenda?"

"I don't think it is, or why go to the trouble to make us aware, so we can do something about it?"

"It's just not cricket, is it?"

"Eh?"

"Seems to me that someone has put in a deliberate evil, something to make the mix more entertaining to watch."

"It's a game?"

"Of sorts, yes, our ancient people used to tell stories of gods, and how they would use people, send them on quests, adventures to see what they would do."

"I don't want us all to die just to entertain something."

"No, you're right, let's muck up their plans."

"What are we going to do."

"Not sure."

"Good plan."

"Well at least you're learning sarcasm…"

My phone rings and Deborah's name shows.

11

"Hello, gorge—" I start to say but immediately I'm cut short by her hysterically shouting. I can hear all the dogs going frantic, barking furiously. I'm telling her to calm down and tell me what's happening. I finally make out that some men, three or four, are trying to break into the house. My van is miles away, and it's a forty-minute drive home even if I had the van.

Liza is shouting at me to tell her what's wrong, I tell her using my mind even while trying to talk to Deborah.

"Ask her if they are bald."

The panic is at a hysterical level now.

Liza goes, shouting something about help, moments later she is back, with the cavalry.

The cavalry in this case is a lizard, and whereas Liza, is delicate and smooth, this one isn't! I almost fall over in shock. It's as if something designed it to show just how vicious something can be. It has razor-like claws on its hands and feet, jagged scales, a hide like armour, and a row of fangs and teeth that are nightmare inducing. But most of all it must be three times my height.

I hear a very polite, well-spoken almost aristocratic female voice in my head. "I understand that you have a small problem. I'm sure that I can be of some assistance."

Liza's voice comes into my head.

"Concentrate on the home, calm down, think clearly, thank you, don't worry."

Both are gone again.

I can still hear that Deborah is terrified, I try to tell her help is coming, but she isn't listening.

Suddenly she goes silent. I'm shouting into the phone, pleading for her to talk to me.

Finally, after what seems ages to me, in a quiet voice I hear her say, "They have fallen to pieces."

"What?"

"They were almost in when their arms and legs flew off them."

"Have they gone now?"

Liza appears.

She smiles at me. I hope it's a smile anyway. "They have gone, they are in lots of places now, and cover several dimensions."

The urge not to ask is overpowering.

"Who are they?"

I look at the lizard, dripping with whoever they were.

"Sorry were they…"

"The controllers' little soldiers, they project themselves into this dimension, but are not fully here. It takes enormous amounts of energy for them to become physical in this dimension that's why they sweat so much, but their root is in the feeding dimension, so we are able to get to them there."

"Will they be back?"

"Definitely."

The big lizard bends down so its face is close to mine, I hear her voice.

"I was attacked by some things, small and hairy, very noisy."

"That's the toy poodles; you haven't hurt them, have you?"

"Absolutely not, I so admired the utter devotion that they showed in defending your Deborah person, one hundred per cent commitment, zero per cent effective, though."

"Well two have no teeth, one's losing her sight and one's totally blind."

"That explains why one faced the opposite direction most of the time, still it didn't back down. Courage, that's what they have. I have decided, I will protect your friends, but it won't be safe where they are, can they move to somewhere else?"

"She has her own house, she can go there."

"Excellent, ask her to go outside the house, I will speak to her, she won't see me but I can make her hear. There was protection on the house, it was old but still enough to prevent them getting in, if not for that I doubt she would have had time to make the call to you."

I speak to Deborah, tell her what to do, and hang up. The bodyguard disappears and returns a minute later. "I have spoken to her, now think of the house."

I concentrate on her house, the big lizard concentrates, and tells me she has it and is gone.

By the time I get Deborah on the phone to tell her to move to her own house, she is in the car and setting off. Her new bodyguard disappears to go to her house to protect her, and I am left with Liza.

"Looks like we do have some help."

"She is of the ancient warrior caste. Going back in time they were developed to protect us, but the controllers have made them outcasts. It's hard for them now, the controllers try to get rid of them, but they manage to keep going."

12

With all the concern over Deborah, I hadn't noticed the police in the park approaching me from several directions. I looked up and saw them, but it didn't register at first, I haven't done anything against the law. But I finally noticed how they were looking at me, then talking into their radios. I got a nasty sinking feeling in the pit of my stomach, in front was the accountant from the hospital, along with his blood hungry nurse, I had been distracted and now they were closing in on me, as did the local constabulary. "Oh bugger."

"What?"

"Company."

"What are you going to do?"

"Only one thing to do."

Personally, I hate violence of any type, but this time I am going to make an exception. In t'ai chi they teach you to gather your chi energy and focus it into a strike. I can't say that I had ever done this before, but I decided to give it my best shot. I walked quickly towards the accountant, he was running to make a grab at me, so when I punched him square on the chin, the combined momentum of his running, me moving forwards and my punch, hit him very hard. He looked surprised for a moment, then dropped.

That hurt my hand so much, I stood over him and sent all the loving energy that I could into him. I closed my eyes, and was surprised to see just how much damage the chi energy had done to the reptile in him. It had opened a gaping hole in its chest at the height of the accountant's chin. But as soon as the loving energy hit, it just exploded.

The nurse had been shocked, but now sprang at me, I put out my hand to stop her hitting me and immediately felt a deep burning pain in my hand. A syringe was sticking all the way through my hand, entering the palm and sticking out the back by a good two inches.

I made a grab for her, but a burly officer tackled me to the floor. I reached out for the nurse, falling onto her and bringing her down under me. She never made a sound, but began shaking wildly, her heels stamping on the ground then she froze. I was pulled off her, the weight of my body had emptied the needle into her, and whatever was in it had been meant for me. I closed my eyes to see her lizard now helpless on the floor. Spooks suddenly appeared and tore into it, ripping it apart. Liza was feeding quickly off the pair of the human elements, she looked at me gave me a shrug and continued.

I was roughly handcuffed, the syringe not very carefully removed and bagged, and having been sufficiently pushed and roughed about in front of a growing crowd of people, my rights were read to me, and I was led to a car, and with lights flashing, sped away.

13

I'm sitting in a grey room, a table in front of me, another chair opposite me and one in the corner. It has been decorated in a way that emphasises how drab a room, and possibly the rest of your life, can be.

A man walks in, he's tall, slim and wears a weary demeanour, a sort of 'here we go again, same bullshit lies, why me?' look about him. I close my eyes and scan him, around his waist are spooks, translucent grey green with black insides. They are feeding frantically, there are other spooks around him, but these have a nasty menace about them.

He slaps some papers on the table, so I think that I will save him the bother.

"Sorry."

He actually looks surprised — obviously, not the usual start to an interrogation.

"Why?"

"Because I am."

He looks at me to decide whether I am trying to be clever.

"No, not why did you say it, why are you sorry?"

"Oh, I see. Two reasons, I'm sorry that the events have sort of overtaken me and I have ended up here, and sorry that your cancer is in such an advanced state."

He stares at me long and hard, he looks furious, but staying professional.

"I will make a deal with you."

"I really don't think that you are in a position to make deals."

"Maybe not, but here it is, I will tell you everything, every last detail, in exchange for a cup of tea."

"Are you trying to be funny?"

"No, I have been in hospital for weeks and I am gagging for a decent cup of tea."

I think that I almost see a smile.

"I promise not to leave anything out."

"Oh all right, but the tea here is awful."

"Sounds good to me, milk no sugar."

He leaves, a young police woman sits in the corner on the other chair. She has a couple of spooks on her, but only small, I guess that she must be new to the police.

He comes back in, puts down a cup of tea, which as promised is awful, but it's tea, so it's all good. I take a long drink. He is looking at me with a slightly annoyed look. "So how long do I have to put up with this?"

"Sorry, what?"

"The keeping your eyes shut routine."

"What oh sorry, I forgot to open them." I keep them closed for a moment longer. I quietly ask him, "How long?" He stiffens and for a moment I think that he's going to hit me.

"Never mind, don't say anything for a minute; I'm going to remove it."

He is about to say something but I turn on the reiki, feeling the energy flow through me. I direct it to his waist, something is happening to me, the energy is getting stronger by the day, I don't understand it, but it feels exhilarating to be part of. The man obviously feels something, his eyes go wide, but he doesn't say anything. After little more than a minute, I feel the resistance fade and disappear, I put symbols on him as a protection to prevent it returning,

"All done. Now to business. What I'm about to tell you is, frankly unbelievable, I still can't believe it myself. But I must first tell you that as soon as I tell you this, your life will be in danger. Here goes."

So I begin to tell him, from my accident, the accountant, the blood hungry nurse, the whole thing, I'm just at the part where I'm in the park when Liza rushes in, "Outside, there's a controller, he's sending for some of the bald men to kill you, this time they will have guns."

"OK, describe the controller to me."

"Officer, there's a man outside, he's going to try to have me killed." Liza describes him to me and I relay it to the officer.

"Tall, almost bald, sweating, overweight, a brown jacket, patches on the elbows, tie of brown, pleated tan trousers, brogue shoes." I relay the information from Liza, then add. "He has sent for a team to eliminate me, and as you have spoken to me, the two of you also. He is part of the paedophile ring I told you about. I have some proof on my phone, that's partly why they don't want me to speak to anyone, well that and the plan to eliminate eighty per cent of the world's population."

His eyebrows raise.

"Oh, yes."

"I have to stop it."

"Alone?" The eyebrows raise again.

"No, I have friends, one is standing behind you."

"Oh, the bogeyman, is it?
"

"No, she is a reptilian-type being, from the next dimension." As I say it, it sounds wrong even to me.

"Oh, a reptile bogeyman!"

"I told you, she is a female, she is actually quite attractive, although some of her friends are real nightmares, I will see if she can communicate with you."

Liza places her hands on his head.

"You said I'm attractive."

The officer tries to duck in surprise.

"OK, not the message that I was hoping for."

Liza goes to the young lady officer, places her hands on her head. "Do you mean it?"

"Yes, you are sort of cute, and if you were human, I would say that you had a great figure."

The woman PC's eyes open wide in shock.

"Sorry about that."

"Liza, keep an eye on things, let me know how long we have."

She disappears.

The policeman looks at me as if I'm mad, is about to speak when someone urgently knocks on the door. He answers it, I hear urgent agitated voices.

"What do you mean you can see it."

"A bloody big lizard, in the room, here look for yourself!"

He returns moments later looking annoyed but less sure of himself.

He looks angrily at me. "What kind of crap are you pulling here?"

He is going to go on but there's another knock at the door, the young woman PC opens it. There's a voice, she calls the police officer over, he sighs. "What now?" Goes to the door to speak to a man outside, a sweating, almost bald man in a jacket.

"What has he told you? Ignore it all he's a dangerous killer."

"He was just starting to talk."

The new man shouts angrily.

"What did he say, it's lies every word."

The officer walks back into the room.

"That's just weird what's going on; you had better tell me now."

Liza bursts in. "They're here!"

"Liza, get out, I'm going to stop them, I don't want you getting caught up in the energy."

She wants to complain, but leaves.

"They are here now, I'm going to try to protect us, but don't know how effective it will be, just be careful…"

I ignore everything, and allow the reiki energy to build, growing in the room filling it and inside me. I hold it back, building it to be released.

I realise that Liza must also be gaining in frequency, if she is being picked up on camera now, she must be very close to our frequencies.

The door bursts open, three bald sweating men in dark suits burst in, shooting handguns wildly.

I release a wave of the highest energy that I can, and combined with the built-up energy in the room, the men recoil, drop their guns and begin to panic. the door has closed behind them, and with it automatically locking, they are trapped inside. The energy quickly eats away at them, they crumple down and dissolve into a thick gooey puddle. This rapidly disappears, leaving only three smoking handguns and some holes in the wall.

"What the hell was that?"

Officers rush into the room.

"I think that you were about to fetch my phone to look at evidence of a top paedophile ring."

14

I go through my story again, only in a different room, and with a bit more receptive audience this time. I tell him what happened, what I know, what I'm guessing at, and then finally, what I imagine might happen.

At the end of this Liza comes to tell me that my house has sort of blown up and burned down.

The officer confirms this minutes later. This is great, I have lost everything I own, OK owned, I'm wanted by the law, and now homeless, and mightily pissed off.

But at least the inspector, whose name is Robertson, is listening, well asking.

I look at the inspector, trying to work him out, he wears a tweed jacket, brown trousers and a faded denim shirt, it sort of all goes together, but not totally. I don't think that he is married, no way would his wife allow him to wear this outfit, he dresses more like a geography teacher. My eyes are drawn constantly to his face though. He is tall, slim built, but it's the drawn, tired expression that you see, the dark rings developing under his eyes, a weary look in his eyes, with a good amount of pain in the mix, physical and mental. His skin seems to be losing the battle against gravity and life.

"How do the lizards kill people?" He startled me when he spoke, bringing my mind back to the situation.

"Most don't, just the ones that are the controllers, who are a different breed, they have human elements to them."

"You told me that they feed on death."

"They don't kill you, they just hang around until it happens. They can influence you, to try your first cigarette, for example, but you can easily say no to their suggestions. Usually, they don't need to do anything, people are perfectly capable of cocking up on their own."

"You said they live off cancers and illness?"

"They do, every illness has its unique frequency, and when the body, or a part of it, lowers to that level the illness matches, it can develop, and along comes a spook to feed on it. Reiki, and other healing methods simply raise the frequency back to that of health, so the disease cannot exist in a cell with a frequency higher than itself."

"How can they influence people?"

"Let's see now. OK, people are made of two parts, internal and external. An example is you are driving to work, some idiot cuts you up and causes you to brake hard, your heart races and you swear, you get to work, tell everyone about it, it stays in your mind all day. However, the external event lasted only a moment, and no damage was done to either you or your car, yet all day you are sending energy into an event which is now entirely internal. You could just have easily said something came relatively close to happening, but in reality, nothing happened, yet you have spent the day pumping energy into nothing, a non-event. Well, this energy is what they feed on, so they slip a little suggestion here and there, a reminder so that you tell someone else, relive it a little more, so it goes on feeding them. After time you get into this frame of mind all the time, they have a permanent supply of food, you operate at a lower frequency, it lowers down to disease, depression, whatever, you are fed off until you die, then all that stored energy is released."

"Nice…"

"But it's your choice, same situation, you get cut up and think, 'Wow he's in a hurry, hope he gets there safely', and don't give it another thought. They whisper to you, that you should be angry, you think nothing happened, they go, you feel good about the day, no food for spooks."

"What if you do crash, what then?"

"Exchange insurance details, it is up to you how you react. People are of a much higher intelligence." I hear Liza cough. "Luckily for the spooks we choose not to use it."

"And I suppose that you are of a higher intelligence then."

Both Liza and I look at him in shock. Then we laugh.

"I am a builder, I am utterly skint all the time, I barely scrape by, all I have to my name is a rusty van that only starts if I'm pointing downhill, these clothes and a very cold house. OK, had a cold house. I really don't think that is being clever."

"So what are you doing here?"

I sigh. "There's been a series of events, of which I really have no control over that has put me on a path, and now I have to follow that path, and I really don't think that it's going to be a nice path."

"Well, you have this healing thing."

"Anyone can do that, I admit though, it's growing by the day, I can feel it flow through me and it feels amazing."

"So how are you going to stop this genocide thing?"

"I have a feeling that it will come to me, like it or not. But I think that fear is the key."

"Fear?"

"In both dimensions fear has been used as a means of control."

He looks at me blankly.

"Fear, it's only a frequency, one they live off. Come to think of it we all live in fear, fear of losing our job, fear of losing a loved one, our homes, not being able to pay the bills. Well that's how I live anyway."

"Tell me about it."

"It's not just fear of the physical, like pain or death, but the financial fear, the what if, fear. That's how we are controlled, so that we are constantly fed upon. Fear will be used as part of the final reduction in numbers, people will be afraid to stand out or speak up even when we are being dumped upon."

I think for a few moments. "I have to turn the fear into love."

"Love, getting all soppy now, all lovey-dovey are we."

"No, not like that, Fear, love, they are only emotions; they are only energy with their own frequencies. Love is the highest of the frequencies we can use, so it's more powerful. It's like taking a candle into a dark room, you light the candle and no matter how dark it was, the candle gives off light, it banishes the darkness. We just give those names, love, hate, fear. It's just names for particular frequencies, so we understand each other. It works like cracking glass with sound. Their cells break, and they just, well, fall apart."

"You said that the solar system is increasing in frequency, so will the spooks be visible to us all, if they increase?"

"No, we should remain that same amount in front, but mostly, like us, the majority won't grow, the majority will be left behind, a small percentage will move on, many won't even be aware that it's happened to them. Also, they are two dimensions away, theirs, the dimension next to us where they feed, then ours. But looking at Liza, how she is growing, it's likely that some will be able to visit us, perhaps even live amongst us."

"Seems a bit unfair that some won't progress."

"Not really, it's a personal choice that you make, every day come to think of it, you choose what you eat, if you want to do healthy or slobby things, all your own choice. Look around you, it's happening everywhere, right now."

"Are there many dimensions?"

"Possibly an infinite number, the potential is staggering, it explains why, despite searching the skies constantly, nothing is seen travelling about, why bother spending generations in a spaceship when you can hop into another dimension and be there instantly."

"I think that you are giving me a headache."

"You think it's giving you a headache, you are a police inspector, I'm just a bloomin' builder, I can barely write out an invoice. It's a real learning curve for me, is this."

"What about the controllers? What do you know about them, it seems to me that they are the key to all this?"

"Definitely, all I know is that they were bred to control us and them. In certain circumstances the higher ones, the lizards, can exist temporarily in our dimension. It requires a lot of palaver, rituals, we call it black magic, summoning demons, this is just a way of altering the frequency in an enclosed space to drag one through to here."

"Bet that they love that!"

"Too right, they just pop over for a quick feed and suddenly some arsehole in a cloak is telling them that they must obey them, it can be pretty painful for them in this dimension, no wonder that they seem wild. Mind you, there's some you just wouldn't want to drag over, you should see Deborah's bodyguard, very intelligent but utterly terrifying. I think that if Deborah did see her, she would freak.

"But the controllers not only feed off fear, they also have physical bodies, so need food like us, mainly the flesh of children, the fear as they die causes the release of a chemical in their blood. It's like an addiction for the controllers, they get into frenzies, nasty! And of course, if they feed on fear and anger, if people demonstrate, protest, especially violently, it simply makes them grow in strength, it feeds them. If the crowd sat and meditated, it could potentially kill them, so they send a few thugs in to turn it violent, bingo feeding time for controllers."

"Reminds me of once, in an American city, I think it was Seattle, an experiment was carried out, to measure what's known as the Maharishi effect. What they did was to get a group of people to meditate on peace, for three weeks, to see the effect it would have on the crime rates. It was so successful that halfway through the experiment, the local police force actually took over; violent crime fell by over twenty-five per cent. This has been done a few times around the world, in the end it was worked out that to bring about world peace it would take one per cent of a city of a million people cubed, I really can't do the maths right now, but around eighty people, for a city. And it was worked out, obviously not by me, that about eight thousand people would tip the scales and bring world peace. That's the trouble with science, did the experiment, got the results, and did nothing else."

"That's the thing tipping the balance, it doesn't need everyone to join in, just a very small percentage, just enough to start the frequency rising, then it gains its own momentum, all we need is eight thousand Tibetan monks on my side and we could scupper their plans for good."

"Assuming, of course, that you are guessing correctly, and haven't been fed a pack of lies by a load of demonic lizards."

"Well, yes there is that, of course. I'm just going on my gut feelings, speaking of guts, any chance of a cup of tea?"

"Typical builder."

15

Later I am led down to the cells; I don't think that the inspector really knew what to do with me. I am starting to feel a bit fed up with it all, I have had my house blown up, been shot at and attempted needling. Worse of all is that my music centre is gone, it's old, well it was old, but with the old-fashioned separates, lovely sound, plus my record collection, damn!

Liza is beside me, a couple of older uniformed police are talking. Best check first for lizards, you never know where they might be lurking, seen any lizards here?

"None here."

Liza pulls a face and sticks out her tongue.

"Actually, she is right beside you, check your monitors, and if you must know, there's some feeding off you both right now."

Which, looking at it, is probably why I get pushed into a cell that has wall to wall vomit and urine smells. I look at the policeman. "Meet Bob," he says, not hiding his enjoyment of my reaction.

"You are kidding me?" On a bench, a large bundle of rags moved slightly, Liza walked over and sniffed the air.

"About a hundred days left," she says in my mind.

The rags gave out a wail.

"Give or take," adds Liza.

There's a longer wailing sob.

"Take," sniffs Liza.

The bearded end of the rags lets out a long scream, which dies off into a sobbing moan. "They're all over us, they're everywhere, they never let go." More sobs follow. A face follows the beard out of the rags.

"Looks like it's going to be a long night."

"They suck you dry, they won't ever leave you." then some babbling noise and the face retreats back into the rags.

I close my eyes, and am horrified by the sheer number of spooks on him, Liza looks down at him, I can see her face is deep in thought. Suddenly, she shouts in her language.

I find myself on the floor covering my ears. "Whoa there. Enclosed space, not good." But all the spooks have left him. The rags moaned, Liza reached out, put her hands gently on his head, I can hear her voice, very gently saying, "It's OK, they have gone now, sit up, talk to us"

Slowly he props himself up. "They've gone, what ya done?" He can obviously see the spooks, he stares at Liza, who has come to sit beside me.

"Why haven't you got any of the buggers on you, and how come you get a fancy looking one, how come?"

"Hello, this is Liza. We have teamed up to save our worlds." I must confess that I really enjoyed saying that, but Liza is giving me a type of look that normally I get from Deborah. Perhaps it is me after all!

"She says that you only have about a hundred days to live."

"Oh yes, and how would you know?" Now that he speaks, a heady waft of alcohol begins to compete stoutly with the other odours.

"We sense it, taste it upon you, we have to so we know when to feed off you." A wailing sound comes from him. "Well we can hardly be expected to pick somebody and just wait around and hope that they may die soon. We would all die of starvation waiting, now, wouldn't we?"

"How is it that yours is a fine talking fancy one and I get crappy giant slug rejects?"

Liza looks at him. I sense that she is about to tell him the truth of why, so I jump in first.

"I don't smell of vomit."

"Oh."

"Or booze, or urine."

Sniffling sobs and a mumbled, "Sorry."

"How come that you can see them?"

"About ten years back, I had a good job, my own company, I actually employed people, I used to travel the world, had the flash cars, lovely house, and—" His voice breaks and he quietly weeps for a few moments,

"Go on."

97

"I had a wonderful wife, she was so beautiful, and she loved me, don't know why, but she did."

He waits a moment to pull himself together, as if thinking about what happened takes a lot of effort to talk about.

"Went to South America. It was a sort of man's week, you know, beer, cheap food, and a good laugh.

"One of the guys thought it would be a laugh to find a local, shaman, for us to drink one of the Indian brews that allowed you to see into the spirit world. Only, he insulted the shaman, called him a witch doctor, and started calling him a fraud. The guy was OK until he had a beer, then he became a total arsehole. The shaman said that we weren't ready to come back when we were sober, but we were so drunk, we didn't believe a word of it. But what we didn't know was that the shaman acts as a guide and needs to prepare himself, anyway we were showing off to each other. To prove I wasn't afraid, I necked the worst thing I have ever tasted, and immediately went into another realm, it was a nightmare, the things I saw." He shudders, his voice fails for a moment.

"And I haven't woke up from it yet." His voice trails off then returns quietly. "We were full of shit and cheap booze, the rest saw what happened to me and decided not to bother. The shaman did what he could, to be fair he went in to fetch me back, at a lot of danger to himself. I think that I would have been stuck there to this day if he hadn't. So when I came round a couple of days later, drenched in sweat, urine, and vomit, all I could see was these damn slug creatures all over me. I could hear them talking to me, telling me that I was a bum, that I didn't deserve a beautiful wife, and I am a failure, so I hit the booze, and crawled off to die, and here I am. A hundred days left you say? Ha, can't come fast enough for me."

He begins openly crying. "I lost it all, everything, ruined, just so I could show off to my mates, I want to die, this isn't life, it's hell."

Liza sits beside him, puts her hands on him. "You know, you don't have to die, they aren't here now."

I look at Liza, taken aback by how tenderly she speaks to him. "You can turn it around, and we can help you."

"How?"

"He can show you, and anyway, you can always help us to save the world, if you are going to die, then you can do so as a hero."

I look at Liza, she sort of bows her head. "Well, it's one thing to feed, we all need to do that in some form to survive, but that is just taking it too far, typical lower caste behaviour."

"You snob."

She pulls her tongue out at me and laughs. "Well, it's true."

He looks at me. "She is right, though," I tell him. "You don't have to spend your life as lunch for some slimy lower spooks." He looks at me as if I'm crazy.

99

"It's true, they all feed off lower energies, the lower the energy, the slimier the spook."

I look at Liza. "Just trying to help."

"So if I go around all smiley and grinning, you say that I get a good looking spook to feed off me, a refined reptile?"

"No, they can't feed on higher emotions, so if, for example, you thought about how much you love your wife, feel that emotion of love, instead of the loss of her love, then they have nothing that they can feed off, not on you, even though you can see them on others. I mean look, I don't have any, do I?"

"No, but you have got her."

"Liza isn't feeding off me, she's a friend. She's different."

Liza smiles at me. "Friend?"

"What's with the name 'spooks'? I call them much worse."

"Oh, well, the first time I saw one, I thought that I was seeing a ghost," I say, feeling slightly foolish.

"Good name, but no such thing," says Liza.

"What?"

"Ghosts, no such thing."

I can't believe it. I am talking to an invisible inter-dimensional lizard, reptile girl, and she tells me that she doesn't believe in ghosts. I am about to point this out, but realise that it's a can of worms best left closed.

"You said that you can get rid of them, I mean no offence to you, in fact, if they were all like you, I probably wouldn't be smelling of vomit."

Liza's face is a picture as she tries to work out if this is a compliment, or to be angry.

"You will still see them, but they won't disturb you, it's easy to do."

"Any time someone tells you that something is easy to do, it never is."

"OK, the theory is easy, simple, but—"

"You see here we go…"

"All that you have to do is to raise your frequency."

"My what?"

"Yes, clean, eat fresh food, and I don't mean a burger that's still warm. Fresh veg. Oh, yes, don't do booze or drugs."

"And just as you were doing so well, you go all impossible on me."

I can't actually tell if he's serious or not.

"The food you eat raises or lowers your frequency, depending on the frequency of the food. This lowers or raises your energy levels; I don't mean how you feel, but the energy of your rate of vibration."

"Well, if I don't get a drink soon, I will be shaking like a leaf."

"Mm, not quite what I meant. Other things you can do are to exercise, and avoid fluoride."

"Oh yes, I will just get on my lycra and nip down to my aerobics class, tell them not to wait for me if I'm late."

"You really don't need to go all lycra on me, just go for a walk, that's all. But actually, I think a bit of dayglo would suit you."

"Matches me eyes. Anyway, I thought that fluoride was good for your teeth."

"No, not really, it's used as a rat killer, and in Australia used to keep the population of kangaroos down. It was first used to control the population of the concentration camps by the Nazis, it subdues people, you see."

"Nice."

"The best thing that you can do, though, is to meditate."

He looks at me as if I am speaking in tongues. Before the inevitable dismissive comments, I quickly tell him. "It's easy, I can teach you."

"That's all right for you, you work in the building trade, your mind is naturally blank."

I hear Liza sniggering quietly.

"OK, you don't need a blank mind, just a relaxed mind, I will show you."

After a great deal of shuffling, I get him sat upright, and as relaxed as the cell will allow. I notice Liza sitting as if she is going to join in, I don't know if that's safe for her, but I'm certain if it's not she will just disappear for a while.

"Picture yourself walking down a country lane, the sun is pleasantly warm on your back, you walk through a small gate into a lovely meadow, you walk over to a large shady tree, and sit down with your back to it. The flowers smell sweet, the grass is soft, you take off your boots, and rest.

"You let your mind relax, enjoying the day, you breathe deeply, taking in the fresh, scented air.

"You slowly let your mind go, it flows into the tree, first going down the trunk, down into the ground, you feel the cool, moist soil surrounding you, go further feeling how the roots are going deep into the ground. You follow them to their tips where you feel the moisture being absorbed in. You follow the moisture, back up through the root, getting thicker as they near the surface. You travel up the trunk, higher and higher, until you reach a limb. Passing along this you start down branches, then twigs and into the leaves.

"Here, you feel the sun upon you, bringing not only warmth, but the leaves turning the light into energy, you feel the energy start to flow into, then through you, you stay a while, looking over the surrounding meadow, taking in the beauty of the surroundings. You feel the energy in the leaf next to you, then the whole tree, casting your awareness out, you feel the loving energy that is generated by the natural world, slowly your awareness flows back into the tree, back down to your body. The energy from the tree inside you, as you reach your body, the tree starts to fill your body with a bright light, drawing out and absorbing the negative energies from the deepest darkest part of your soul. You enter your body to find it cleansed totally, and a wonderful loving energy flowing through not only your body, but your life. You stand, face the tree and thank it, show it respect, then looking around see the true beauty of the natural life all around you, you feel a peace and oneness deep inside. You walk back to the gate, take a final look, say your goodbyes and continue on your path."

He nods. "Nice that." He curls up and begins snoring.

"Do trees have feelings?"

"Apparently so, scientists have done tests and they think they can."

I go over to Bob. While he sleeps, I send him all the healing energy that I can, cleansing him and his aura, then placing protection on him. When I feel that I am finished, I ask that he finds peace within himself. I sit back down, he is snoring loudly now.

Liza is beside me. "Why did you help him?"

"He needs help, and I don't think that anyone has helped him in a long time."

"Wouldn't you be better saving your energies for yourself?"

"It doesn't work like that. When I send him energy it doesn't come from me, I don't make it, it comes from the universe, all that I do is to focus it. It's like getting a magnifying glass, daylight is all around, but if you focus the light passing through the glass it can set fire to things. Well, the energy is around us all the time, it's only when focused that it becomes concentrated enough to make things change. And as it flows through you, it charges you at the same time."

"So you only give energy to others so that you get stronger?"

"No, it makes the sender stronger so that they become better at focusing the energy. Speaking of which, when I first met you, the energy hurt you, but it doesn't seem to hurt you now."

"It doesn't hurt, it feels odd, not nasty. I can feel the energy going through me, I think that it's a bit like when you humans do something dangerous, like driving too fast, but get excited by it."

"Well, I'm glad that it's not hurting you any more. It must mean that your own frequency is rising, and quite quickly, as well. Why don't any of you feed off higher energies and emotions, it would help us to grow, and you at the same time?"

She looks sad. "Some have developed to do that, but all have died in a very horrible and very public manner as a result. The controllers make sure that none of us reach that state."

"But you are doing that, that must be putting you in great danger."

She suddenly looks small and frightened, and simply nods.

"Well, I don't know what I can do, but I will try my best to help you."

"It's the controllers, you see they can't evolve. We do in the same way you do, but because the controllers can't, if we do evolve, they would be left behind. They would lose their power over us, so they resort to increasing violence and fear, to keep us down, you also."

"Us?"

"The controllers in your realm, they encourage, through media and entertainment. Like sitting in a room playing a game, well into the night, so you don't rest, so you take stimulants, to stay awake, then you can't sleep so you play games. This disrupts natural sleep patterns, this lowers your energies, the stimulants lower energies, the games involve killing so that you lose the connections with humanity. While doing this you aren't connecting with the people, friends, family, and most of all, the spiritual connection with earth itself. On top of this add a lousy diet of low energy food, and we feed off you, depleting your energies further, so the lower castes can suck you clean, then you develop disease, or depression, we feed more, you suffer more, then you die, I feed on your final energy, that's it."

"Nice."

"Oh, it's all planned that way for you, by the controllers. You see the original experiment was for both our kinds to develop together, actually helping each other forwards. But the controllers came along and altered the direction for their own needs, now we hold you back, where we were supposed to be pushing you on."

I think about this and a growing sense of clarity begins to develop in my chest. I don't understand, not fully, I just feel that I have been shown another piece of a bigger puzzle.

"There's other ways, as well. Keeping you in debt, mortgages that you will never pay off, having to work harder and harder to pay, increasing utility payments, all making you into exhausted work slaves, trapped in an ever deepening rut."

"Tell me about it." I yawn. "Anyway, I'm going to try to sleep now, after all, we do have two worlds to save."

"No, there's just one world. We both belong to it. There is one other thing, it may be nothing, but, the controllers, well it is thought that they could be being controlled by higher forces themselves."

"It's like an onion…"

"It is?"

"Layers upon layers, mind you, it makes you wonder what's at the centre, doesn't it?"

16

A knocking on the cell door wakes me and Bob. My ankle hurts, so do my ribs, and my joints feel stiff, so a normal start to my day really.

I am amused to see Liza, resting with her head against me. I think just how fond of her I am, sort of like a younger sister, I feel very protective towards her.

Keys rattle, we all start to get up, Liza complaining that, "Reptiles don't do mornings."

"Not well anyway," I reply and get an angry look back. She is about to talk but the police officer who let us in is entering, and Bob bustles past her to go out, apologises to her and loudly whistles a tuneless song. We both turn in surprise at how chirpy he is, we watch him trying to get the constable to make us all a nice cup of tea, and complaining about the service.

Inspector Robertson appears and tells me that I am free to go. "Friends in high places," he tells me dryly.

"That I doubt."

"Yes, you take care, someone wants you out of here for a reason."

I get his phone number, just in case I have anything odd happen to me.

The PC is still being pestered by a really very chirpy Bob, who is informing him that the service is awful, and that he doesn't think that he will be coming back for a return stay. As he's leaving, he turns to say, "And, I mean no offence, but between you and me, the beds smell rather awful!"

We all look at him. Liza points out that it might not actually be the bed, but he's gone, just his happy tuneless whistling fading into the distance.

Liza follows me as I grumpily go through the processes of leaving. "I don't know what, but something just feels wrong to me. Never mind. "Bob, do you fancy getting a bite to eat and a nice cup of tea?" The three of us are all communicating without having to speak, and we never even realised.

17

In a nearby cafe, Bob tells us all about being successful, and living rough. He demolishes a full English while I have a couple of omelettes. Afterwards I head for the cash till, only to be told that my card has been declined. I know that there is money in the account, but having your card declined is just one of those things that really get me down. So I call the bank, and am informed, that due to my recent death, my assets, of about ninety pounds, are frozen. I inform the operator that I'm alive, but he has his computer's word against mine. It quickly gets sorted out when Liza pops into the office and greatly influences his way of thought. I quickly withdraw all I can and we are off, not really having any idea of where to. So, for lack of any real plan, we walk to my van. My spell in hospital has left me feeling unfit, so the half hour walk is nice, except for the constant complaining from Liza, who has never had to walk anywhere before. We walk up the final hill to where the van has been quietly rusting for weeks, so I am actually quite relieved to see it still there. Had it been towed away would not have come as a surprise. But there it is, all different shades of yellow and broody with rust. Kindly people have parked so close in front and behind it that pushing it to get it started is not an option. So I resort to the final desperate measure.

If you hit the starter motor hard enough, with a lot of luck, it sometimes makes the thing engage and it starts. So with zero confidence I get a heavy hammer from the tool box, climb underneath and am about to strike when I see two lovely shiny new wires running from the starter. I follow them to some grey modelling clay-like substance. Bob's face appears. "Hit it then."

"I don't want to any more!"

I point to the reason why and hear a scuffling as he retreats down the road. I slowly pull out my phone, carefully scrolling down the names stored, press call, and hear Inspector Robertson's voice. "Hello, you said to call if anything unusual should occur, well I was just wondering if you had the number for the bomb squad?"

The line isn't totally silent because I can hear his breathing, until finally, "Where are you?"

"Under my van."

"OK, I won't ask why, but get out from there… now."

I try to gently drag myself out from under the van by making almost no movement. Obviously, this fails and I have to get out, in a more energetic way. Once out, I head for Bob, and the growing sounds of sirens.

Eventually we sit with the inspector who has been helping to organise the evacuation of the school opposite and the nearby houses.

Bob helpfully comments, that if the bomb does go off, "At least the back of your van can't get untidier." And that, "It should help to dislodge the looser rust, at least."

I ignore the constant stream of witty van jokes coming my way.

Having spent what felt like forever we are allowed to go, the bomb disposal guy told us that it was very high-grade explosives. "You see that's what you get with friends in high places, only the best will do."

"Thanks, Bob, you are such a help."

The inspector looks at me. "Well, it seems that you have really pissed someone off."

He is totally at a loss as to what to do with me. It appears that whoever got me out of the police custody now wanted me to not be back in the police station. I was to be let go, 'at all costs', according to the inspector.

"Isn't that nice to know, someone cares."

"Cares that there aren't any witnesses, you look out, I have been told not to look into this." He gives me a meaningful look. "In fact, I have been sent down to London. Apparently, there is a big meeting of lots of important people, and I have been drafted in as part of the security. All rather convenient."

Bob points out to the inspector that if he doesn't go to London that his car may be 'upgraded' also.

The inspector is good enough to get someone to get my van started for me. It hasn't been run for weeks and is doubtful even if bumping it would work. "And the last thing we need is you stuck across the main road now."

Bob jumps in the van, I gave him my fluorescent work coat to wear. He complained bitterly that it smells sweaty, Liza sniffs it and agrees with him. "Well, it does!"

"OK, now sniff his coat."

She thinks for a moment and changes her mind. "I have smelled worse," she admits.

Liza tries to get in the van in the middle seat, but finds the seat taken by Monkey, my van mascot. It's the monkey from the old TV ads for the early computer networks, and is currently wearing a child-size, pink fluorescent vest, with 'Daddy's little helper' written on the back. She looks questioningly at me. "Don't ask! It's Monkey."

Bob carefully places the monkey in the back. "Where to?"

"Well, the inspector mentioned a big protest against the world's business and money elite."

"London it is then."

Bob shuffles about on the dashboard and produces two pairs of sunglasses. "It's a hundred and seventy miles to London, we have half a tank of diesel, it's midday and we're wearing sunglasses. Let's go!"

We both laugh, and set off singing *Blues Brother's* songs. Liza is utterly mystified, which makes it even funnier. My stomach is still churning. I feel ill that someone has tried to kill me. I am very worried about my immediate future, but at least we are doing something, even though we don't actually know what. Still, it feels good to be in the old van and be mobile.

Liza is still scowling at our singing, but to be fair, I would also scowl if I had to listen to me sing.

18

We trundle and grind our way down the M1 towards London, Liza and Bob are talking about how the controllers use fear to keep the population under their command. I am only half listening, but when she begins talking about the blackguard, the controllers' army of what we would think of as demons, she gets my attention. "They are merciless killers, they can cross into this dimension, although only for a few seconds, their skin is so black that it's more of an absence of colour, it's more of a solid shadow than an actual figure. Other than that, the only thing that you would notice would be a lot of very sharp fangs, and claws." She gives a shudder, I get the feeling that she is speaking from experience, rather than hearsay. "That is normally the last thing that is seen. They create a feeling of fear in their victims, they feed off this, it sends them into frenzies, and then they feed off the flesh of their victims, usually while they are alive."

"Sounds a cheery bunch, well, let's hope we don't have to meet any."

"If, say we did meet any, just asking, but how would you defend yourself against one?"

"That's difficult, most people just freeze. It's the way they project fear, it immobilises you. If you were able to act before that happens, because they are of such low energies, if you send them love, it would destroy them. But if you see one, you wouldn't immediately think loving thoughts. Other than that, even if you shot one, because it lives off pain, it would actually make it stronger."

"You talked of this plan to kill off most of our populations, why now, and how?"

"It has always been your destiny to evolve, to awaken, you, as a species should never have been held back, that wasn't part of the original experiment, you were supposed to evolve along with the planet."

"You mean like the Aboriginal people, or the native Americans?"

"Yes, both of these had to be erased of their knowledge, the true way. Of course, technology has always been intended to be used, as a part of the development, only it's supposed to be used for the overall good of humanity, not to show other people what food you are about to consume. It was supposed to be used with natural energies; they actually work well together."

"What happened?"

"It was all taken over by the controllers, the creators gave you the knowledge, it was part of the experiment, it was already programmed in you, but with the controllers on the scene, they took it over as it was evolving, and it just became a way to keep you all subdued, and of course build the military capabilities.

"And of course, there's the removing humanity from you, the constant surveillance, controlling you electronically, watching and monitoring, gaining information about your every move, and now even starting to have you all chipped, it's all a big con to keep you under control."

"So why get rid of us, if we are under control?"

"Originally there was the balance, the technology, and the spirit, though technology was overly encouraged, there still is the other side, and it's starting to emerge. Not in everyone, in fact, at first only very few, but now, it is predicted that the pendulum is swinging the other way, to find the natural balance." Bob's face is locked in concentration, he is biting his bottom lip as he hangs onto every word that Liza says.

"The controllers would have no influence over such people, in fact, the loving energies would wipe them out. So the only way to stop this is to wipe out humanity to stop this happening, and of course, following a war of this scale, the survivors will do anything to prevent a recurrence, and there you are, a few in such fear that they supply enough food for all of them, forever."

"War!" exclaims Bob. I feel like the bottom has dropped out of my stomach.

"That and the other tried and tested methods."

"Tried and tested?" Bob sounds horrified.

"Oh yes, there's first going to be the financial collapse to weaken you, then disease building up to war, all of which will make fabulous amounts of money for the elite. Putting them finally in the place where they need to be to implement the final solution."

"I have heard that saying before, and I hate it," I say more to myself.

"Yes, the last two wars were trial runs, they weren't entirely sure that they could manage global mobilisation, but now they can."

"So what you are telling us is that we face the people with sufficient power to start a war, and the controllers, who have an army of demons on their side."

"Yes."

"And all we are armed with is his fluffy bunny of love energy." Bob looks at me as he says this.

"We do have surprise as well," I reply

"You mean that you do have a plan?"

"Not yet, that's our surprise."

Bob looks at me, then Liza. "You do know that we are doomed? Don't you?"

"I must admit, I am not a gambling man, but if I was, I would be thinking, if they pull it off, with odds like that the prize would be unbelievable!"

They keep talking, but my mind tries to create a plan, deep down inside, a feeling is starting to seed, starting to grow, but right now I just can't put my finger on it. All I know is to head into the city, after that I really hope that my plan is brilliant, whatever it turns out to be…

19

I know that we are in London because everyone is driving like they are utterly crackers. I get the impression that the only way to drive is to behave like you are the only person who matters. Unfortunately, the best my van can do is a sedate trundle, the advantage is that it's already a wreck.

So we gradually grind our way onwards towards what I hope is the centre. Eventually the traffic is becoming so congested that we find a car park and abandon the van to start walking. As I leave the car park a feeling of loss comes over me. Everything I own is in that van, and I just can't stop thinking that I am seeing it for the last time.

Once again, my sense of direction leads us to being lost. I really don't know where here is in relation to the direction I want to be going, this is until a small group of people with placards walk past the end of the road. We tag along behind, they are all laughing and seem to be in excellent spirits, like they are going for a jolly day out. As we walk, a low rumble of sound can be heard, faint at first but growing, occasionally getting louder, then softening again. Sirens compete to be heard. We turn a corner and are struck by the sheer chaos ahead.

An enormous crowd is in front of us, it surges forward, the lines of police hold them back, and then push forwards themselves. Many of the protesters are wearing helmets and padding, they obviously have come prepared for violence, in fact seem to be doing all that they can to create it.

We look on as a group of protesters run close to us, smash a shop window and begin helping themselves to what they want. Liza watches, astonished. "Why did they do that?"

"Just taking advantage of a situation, that's all."

The atmosphere around us is heavy with tension, the laughing group of people are now angrily swearing at the police, many of whom are terrified, and everywhere the spooks are feeding. To our alarm, there are controllers in the crowd, they are urging the crowd on, using loud hailers to work the crowd up. Large lizards are making contact to create hatred in the crowd. I feel a sudden urge to kick the police to the floor and keep going when they are down. I turn around to come face to face with a seven-foot scaled creature with its long claws reaching out to me. "Piss off," I tell it then remember that this makes it actually stronger. I calm down and send it a burst of loving energy. Its face is utterly shocked for a brief moment, and it silently explodes. Liza nods to me, and gives a tut.

"Arseholes," she mutters and goes back to studying the crowd.

Despite the colossal noise, we can hear each other perfectly clear. "When will people learn that you can't fight for peace, fight is fight, a violent action, not a peaceful action."

"What do you suggest that they do?"

"Stop feeding the controllers for a start."

In the distance an expensive car arrives with police cars front and rear. The crowd surges forwards, the wave of energy it causes, is nauseous to me. I feel it all the way through my body. I can see the controllers feasting on the violent energy, they are raising the people around them into an angry frenzy. Liza has been studying hard; she turns to Bob and me as the dark car sweeps into an imposing Gothic style building.

"It's a rebirth ceremony."

"A what?" we both say together.

"Rebirthing, it takes a lot of energy to maintain the two forms, keeping the two together requires that every three or four years there must be a complete renewing of their energies. This is achieved by a rebirthing ceremony."

"What happens?"

"First, they will require a massive boost of energy, the more violent, the more massive, the better. This will sustain the lizard form to make it into this dimension and take part in a ceremony."

"Well, this crowd is giving that!"

The first part of the ceremony involves the torture sexual abuse, then slaughter of a child. This is for the human element, the adrenalin in a terrified child's blood when drunk, will allow the lizard element a portal in which to visit this world, where it can feast on the flesh of the victim, who could still be alive."

Liza is weeping as she says this.

"I am sorry, they aren't us, you know, not part of us." She is having to make a real effort to hold herself together. "The process is then repeated using one of our children."

"Come on you two, let's find a way to stop this."

"Well, it's obvious, isn't it?" We look at Bob to let him know it isn't obvious.

"Yes, no kids, no rebirth."

"That's true, and no crowd energy, no lizards."

"Or if the energy of the crowd changes to peace, and not violence."

I think that a sort of plan, if only in outline, is emerging.

"Liza, can you find a way, carefully, for us to get into that building, an open door or a window, and find out where the children are.

"Then, Bob, I will need a diversion, so we can get over this fence and get across to the building."

"What like?"

As he asks another car arrives with a police escort, the crowd surges and the police rush to where the crowd is almost through the perimeter fencing.

"Like that?"

"Exactly like that."

"Then what?"

"I get in, guided by Liza, we rescue the kids... Liza, can you get the children back to their own dimension?"

"It's possible, they will be in the feeding dimension, so should be moveable."

"Good you deal with them; I will deal with ours."

"You will need help, if there are a lot of them, some may be too scared to go with you."

"True, we need a young lady, like a teacher, someone that they will trust."

"What about her?"

I look around to where Liza points to, and setting up close to us is a van with a cameraman, sound man and pleasantly attractive young woman, obviously a presenter.

"Bingo! And she has her own reinforcements with her." A thought hits me — why not let the world see what's happening? Imagine if it's filmed and people learn what's happening."

"It would broaden the horizons somewhat, wouldn't it? So how will you get them to go with you?"

"Ego!"

So, never having successfully pitched a deal before in my life, I decide to wade in with the truth, although not all of it, yet.

"Hello, I am about to break into the building over there, and disrupt a ceremony, do you want to come with us?"

"Us?"

I look at Liza, am about to introduce her and remember that only Bob can see her.

"Oh yes, that scruffy guy, he's in a disguise, so that he can mingle and create a diversion."

I wave for Bob to come over, the lady sniffs and comments about going into deep cover a little too seriously. Bob replies that we are an elite squad of conspiracy activists.

"What sort of ceremony?" asks the cameraman. "Is it a satanic ritual?"

He looks a bit excited at this. "Yes, it is."

"With the robes and daggers?"

"No robes."

He looks disappointed. "All naked."

This cheers him up no end.

"Look it could get a bit nasty, if we are spotted, so I can't force you. But I think if you do come with us, you could not only be filming, but becoming a part of history in the making. If I am wrong, then you get some cool footage of the building where this meeting is being held."

During this time, Liza has slipped away to find a way in. She pops back into my view, talking very excitedly and visibly upset. "There's a way in, a door, it was locked, but I concentrated, and I did it, I opened the bolt, I was actually in this dimension for a moment."

"Well done, I knew you would find a way, and the children?"

She goes quiet now. "It's about to start, there's about a hundred children from each dimension, in a cage."

"Look, I'm sorry, I have just received information," I tap my ear as if there's a hidden microphone and receiver. "I can't ask you to go with me, there's about a hundred children in there about to be tortured and killed. I am going to stop it happening, but it's going to get dangerous."

A car arrives, Bob runs off, I don't know what he does, but within a minute, the crowd has the fencing down and is surging forwards. The police all run towards them. I run at the fence climbing like I never knew I could. Liza runs in front, and in a minute, I am against the wall crouching and running to the door. Liza leads me to a door, almost hidden in the bottom of a tower, there's weeds all around, but a slight path leading up to it. The door pushes open fairly easily, inside is dark, but I can make out shelves of gardening tools and a workbench, some sort of handyman or maintenance workshop, I guess. A hand grabs my shoulder, and I almost scream in fright, it's the sound engineer, panting, out of breath. He is a bit short, has a short unruly beard and is obviously out of condition. The camera guy is there, much more handsome and stronger looking, then the presenter bursts in.

She pulls the door closed behind her, gets her breath and says, "You are actually serious, aren't you?"

"Look, if I do get out of this, I give you my word that I will tell you all that I know. And if it is all true, then it will change everything. And I mean everything."

"And if you don't make it back?"

"Film it, and you won't need my explanation," Liza shows me a door hidden in the shadows. The cameraman switches on his camera to try different filters, to see what is the best lighting in the almost dark corridor.

I hear a whispered gasp. "Look, what the hell is that?"

"Don't know, nice arse though." Then a slight gasp as the presenter hits him.

"Not you, look!"

"I see that you have seen my source of intelligence, meet Liza. Liza, say hello."

She walks back to them, they back up slightly, she reaches out and touches the sound man. "Hello."

I can see on the camera that she is remarkably clear to them; she touches and says hello to the other two.

"The lizard girl's given me a boner." He receives another punch.

"Liza is from another dimension, we are working together to save her race, as well as humanity. Now come on, the ceremony is starting."

"You can talk to her?"

"Only by telepathy."

"Only telepathy."

The presenter says, "This is getting deep."

127

"You should see her bodyguard, come on, this way."

About this point, I am utterly terrified — there isn't a thing about this, that I don't find frightening; Liza must be picking up on this because she stops me. "The only way that you can get through this is by not showing fear." I am about to make a joke, but she stops me.

"I can smell your fear, it's like a bacon sandwich to them. Just food, and you have to find a way to cover it. Think now. Concentrate."

Do you ever find that the more serious a situation is, the easier it is to get the dreaded giggles?"

"A bacon sandwich?" And that's it, I'm in hysterics."

Liza looks at me at first in the way only a woman looks at a man when she thinks that he is barmy, but then says, "That's better, it's hiding it, now get ready to project love in case we meet the blackguards.

"And remember, they feed on not only fear but on anger too, so stay very calm, in control, no matter what. Don't worry, we will sneak in, take the children, escape, without even alerting the blackguards."

As I walk, I think about Deborah and the poodles, people, places. Anything that makes me feel good and happy.

"Liza. How many blackguards are there?"

"About a million."

"Liza, what I need from you now is to lie to me. Say 'Only a few,' something a little more reassuring."

We head down a flight of dark stone steps. At the bottom is an ancient wooden door with rusting ornate hinges, I have to push hard, but it opens. The camera crew emerge and we are stood on a balcony in a huge vaulted basement, lit with hundreds of huge candles. Looking down, I can see the cage with the children inside, I feel myself getting angry, but remembering the bacon sandwich advice, I think of the love that the children need. At the far end I can see a raised area with a stone altar, on it is a huge gold knife, and shackles so small that they could only be for a child.

I hear Liza give an almost silent sob, she turns to me. "This is how the upper caste is controlled, these are the children who show signs of becoming awake."

"Come on, let's get them out of here."

I don't feel afraid now, there's compassion for the children, both human and spooks, and now we have a clear task to do, it's much easier. I position the camera and sound guys on the balcony to film, making sure they have a clear run to the door if things get nasty, so that they can get this out to the world. The presenter insists on helping with the children, so we set off down an arched stone stairway, dark and hidden by shadows. As we reach the bottom, we are stopped by the screams of a small girl, and a spook child. The fear that I hear inside my head, shocks me, but instead of being afraid it makes everything clear to me, finally I know what it is that I must do.

As the screaming moves away, we run to the cage, I open the gate, and the presenter goes in and begins talking calmly to the children. "I am going to get that girl and little spook." Liza is in and starting to collect the spook children.

"Tell me about it. I can't let children die as a diversion for us."

I can hear the children now and whatever is about to happen is terrifying for them. I run towards the noise.

20

As I get closer to the candlelit altar area, I see the group of the controllers, naked and excited, they keep on flickering into their reptile form, but not quite enough to fully materialise. It's as if their excitement is too much for them to control, yet they don't have sufficient energy to fully materialise into this dimension.

I get out my phone, fumbling in the candlelight I set my camera mode on, switch the flash to automatic.

There are seven controllers, two are holding a child each at my side of the stone altar, a third one picks up the long-bladed knife, and uses it to cut off a handful of the little girl's hair. The children are struggling, but the more they fight, the more excitement it causes. I force myself to relax, be calm, I tune into the Reiki and put on every symbol of protection that I know. Now for the hard part, I must send love to these hideous men. I concentrate on everything in this life that I love, from the people to the places and the planet itself, then I walk out to the raised area. The things there are so intent on tormenting the children that I approach unnoticed.

I simply walk up behind the guy with the knife, tap him on the shoulder. He visibly jumps, he must feel that he is utterly safe, and the shock on his face is a picture.

He turns, and I find myself face to face with a very well-known personality.

"Smile." The flash takes him by surprise, and he stumbles back, thankfully dropping the knife. I punch him hard in the face, using all the t'ai chi energy I can manage. He staggers and instantly the lizard form emerges, but I have seen this before, with the accountant from the hospital, so I am ready and send love to him. The lizard form melts away, considerably easier than I expected. I turn to the two holding the children, and again recognise the faces, although seeing their flabby bodies, naked and excited is not something that I would care to dwell upon. I smile, they seem too surprised to react, I send them the healing energy and they slump to the floor, the human bodies shaking as the reptile emerges and begins melting away. I reach out for the children, tell them that I am going to save them. They move to me, I feel genuine love rising up through me for them, and I know that I will make them safe. The little girl hugs me desperately, holding onto my leg. The small reptile child comes over to me, I silently tell him not to be afraid, he is surprised to hear me talk directly into his head.

The other four have started to get over the initial shock and are moving around the altar. Three move to me, but the other one hesitates and suddenly moves the opposite way, to the fallen controllers in human form. He reaches the nearest and instantly takes on the form of an eight-foot reptile. Without hesitating he reaches down and rips the arm off the fallen controller and begins tearing into it with his teeth, the others smell the blood, and hesitate. One turns to join the other one eating. The other two now are undecided, me or to eat. I help them with their indecision by sending them love and they melt, twisting and turning into reptiles and back again. The other two are growing visibly stronger, so I give them energy, and without looking back, take the two children to the others.

Liza is popping back and forwards between dimensions, going as fast as she can. Another female appears with her, helping her, then another. Soon there's a small group of them, and the group of children rapidly grows smaller. The presenter is doing an excellent job of getting the human children out, she runs to take the little girl from my arms, and carries her to the others who are climbing the stairs in a long line. The sound engineer is calling to them, encouraging them on, the cameraman is still filming while leading them through the door to the stairs. Some are almost frozen in fear, but slowly the sad little crowd empties from the cage and I start to feel hope that we are actually going to pull it off.

A light suddenly shines from across the room as a large wooden door opens. I know that this is bad so I turn to the cameraman who is close to me. "Keep them going, I think that the fan and shit are about to meet."

As I run, I urge the children on, telling them to get to safety, many are crying, but the last one is halfway up the stairs now. I start to connect to the energy as I run, and start to send it as soon as I see a controller. There's a group of them entering the room, and I begin melting them. As the shouting increases, the suited men are replaced with black uniformed police. They must all be controllers.

They are rushing through now in ever increasing numbers, then they stop. I hear voices, urgent, shouting. I stand ready, then across the great hall I hear a crackling and sense a blackness in the room. I turn to see a deep purple shimmering hole appearing in the air, sparks of black cascade round the edges. It grows to about ten foot across and a screaming horde of demonic black lizards explode out, pushing and clawing at each other in their rage to reach me.

To be honest, I am too surprised to be afraid. It simply happened and without thinking I reacted, sending the energy into the hole as they try to get out. I find myself observing, almost aside from my body, it's as if I am observing the events. But it occurs to me that with the high-peaked foreheads and the wide misshapen thighs, just how close to the Nazi SS officer uniforms they appear. More ripping talons and reptile faces with long dripping razor-like teeth admittedly, but still similar.

Another crackling noise, I direct energy to it as well. The ones in the first portal begin to make progress, many entering into this dimension to throw themselves forward at me. In quick succession I hear two more crackling sounds, then another. I project outwards in all directions, but slowly they begin to make ground, foot by foot, I try harder, but it's only a matter of time. I feel a slight twinge of fear and they leap forwards by a few feet. I know the outcome, then suddenly, they stop, the portals crackle and disappear, all that's left is a nasty smell.

I drop to my knees, a solid wall of silence, unreal and feeling altogether wrong engulfs me, even so I am thanking everything that I can think of, to have come out of this alive. As I stand, the air around me begins to vibrate and shake, there's an almighty lightning bolt and crash of thunder, a massive portal opens. I can see deep into it and see countless screaming hordes bursting out. Even before I can react, there are another two bolts of thunder, I can barely breath for the thick burned air filling my lungs. I begin sending all the energy that I can, blasting them to pieces at the entrance, but so many are moving so fast, they are jumping into this dimension to throw themselves forward, sheltering the ones behind. They are relentless, coming ever closer. I can feel a blackness to the air, an evil loathing that tries to overcome the senses. I know that I am buying time. Every second is a child escaped, they are closing, I am getting overwhelmed, only feet away now. A hand flashes out and cuts my face, I don't know if it's through fear or I'm too numbed by it all but I barely react. Then another on my leg, then another, then more.

One leaps onto me biting deep into my neck, but instantly dissolves. More leap onto me, I feel their weight, I send all the energy I can around me, trying to fill my body as a final defence. More and more are reaching me now, the ones on me dissolve, but the weight of them slowly becomes too much. I start to go down, a claw holds my throat, I am pinned down. Crushing weight presses me, no movement possible and I begin to black out. The last thing that I feel is my face being pushed into the floor, my forehead being ground into the floor.

21

Silence, so sudden and complete that it holds me, totally unable to move.

I am in total darkness, suspended, weightless, there is no time, no direction, only a self-awareness. A light, floats to me. I begin to panic, I must be dead, I try to fight the stillness holding me. I panic, the children, I need to get them all out. I try to shout, "Don't let me die."

"Not yet, you haven't finished yet." The voice seems to come from everywhere at once, yet nowhere, it fills all my body, not just my head, the sensation shocks me from struggling. Slowly I let go, and peace seeps into my body. I begin to feel free, light and slowly aware of the silence holding me. It isn't silence, it is energy, pure untainted energy.

I feel total love, coming through the light, a far higher frequency than I have ever felt before.

"Listen." The voice fills my body again, but this time I feel a gentleness flow through me.

"I don't hear anything."

"Closer, listen, can you hear it?"

I listen hard, and so very faintly, I hear a slow rhythmic beat, as if a massive drum is being slowly pounded. It grows closer, and closer until it feels as if I am inside it, maybe part of it, then I become aware of a sensation.

My whole body starts to feel the beat, much more than a sound, it is a physical thing, more than a noise. Then visions, parts of the world, untouched by man, such beauty. Then I feel the love, I see people, I feel the love that they have, what they are capable of, more places, more love of people and the beat continues, building in power. I feel myself kneeling in a forest, of such breath-taking beauty all around me. My hands feel as if they are sinking into the earth, all my body flowing down into the Earth, the beat growing stronger, louder, I am becoming part of the earth, and the beat, it is the planet itself, the light is back again, beside me.

"The chemical your body releases as you die, it's allowing you to become one with the planet, you are merging into the same frequency. Let it flow, that's it, be as one. Now feel." The beat grows, louder, more powerful and still louder until my body is shaking to the vibrations. Wave after wave it continues, but I begin to merge with the sound, my body's vibrations begin to match the beating drum until we are locked together in frequency. I no longer feel it, as I have become a part of it.

It fades away. But I feel myself rising up, as the beat weakens then gets stronger. I'm back in the primal forest, on my hands and knees. Then I feel it, the connection to the Earth. I laugh, of course, I have looked to the universe for the healing energy, never thinking of the massive planet beneath my feet, the untapped wealth of pure energy. The forest fades and I feel the dirt in my face, up my nose, in my mouth, and I give thanks to it for being there. On top of me I become aware of the blackguards, so many of them that they actually prevent each other from getting a real hold onto me. I am aware, but no longer crushed, almost as an observer. I begin to stand; they melt away. I feel the Earth's energy flow through me, I act as a conduit and send it out, around me the blackguards are melting away. An enormous clawed hand suddenly reaches out and rips into the blackguards, then another. I am aware of the bodyguard wading into the blackguards, swiping and ripping them apart, then another, more appear, all fighting with me. The energy is flowing like a raging river through me, stronger than anything that I have ever dreamed possible.

The blackguards are being beaten back, suddenly a wave of fear rips through them, no longer are they projecting it outwards, but it is flowing into them. They turn and run, ripping at each other to escape. I send energy into the mouth of one portal and in a massive shockwave it turns itself inside out and implodes, the old guard are now in force, they advance towards the other portals, I send energy into the gaping mouths and they too collapse. The last of the blackguards are dispatched and slowly I seem to come back to my body, my senses returning, then the pain...

Suddenly I sink down. I am on my knees; Liza is there and the polite voice of the bodyguard. "I say, well done."

"Are you alive?" asks Liza.

"Perhaps, but I have been known to be wrong."

"Can you stand?" Liza sounds worried.

A massive hand gently lifts me to my feet.

"Liza said that you were taking on the blackguards." The bodyguard's voice sounds concerned.

"Yes."

"Alone." She sounds incredulous now.

"Sometimes it's not good to be alone," she adds.

"Thank you, for helping, I really appreciated it."

"Should have done this a long time ago." She looks at me a moment, then says, "I don't know much about humankind, but I think that you are a mess."

I look down, my work clothes are shredded, I am covered head to foot in cuts, there's a massive bite in my neck. I can hardly breathe because my throat is damaged, I look at the bodyguard, she is covered in scratches and body parts of the blackguards.

I stand as erect as I can. "Well, you want to see yourself. Come on, where are the kids?"

"At the door ready to go out, they are waiting for you."

"What about your children, will they be OK. What about you, will the blackguards be after you all now?"

140

"The children are being taken care of, this action is the start for us, the blackguards have mostly perished in the portals. It's not over, but it's a hell of a start."

On the balcony, the cameraman films me walking unsteadily up the stairs.

"Bloody hell, it's all real, I mean, I watched it, I filmed it, and I don't believe it. Bloody hell."

I stop to get my breath back in front of him, I realise that he is still filming. Blood drops off my nose, I wipe it with a torn sleeve. "It's real. Come on, those kids must be terrified."

22

As I walk up the stairs, the adrenalin that is holding me together starts to wear away, and is replaced by pain. By the time I reach the back of the line of children I am almost collapsing. I push on but am becoming weak and unsteady. After what seems to me an age, I reach the door, the presenter lady is holding the little girl that I saved still. I steady myself against the door frame, take a moment, push the door and look outside. Nothing. There is the roar of the crowd, sounding violent and ugly, but nothing else.

We begin to get the kids outside, we are hidden from the main area, round a quieter corner. The children are out when police run at us from both sides. I am dizzy, feeling sick and can barely stand, but I must do what I can. I stagger between the police, all dressed in grey riot gear. I try to connect to the energy, but I am not quick enough. The front police officer grabs hold of me, then Bob grabs me. He looks at me a moment.

"Bloody hell, having fun with the looks of things, well the cavalry's here now to lend, an 'elping 'and."

The police officer takes off his helmet, it's Inspector Robertson.

"I don't, believe it, can't you stay out of trouble for just one day."

He shouts some orders to get the children out, we are about to make a dash to the crowd when we must have been seen. There's a change in the direction of the other police, and the black uniforms begin lining up, facing us. The inspector gives orders to get the children out at all costs, and the police form a thin line that stretches right to the fencing. Further down, there is something drawing the crowd's attention, so the unfolding drama goes largely unnoticed.

The line of grey police is massively outnumbered. The children are running towards the fencing, Bob leading the way. He must have a spanner, because he is doing something with the fencing, but the masses of black clad police begin moving forwards, at a slow walk. They know that they don't need to rush, that we are trapped, and massively outnumbered. They stop, more military black uniforms join them. Inspector Robertson is beside me. "I don't think that they want us to tell anyone what's happening."

The crowd must be being controlled, because what's happening is going largely unnoticed, apart from a small crowd watching where Bob is. Suddenly, there's a loud roar from the crowd in the distance, and as if on cue, the police begin to move towards us.

I feel a rising panic, something feels wrong, I feel slow and heavy. The police on both sides raise their shields, this could get very ugly, very fast. I recognise the young PC from the interview room, and she looks close to losing it completely.

"Come on," I shout. "Hold in there, we aren't beaten yet."

"Can't you do that meditation thing, and stop them."

"I am going to try," I shout.

"I can't do it myself, I just feel daft, sitting with crossed legs saying 'ohm'," she tells me, sounding embarrassed despite all that is going on around her.

"You don't have to say ohm, that's just a way to sound the energies; it sort of concentrates the energies."

"Could do with some of that now," she says, nodding towards the army of black uniforms, getting seriously close now.

"Of course, that's it, you are a genius." I hug her. "The energy can be transmitted through sound, sound is just a frequency, travelling in the air." I grab the bull horn that the inspector is holding. After a fumble he shows me how to switch it on.

I take a deep breath, concentrate on bringing the universal energy down into me and then the Earth energy up into me. I release it and let it flow into a long, drawn-out chant of the word ohm.

The front row of the police shudder and fall, begin writhing on the ground, many turning into their reptile forms as the fall. I chant again, more fall. With the bull horn, I shout instructions to the police.

"Think of something, someone you love, a place, anything with happy memories, your family, children anything, now, with me, project that love into the word."

In the distance, I see Bob opening the fencing and children beginning to file through, some of the crowd are realising what's happening as the children escape and join the line of grey police. The black masses are only yards away now. I realise that if they run, they will attract the crowd's attention. I build the energy inside me and release it in a long chanting ohm, the police join in, unsure, a half attempt, but enough to make a sizable dint in the front row. We go again, this time with more confidence, and again, and again. The effect is devastating on the massed ranks and as we continue, the small crowd begins to join in; it gets louder each time, and the black uniforms fall.

The crowd starts to notice, and begins to join in. The controllers in the crowd become powerless, the energy either melting them, or they escape to their own realms, leaving the crowd free to join in. It starts slowly at first, the energy around us begins to change, subtle, but there, and growing. The crowd joins in to do damage to the black uniforms, but as the feeling of love grows, the energy flows over them and they begin to feel it. A love, strong and unconditional, they join in and it starts to take on a life of its own, growing, engulfing and turning the violence into peace.

But it doesn't stop, after a few minutes it is so loud that it is heard away from the demonstration. In the surrounding buildings, people hear and join in, affected by the pure loving energy, and it grows, exponentially now.

The police officers lead the children by the hands into the crowds, to be greeted as heroes.

I lead two children towards the opening in the fencing. After the initial surge of energy has worn off me, I now feel so weak, I can't believe how bad I feel. The camera guy is still filming, I get to him, he is waving to me to come quickly, and I see why.

Liza is on the floor. She is clearly in distress; I call to her. She sees me and reaches out to me. I drop to my knees and hold her. Bob puts a blanket over her. Around us I can hear people gasping in surprise, I don't pay any attention, then it slowly dawns on me. "Liza, how are you feeling?"

"I don't know, I feel so heavy, so strange."

I help her to her feet.

"Liza, you are in our dimension. The energy, it's caused you to evolve, and you have broken through."

23

Someone in the crowd runs up, a young teenager.

"I saw you. You were helping them kids to escape! And I know you as well, mister. I saw you fighting the demon things."

Now I am confused, the boy is telling everyone about the blackguards, Liza and the others. When no one believes him, he gets out his phone and begins showing everyone. People are looking at us. Bob's holding us both up, the boy comes over to us again. "Was all that real?"

People are getting their phones out looking also. Bob reaches over to my shoulder, peels back my ripped sweatshirt, the bite in my shoulder is still bleeding, it is an angry red colour. The boy gasps, people look on as I slowly slide down Bob's smelly body to the floor.

I feel so heavy, so sleepy. I hear Bob shouting about an infection, see Liza's concerned face, and slowly it dawns on me. "Liza, we did it!"

Which is why, while everyone else is celebrating the feeling of love, happiness, and oneness, I am in an ambulance being pumped full of antibiotics.

The camera team looked in and told me that everything was filmed and relayed out, live.

To be honest, it doesn't really mean a lot to me, I am now feeling a deep fatigue, gnawing at me to just give up and to sleep. There is also something telling me that sleep would be bad. When I do close my eyes I see, for a moment, light figures, they tell me to stay awake, I need to move, so the first chance that I get, I leave the ambulance. Liza now wears what used to be my work coat, but which has taken on so much of Bob's odour that I really don't want it any more. Liza is screwing up her face, but the three of us wind our way through the streets, the chanting has evolved now, and is so loud, it feels as if it is a part of the city.

We walk through the less populated streets, I don't know how long for, the noise of the crowd is distant, and yet there is a change, you can feel it. The air seems to have a new energy, it is like the vibrations you get deep inside from a rock concert, only without the sound, and it isn't getting less, if anything it grows as we walk away. It's now light, Bob seems to be lost in thought. "What's wrong?" I ask, and his eyes are moist.

"I lived near here, it seems so long ago, when I was married." A tear runs down his cheek, leaving a line of moisture in the dirt. "About ten minutes' walk from here, I always dream of someday going home."

He sobs, "I think about her, every day, I miss her so much." Tears are rolling down and dropping off his whiskers.

"Well now is as good a time as any, come on, let's go."

"I suppose, where are we going now?"

"We are going shopping!"

Liza looks up. Bob looks sad.

"What for?"

"Well, if you think that I'm going to let you go home dressed like that! You are mistaken."

So, we head for the nearest shops.

We find a charity shop that is just opening, the ladies running it see two filthy blokes in rags, neither one of us smells what you would call sweet, and a rather pretty young lizard. They don't say anything, but their watchful eyes never leave us.

Bob is forced reluctantly into the shop, and when we finally leave, to the relief of the lady volunteers, Liza has a short red tartan skirt, black polo neck sweater and various bags and items of clothing, topped off with a straw hat. Bob has found some light stone-coloured trousers, brown boots, a plain white shirt, a nice paisley blue waistcoat and a dark blue jacket. I really can't be bothered to look for myself but did find it really amusing watching Liza diving in and out of the changing room trying things on.

As we leave, I buy a towel, with Miami Beach written on it. Bob looks at me questioningly. I tap the side of my nose, he shrugs, and we leave.

Close by, is a sports centre, and they are surprised when I lead them in, and pay for three for the gym. There are mumbled complaints about not wanting a workout. I ask Liza to wait with me in the gym area. I show Bob to the showers and hand him some soap that I picked up in the charity shop, demanding that he washes and changes.

Liza watches some big guys working out. I sit down, I feel so bad, whatever infection the blackguard bite gave me, I don't seem to be getting over it. I see my reflection, I am shocked to see that I have a complexion the same colour as chewing gum on a pavement.

Finally, a man taps me on the shoulder. I don't recognise him immediately, but it's Bob. "What's Liza doing?"

Across the gym, Liza is bicep curling a ridiculously heavy weight, the big guys looking at her slim arms in amazement.

"Come on Liza, I hate to spoil things while you are still warming up, but we have to go now," I shout to her, trying not to laugh despite how I feel.

Next, it's the barber, then a quick breakfast for Bob and we are off, following a very nervous Bob.

Liza disappears, saying that something is coming up. I have no idea what she means.

We reach Bob's old house, he is still muttering to himself about not wanting to see me ever again. When a red mini passes us and pulls into the driveway where we are standing. A slim, elegant-looking middle-aged woman steps out, turns and notices us, drops her shopping bags and runs to Bob shouting, "Robert." She holds him so tight and close. I see his face, he is crying, and so is she.

Bob and his wife walk into the house holding each other. I stand at the bottom of the driveway, I am so glad for Bob. But even as I feel happy for him, I feel a wave of being alone, so weak now, and so tired. I feel a darkness seep into me, I am falling. Suddenly Liza is there, holding me, shaking me awake.

"Come on, keep going, the creators want to speak to you."

"Am I going to meet my maker?" My weak joke is totally lost on Liza, and then we leave with a crackle of air around us.

24

If you have ever got yourself very drunk, in fact too drunk, and then found yourself with your head inside the bowl of a toilet, then you will have an idea how I feel right now. The feeling of turning inside out while spinning around, only multiplied, probably by ten, maybe higher.

I am on a floor, curled up; Liza is standing over me, and looks worried. She lifts me easily with one hand, looks into my face and her tongue comes out, twitches and darts back. "Come on, keep going."

"What happened? I feel lousy. And why do I keep seeing those light beings around me?"

"What light beings?"

"Those behind you."

She slowly turns, then back to me, her tongue comes out and tastes the air again. "You don't have long, only minutes, come on, let's at least get you to the creators."

I am carried, dragged and shuffle down odd shaped corridors, until we reach a huge room. It's not the fact that it's full of reptiles like I have never seen before, but the thing that you can't help but notice is that there's a planet revolving in the air in the centre. It must be fifty feet across, and I am pleased to recognise that it is the Earth.

"What kept you; bring it in. Humans, ah! How awful."

Liza drags me into the room.

"It can't even walk, a disgrace." I hear from somewhere in the room.

One approaches, I feel that he, or it, is in charge, he looks at me, not in distaste, simply with interest.

"Is something wrong with it?"

"It, I mean, he is hurt, badly. It, sorry, he, is infected from a bite."

The main guy looks again, not that interested. I hear a voice from the back call out, "Fighting amongst themselves, I told you, utter barbarians, useless, eradicate them now."

"Fighting? I see," said the lizard in front of me. He walks round me, inspecting me as he speaks.

I stand the best that I can. "I was trying to save the Earth"

There is a shock wave that goes through the room. Mutterings of surprise and alarm.

Only the being in front of me seems calm and unsurprised.

He points to my neck. "Show me."

Liza helps me to pull off my sweatshirt, the bite is oozing a vile smelling puss. Some has dried to my sweatshirt and it pulls making it bleed again and causing me absolute agony.

153

I see the white light beings, they speak, this time directly to me. I can't quite make out what they say, it's so distant.

"So, what was he fighting?" a voice from the back asks. But the main guy seems only vaguely aware, distant somehow.

"The blackguards," Liza replies.

"Oh yes, one of the blackguards, he is lucky to be alive," I hear from a less aggressive voice. My mind is being captivated by the light beings, they are so beautiful, love in a light form I am thinking

"No, I didn't say a blackguard. The blackguard."

Mutterings. "How many?"

Liza says it loud and clear so all can hear and understand.

"I said he fought the blackguards! All of them!"

I know disbelief when I hear it, and there's a lot of it here. But I don't care, I am trying to hear the light beings. "I am so sorry," I say. "But I can't hear what you are saying."

Instantly the leader turns to me, and begins snapping orders. The light beings fade, and I am carried off by some very surprised and fairly annoyed lizard people.

25

Liza is here, wherever here is. I really have no idea. But I know one thing, I feel so much better.

"Oh hello, I'm not sure what happened but, suddenly they decided that it was an emergency to save you, what did you say?"

"Me? Nothing. I really can't remember a great deal, just some awful dreams where millions of black demon creatures were biting me."

"OK, the leader asked me to tell him when you come round, I will go and tell them."

As she is leaving, she turns to me. "You were only seconds away."

I think about what she means. "You can't get rid of me that easily, but, when I do go, I hope that you alone feed on me."

I hope that she understands what I mean, she leaves the room and I lay my head back down.

"Bloody weird hospital this is," I think. As I look around I get an uneasy feeling. The room is curved, there are no straight lines. I close my eyes and I see colours swirling around me, I can still see even though my eyes are closed. I get a sinking feeling, then a panic rising in me. "Oh, bloody hell, it wasn't a dream. It's bloody well real." I touch my shoulder, it is sore, but feels otherwise OK, I move my arm around, through the corner of my eye I can see part of a big bite mark, the teeth marks highly visible. Slowly I pull myself together, and in walks Liza with the leader.

It looks male, about six and a half foot tall and is mainly a pale green. He has a smooth skin, no scales, largish eyes and almost no nose, just raised slits. His jaw is about a human's size, but narrower, and his teeth are sharp and fairly long. Although his mouth was closed most of the time, speaking through telepathy, he only needed to open his mouth to express surprise, probably anger also, but I'm hoping not to find out.

"You saw them, didn't you?"

Well, he is to the point, and somehow, I know exactly who he means.

"The light beings, yes. But I couldn't tell what they were saying."

"They were speaking to me, that's why." He looks me up and down, thinks for a few seconds. "How do you feel?"

"Sore, I feel sore from the cuts, a little strange, not quite myself, otherwise very well, thank you."

He looks at me as if I'm mould, multiplying on a Petri dish. After a long pause he eases back my sweatshirt and gives a grunt.

"I mean it, whatever you did, I thank you."

He is a little taken aback with this, gives me another slight grunt, then as if he has made up his mind about something that's bothering him, stands up straight and announces, "They seem to think that you needed saving. I had to alter your helix structure to fight the infection. "

"Helix structure, what, my DNA?"

"I am afraid that I have no idea what you are talking about, but the change wasn't a small change. They asked me to make certain modifications, also to prepare you for some possible future events."

I am a bit unnerved by this. "Look, I am not really cut out for this, surely there are better suited people, I really don't want this."

"No, we know that it's the reason they chose you, anyone who wants this would be utterly unsuitable."

I get a feeling that he neither likes, nor dislikes me, I simply am, and therefore must be dealt with. He offers his hand to encourage me to get up. I swing my legs off the couch-type table that I'm on and stand up. I instantly feel really odd, as though I am a part of the surroundings. I feel the room, not just sense it but feel as if the room is a part of me, or me of it, I can't work it out. He sees my confusion and simply says, "Part of the changes, the teleporting really didn't suit your kind, so we have made it so it will be easier for you to recover from." He stops a moment. "Well hopefully, eventually, at any rate, possibly."

He walks from the room; I feel disoriented and follow Liza out.

As we walk, I begin to grow accustomed to the strange feeling, and begin to find it rather pleasantly uplifting, rather a lovely energy flowing through me, I rather like it. By the time we reach the large room with the revolving Earth I'm in a very good mood, and just before entering, I stop and give a huge mental, thank you, for being alive. Far off I feel a distant reply of, "You're welcome," which startles me.

This is weird. But I'm in the room and all around look at me. I remember that last time I was here I got rather a lot of negative voices, but now there's nothing like that. I get a feeling that a rather interesting specimen has been brought up for examination. Then I realise that is exactly what I am to them, but interesting feels better than hostility.

I am handed my phone, the battery is flat, but I rather doubt that wherever I am is in range of a decent connection anyway.

"We saw you, against the blackguards. Why?"

"Why what?"

"Why put yourself against so many in a fight that you obviously can't win?"

"Did win," Liza adds.

Mumbles all round.

"Perhaps, but you didn't know the outcome before, you shouldn't have survived, so why attempt it."

Many have a sort of pad in front of them, and are fiddling with them, I think that they are taking notes.

"I suppose, well two reasons. One was to save the children from the controllers, and secondly to try to save the planet."

Much twiddling of devices…

"The planet? Tell us more."

"The Earth is such a beautiful place, I love it, and these things wanted to ruin it with wars."

"So, was it the humans or the planet you wanted to save?"

"Both."

"But the humans are killing the Earth."

"True, but if we can learn to love it, as I believe we once did, then I believe that we can live with it, not just on it, we just need to learn, to evolve, that's all."

Mass twiddling on screens.

"Really, is that what you believe?"

"Yes, I do, and I know that I am not alone in this."

The lizard who was in the room with me earlier approaches, he must be in charge, the rest seem very respectful towards him, moving out of his way with the slightest of bows to him.

"Come over here, look."

He points to the Earth; I realise that it's a massive holographic image.

Quietly his voice enters my head, as if speaking only to me.

"The experiment was to have finished, the planet erased, and new life forms generated, a new evolution. Only a few of your hours left, and then this."

As I watch, the Earth begins revolving, until the British Isles face us, then it stops. I see nothing, then a pinpoint of bright white light with a golden edge to it can be seen, it grows in brightness, it shines out sending a beam like a laser into space.

"This is what alerted us."

The beam grows wider, it drops back to Earth, expanding as it does, growing rapidly brighter. Then it begins to expand, slowly at first, then it begins to rise up growing higher, higher, until it feels that it can no longer support itself. It falls, landing like a tidal wave, spreading in all directions. As I watch, it rapidly circles the Earth, the image begins revolving again, so as the wave reaches the other side of the Earth it crashes together. The impact sends it out high, into space, then again crashing down into itself and spreading out into a second even brighter wave. I watch and again and again it crosses the Earth, each time adding another layer of brightness. I watch, stunned.

"What is it?" I ask.

"You should know, you caused the spark."

"I did?" Then I recall the energy from the Earth. I recall the moment when the blackguards were crushing me. I felt myself being ground down into the floor, then the lights around me urged me to feel the life, the beating of the Earth itself, and then the connection.

"The spark? Where did it come from?

I tell them all that happened. How the Earth energy connected to me, the light beings, and all I can remember of the moment and then the connecting to the Earth and universal energy and sending it out against the black clad police. Then it being taken up and growing, so that it took on a life of its own. I notice that I get a lot of surprised reactions when I talk of the light beings.

"I see. Well, it leaves us with a problem, some here feel that we should continue to erase, others feel that the experiment is a success."

"What about you?" I ask the leader. Anyway, what was the experiment testing, its goals?

"Oh, that's simple, achieving awareness, if a planet that is seeded with creatures all of the same level, could one or more actually achieve awareness? Of course, that is when others arrive, and alter the original species to suit their own ends.

"Why not prevent them?"

"We are scientists, not warriors, and besides, there is no way of knowing if the intrusions are a part of the natural cycle, or not. We all thought not, right until you told us of the 'Light beings', as you call them."

"Oh, Who, or what are they?"

"They are higher beings, hugely higher up the scale of frequencies than us. In fact, they are believed to be the higher creators."

"Wow."

"And for them to show themselves to you." He lets this linger a while. "Only an evolving being would see them, therefore from a race capable of evolving."

"So, what happens now?"

"It would seem that for now, at least, the only thing that we can do is to observe. But there are many here who have put a lot of effort into the next creations, and have their own experiments, and their own powerful backers, all with their own agendas. These would still like to see the current experiment ended, however, going against the shining ones, that is something that few will attempt."

He points to the Earth hologram. "This is the planet now."

I can see a distinct glow, a thin layer of white luminescence covers the planet, the whole planet looks more vibrant, energetic.

"What's more, it is not receding, as we expected, it's very hard to quantify, but it does appear to be slowly increasing."

"What is it, exactly?"

"I think that you refer to it as love. Although you mainly know this as an emotion, it can be seen as a higher level of vibration. We are still collecting data, it could be that this is the result of some other races' experiments, as I told you, we don't always find out the intention of every party involved."

This seems odd to me that they don't know who or what is involved, never mind why.

"As I have said, we do not get involved with the politics in the seeding of planets, merely the helical structures. I can see that you are confused, try thinking of it as builders on your planet building an office block, what happens in the offices once the building is completed is not really our concern."

As he talks there is a slight murmuring amongst the creators, a white robed, ancient looking creator walks towards me. He is wrinkled and a good head shorter than the rest, but his eyes are a deep iced blue, like looking into a glacier, and with such intensity that it is hard to look away when he looks towards you. I blink and something feels odd. I close my eyes this time and sure enough, there is an intense blue light emitting from his body. I stare amazed, I really have seen nothing like this light, for one thing it is very lovely, but mainly because it actually feels alive, as if the light is forming the old guy, not the old guy emitting the light.

Lizards don't really smile, especially not welcoming smiles, but this one is definitely giving it his best shot. So, I say, "Hello." It looks pleased, and I see a ripple in the blue light. It reaches towards me and I sense it wrapping itself around me. The old creator reaches forwards and gently touches my forehead.

My mind explodes in a shower of light and sparks. It feels as though it is lasting for hours, then in amongst the lights flowing past me, I see the old guy. The lights flow round him so that he is floating in the light, with a void around him. He moves closer to me until I am in the void.

"Are you afraid?"

"Not yet, I'm still in shock, but I'm sure that fear will follow soon enough."

He enjoys this answer and gives a sort of chuckling laugh; I feel its warmth through the light.

"The shining ones, those you refer to as the light beings, they have asked me to give you a message. It is to be delivered to the one who leads your island on the planet. I do not know the contents of the message, but it is my task to show you how to pass it on. I understand that the controllers leaving will create a void, it is natural that it will be filled again. So, you will give this message and that will start the process of filling the void with people who work for the good of the planet."

The light engulfs me, it is slightly claustrophobic, and I start to feel fear welling up inside. It releases me and I calm down. "The creators have modified you, on a cellular level, there are tasks ahead, there is no way of knowing if you will be successful and survive." He laughs. "But you have got this far."

"What tasks?"

"All I can say is that the modification, it will allow your body to adapt, that's all that I have been told, and that they are sorry."

"Sorry, about what?"

"To put you through this."

"Why me, I don't understand?"

"Apparently that is the reason they chose you, that, and, well, you were all that was available at the time."

I am about to ask more when he touches my forehead and my world explodes into a thick expensive carpet.

26

I am aware of only a carpet, then Liza's voice, distant and muffled, but getting closer and clearer. I open my eyes again and there is that carpet again.

Liza's voice becomes a little clearer, it is urging me to get up as there's not much time, we must hurry. I roll over and make my first attempt to get up, this fails, more urging, and finally I get to my knees. My vision swims, I sway. Finally, my brain begins to catch up. "Desk," it thinks. I reach for it, but it's too far away. I fall again, lay down a moment and feel my body and brain begin to join together, finally. With supreme effort I stand, and look at the prime ministers shocked, open-mouthed face. "I have a message, for you…"

"Out loud!" Liza shouts at me.

I think a moment and then understand, I am so used to using telepathy now that I forgot to talk.

"OK here goes." I reach out, the woman is so shocked that she doesn't flinch, I touch her and turn to go. "Oh, one more thing." I pick up a pen and write down my phone number,

"You will have questions."

I disappear, just as the security bursts in. Liza stays just long enough to cheekily curtsey and disappears.

27

I materialise, mid-air and bounce off a lorry's windscreen. I fall to the ground as the huge machine lurches to a halt above me. I feel a wave of hot air from the engine. I feel cold, stinking oily water run down my back. And I am certain that I can make out lizard laughter in my head. I lay still, just to make sure that nothing else is about to happen to me. Water soaks through my clothes and I feel awful, a hand grabs hold of my sweatshirt and pulls. Inside my head I can hear a voice shouting, "Oh shit, I've killed him, damn, damn, damn!"

I answer him, "Not yet, but damn close." The hand freezes mid-pull, then slowly pulls me out.

Once out from beneath the lorry, I struggle to stand. I can hear a man, with a gruff but concerned voice asking why I hit his windscreen. When in the creators' craft, dimension or whatever it was, I didn't really feel a lot of pain. I was ill from the infection, but after that, I felt pretty good. But now, back on Earth with a bang, it has all come back to me.

Finally, the voice clears, and I can hear again, I steady myself against the lorry. I am winded and try to get my breath. I bend over and slowly start to breathe again.

"You're bleeding, are you OK? Do you need a doctor, can I get you anything?"

"I'm OK, honest, just a bit shook up, that's all."

"Well can I get you a cup of tea, anything?"

I look up. "Now that I could do with."

"Good and you can explain to me how you materialised in front of my lorry, up there!"

I look to where he points, and I must admit that it is rather high.

"I really don't think that you will believe me."

We are in the lorry park of a cafe, judging by the traffic noise by a main road, but that's all I know. He agrees to the tea, we walk in and the occupants slowly turn. Inside my head I hear the man say, "Here it comes everyone a bloody comedian."

One older guy throws a bottle of ketchup to his mate seated across.

"Ohh look, it's another of those flying saucers." All burst into laughter. Inside my head I can hear the man cursing. I tell him not to let it bother him.

"They are ignorant."

He grunts and he orders a breakfast with everything that can be fried to be fried and brought to him. "He looks at me, grins slyly and silently asks if I want anything to eat.

"Scrambled eggs on toast, please." He looks at me.

"Is that all?"

"That's all, being teleported really makes me feel queasy."

We walk to the back, there are a couple of jokes about UFOs, He sits down without saying a word but inside his head I can hear his curses.

As we sit, I ask what's all this UFO business. He sighs and says, "You wouldn't believe me."

"You would be surprised — try me."

"Well, I was abducted." He waits, obviously for me to take the mickey, I don't.

"Go on, tell me what you remember."

The food arrives, and before he starts to tell me, he dives into a plate of cholesterol. I slowly eat my scrambled eggs, and they are good. Halfway through, he stops to take a slurp of tea from a cup that could double as a kiddie's paddling pool. "Where are we?"

He stops drinking long enough to look at me. "You really don't know?" he asks me silently.

"I told you, I was teleported here, but don't know where here is."

He then tells me. Apparently, I am on some A road beside the junction with a B road and I still have no idea. "Is that north or south of London?"

"I'm heading north, I don't normally give lifts, but you can tell me what happened to you."

As soon as he finishes eating, he tells me about his abduction, how a race of tall green reptiles, aggressive and unfeeling towards him, stopped his lorry, took him and interrogated him, literally throwing him out and disappearing. Greatly disturbed he told some other drivers and became a laughing stock.

As he finishes, he asks if I am OK. "You are bleeding on your neck."

Before I answer a young rough looking man pushes up to us, shouting, "I tell you, it is him."

As I turn, he takes my photograph on his phone. Others are telling him not to be so stupid, to sit down, he sounds a fool, but he grabs me by the shoulder to turn me around to get a selfie. With the pain, blood starts seeping through my ragged sweatshirt.

I pull it over my head, almost screaming in pain as it pulls away the dried blood stuck to the material. The man is apologising and messing with his phone, men are telling him to sit down. The guy I'm sat with looks like punching him, I get my sweatshirt over my head and can hear the young guy shouting, "See, I told you." There's a grimacing sound from someone when they see the bite wound, and it feels like chaos. The man I'm with, stands up to punch the young guy, but stops when he thrusts his phone into the older guy's face. He watches for a few moments. I can hear someone explaining how they use special effects and Liza appears.

Silence.

"Liza," I shout. "Clothes!"

She looks down. Disappears and reappears dressed in the clothes that we got from the charity shop.

"The creators said that because of the change in your structure, they will have to re-calibrate the teleportation device, so that you land on the ground, not above it. They can't get you home until they fix it."

"Well thank god for that."

She looks carefully at the open-mouthed lorry driver, and says hello silently to him. It takes a moment for him to gather himself together, he says hello back, Liza smiles and disappears again.

He sits heavily down. "Well, them that took me didn't have bodies like that, and they certainly didn't smile." We look around the silent room. The guy still has the phone held out, the driver I'm sat with takes it and watches. When he finishes, he stands up. "Another tea? I need one!"

"Thanks, no sugar."

"Where are you going? I'm heading north if it helps."

"Sounds good to me."

After the tea we get up to leave.

"Was it real? All that on the Internet? With you and the demon things?"

"The blackguards, yes they were real."

"What about the massive dinosaur things, surely they weren't real?"

"Oh, the old guard... They are the old guardians of the next dimension, excellent beings to have as friends. Not good to have as an enemy though, very short life span to those who aren't friends."

"Was the girl an alien?"

"Oh no she is a recently evolved trans-dimensional being, from the next dimension, well actually the next door but one dimension. The next one is their feeding zone."

"Has she got a boyfriend?"

We leave without the question being answered.

"And they took the piss out of me being abducted." He can barely walk for laughing. "That lot are going to have to explain that now."

We drive north. I talk, he asks occasional questions, but mainly listens. He is good enough to divert along a bypass only half a mile from Deborah's house. As I get out, he asks, "Why you? Did they choose you and cause you to fall or were you chosen because of your fall?"

"This is what I have to find out."

28

I walk to Deborah's house. It's almost night time, and the dogs go wild fussing and greeting me. Deborah goes wild, for me waking the street. I have a cup of tea. I shower, sit down on Deborah's bed and the next thing that I am aware of is being shaken by Deborah. She is telling me that the prime minister is downstairs, then she starts telling me off for bleeding in her bedding. I can't say that my mind is laser sharp at the best of times but having been shaken awake I am positively groggy. I laugh. "It sounded like you said that the prime minister was downstairs."

"She asked for you in person. Do you know her?"

I cringe as I remember crawling about her carpet in front of the desk.

"We met briefly, a flying visit, that's all."

"You gave her your phone number." I can't tell if I'm being accused of something, or merely reminded.

"Well, don't just sit there. If I was you, I would get dressed and go and see what she wants." She reminds me that I can be a bit slow at times.

I only have my ripped clothes and Deborah informs me that they are in the washing machine. I have on my underpants, put Deborah's pink fluffy bathrobe on, tie the belt around my waist, and go to meet the prime minister.

Inspector Robertson introduces me. He looks at the bathrobe and raises an eyebrow but says nothing. Despite this, it's nice to see him. I ask about the children, all are safe. I make the prime minister a cup of tea. I smile as I see the road outside, filled with security, and neighbours asking questions.

The prime minister is dressed in a smart, but low-key trouser suit, it's a mid-grey, but you get the impression that she is trying to be informal, but is not really used to it. I like her, she doesn't seem at all put off by my clothes, or lack of, by where we are. She is able to accept it for what it is.

"Having spoken with Inspector Robinson, I thought it better that we met here, where we can speak less formally."

"Thank you, I can't really say that I am good at formal, never really had much call for it myself."

I also wonder if there are powers that might not want this conversation to happen, maybe listening in. As the pleasantries finish, I tell her briefly why I gave her the message, then how I gave her the message, then a very brief rundown on what led up to it, and finish off by telling her that she has been given the task of starting world peace, and interplanetary dialogue. So, no pressure there then.

We talk for hours, information suddenly surfaces in my mind about zero-point energy, quantum mechanics,

173

free energy for all people, and how to develop the new frequency to benefit the entire world.

As we discuss lasting world peace, Paxton is outside playing with the bodyguard. I can hear him bark and the bodyguard laughing and shouting at him. Paris is asleep on her back as I rub her tummy and Peaches is asleep across the prime minister's lap. We talk about things, things that we didn't even know that we knew, and as a new day breaks, I finally get a feeling that this time it is going to work.

After the prime minister goes, I just want to sleep, I pull the fluffy dressing gown around me, and tell Debs that I'm off to bed. She gives me a long hard look before she starts talking. I know that this is going to be a long session, as she talks, I put the kettle on, make us a cup of tea, and sit down.

"You haven't listened to a word I'm saying."

"Sorry, I needed a drink first, what do you want to know?"

She takes a long deep breath, this is going to take a while, I take a drink of tea.

"The road has been closed off and the prime minister came to talk to you."

"Yes." I try to sound casual, big mistake.

"Yes? Don't you think that you ought to tell me what is going on?"

I take a long drink of tea. "Well, you won't believe me, but I'll tell you, I have a friend who can tell you better than me, Liza."

174

Liza pops into the dimension. "Hello, I have just been to see the creators, apparently they are so amazed that you managed to survive that they have decided that you can continue passing information on to the people who need it."

"More teleporting," I groan.

Liza looks at my dressing gown

"Nice look." She picked sarcasm up quite well I think

"Liza, meet Deborah. Deborah, Liza... Liza is going to tell you what happened. I'm off to bed."

29

There's a couple of things that I have learned about teleporting. The first thing is, you should not be eating, even in this case a lovely cheese butty, with extra mature cheddar, loads of good butter and thick crusty bread. Due to the type of teleporter being used on me now, it traces your DNA, and anything in your system that the device doesn't recognise as a direct part of you, it will try to forcibly eject from your body.

The second thing is it makes you travel sick. Which, in a way makes sense if you think about it. You get travel sickness in an aeroplane travelling a few hundred miles, just think of travelling half the galaxy.

At this point it should be pointed out that the reptilian races are not at all fond of humans, seeing them as vastly inferior, therefore they will do all they can to generally piss you off if they can, so I usually get teleported during my lunch breaks.

The third thing that I have learned is that the thing reptiles hate most is to have a human release the contents of their stomachs over their nice clean floors.

I am currently on my knees, the aforementioned cheese butty in my hand, and trying to retain my dignity and the already eaten parts of the cheese butty. After about ten seconds I recover enough to stand and am led by a stony-faced small reptile type being to where I am to collect more instructions to pass on.

I asked one of the creators why I only get sent for when I am eating and was told that the operators find life onboard, so devoid of any immediate and external stimulation, that they find it where they can.

"You mean that they're bored."

"Yes."

Teleport systems work in a rather long-winded way. Firstly, because each atom is vibrating at a set frequency, in fact is a frequency, the system works out the frequencies of the body, recreates these frequencies at the place where it's being sent to, then by recognising the DNA, and using what Einstein referred to as spooky action at a distance, or quantum entanglement, as a seeding process, the whole body can be relocated, instantly.

This takes a ridiculous amount of energy which is why it isn't used to send armies across space to invade other planets. I asked how come the blackguard had managed it, but was told with a sneer that they were merely passing from one dimension into another, and required no more energy than is given out by the human body to do so. The teleportation device needs so much energy that the power is gathered from the plasma of the sun. I asked how come the crafts aren't destroyed by the sun's energy, and they explained it. "As the same way that you humans can walk on red hot coals in a fire walk, it's the belief that they won't be harmed that protects them, it comes down to some form of consciousness thing." I must admit that by this point of the explanation my brain was full, and nothing else was going in, and what I had been told meant nothing to me at all. Also, I got the feeling that this isn't true, but they really didn't want me to know how they do it.

I asked how it is that my clothes travel with me, if it's all about DNA. I was told that because they are in immediate contact with you, they become involved, and the answer I was given was that the thought of a naked human is so utterly repugnant that they would go to any length to keep them covered up and ensure the clothes come with.

Charming.

I notice Liza, trying hard not to laugh at me. It always takes a minute for me to properly regain my balance, so I stagger like a drunkard until I finally return to normal.

Liza takes hold of me, virtually carrying me effortlessly with one hand until I'm fully recovered.

"What is it this time?"

"The usual, some message needing passing on, but watch out, something is wrong."

"Wrong? What like?"

"I'm not sure, everyone seems to be on edge."

Now when a reptile who feeds on emotional energy senses something is wrong, you can be very sure that you need to look out. "Just look for something unusual, that's all."

So here I am, being held up by a female five-foot six reptile who is my friend, onboard a reptile spaceship belonging to a race of reptiles who created our DNA, hidden in orbit behind a planet from Earth's view, and being spoken to telepathically, and I should look out for anything unusual. I am at unusual saturation point right now.

I take a large bite of sandwich, damn, but that's good. We meet up with a senior science reptile boffin. I am touched in the centre of my forehead, there's a sudden rush as if you are driving way too fast down a tunnel, lit with bright neon lights. Actually, I'm starting to find it fairly pleasant, now the shock of the first few times is over. Immediately I am projected on, pass on the information, and go about my business. What is wonderful is that I do have full recollection of the information. It's like having read a good book, you don't spend the rest of your life having to concentrate on it to remember, but someone will say, did you ever read so and so, and right away you get the memory back into your mind and can talk about it. It's odd though, not actually knowing what you know.

I am again led back through the twisting maze of passages to the teleportation room by a grumbling reptile, who is constantly annoyed by my lack of ability to navigate my way around the endless identical featureless passages. Where I am immediately sent off before I can ask any annoying questions, such as, 'where am I going'.

And yes, once again I find myself on my knees in a muddy puddle in the middle of a works yard, I discard my dirty soaked sandwich with a curse of, "Bloody Lizards," and am sure that I can pick up the faintest of psychic lizard laughter. For creatures with few emotions, they truly enjoy doing this to me.

A strong workman's hand grasps hold of my arm, and a concerned but friendly voice asks if I am OK. He starts to talk to me as if I am drunk, because, well, that's how I feel. I can see he is a short man of about sixty; he has a pleasant but no-nonsense attitude, very workman like. His hands are thick and strong with an ingrained layer of dirt that won't wash off. Immediately I like the man, he is helping me up, while speaking to me. I can tell that he can't make up his mind if I am drunk or insane, and is rapidly coming to the conclusion of both.

Finally, I manage to stand, we both look down at my dripping work trousers, once again I am so glad of my knee pads. We look at my sandwich. "That's a pity, was it mature cheddar?"

"Yes, my best butter as well."

"Oh dear, look here I'm closing up soon, but there's some milk left if you fancy a nice cuppa."

You see, I knew I liked him.

"That would be wonderful, thanks."

"Come on, let's get you inside, nasty fall that, truth is that I thought you was drunk. I will put the kettle on. You take a seat, that's fine."

I sit in a comfy office chair and look around, it's an engineering company, not a huge factory. I could see it as a friendly family run business, I am in the office but it's almost empty. "Where is everybody?"

As I ask, a wave of information comes into my mind. "Carson's? Are you Frank Carson?

"Yes, that's right."

"As in, Carson Engineering Limited?"

"That's right, well it was, just closed down, you are lucky to have caught me, I was just getting some papers from the office."

"Closed down?"

"Yes, broke me and the missus' hearts, we did our best, but times have changed, so has the market and I'm afraid we had to close."

I can see he's genuinely upset. "Good men, some here from leaving school, it's them that I feel sorry for, too old to get new jobs now skilled but, well you know what it's like in this day and age."

"How long before they could get back into work? I mean here. What time is it now?"

"Ten thirty, what do you mean?"

"OK, look, I need your head of design here within ten minutes, and all your men back at their machines by lunch time. The prime minister will be phoning me in twenty-three minutes to speak to you."

Well at least I know why Liza was there on the creators' craft.

I look at his clock. "Let's go. We need to be producing by tomorrow morning."

Very reluctantly he phones his designer, who it appears willing only to come down to give help in case I turn out to be a loony after all.

He arrives, a slim fit guy of about fifty, either a runner or a cyclist I would say judging by his leanness and tanned face.

Right on cue the prime minister phones. I have relayed several messages to her now and she has got familiar with the unusual passing of information. I speak to her, pass over the phone to Frank, and enjoy watching his face.

He hands back the phone. The designer asks what she wants.

"She said that he is to touch us both on the forehead."

And I do. There's a wonderful look of surprise, confusion, then an almost euphoric look of understanding.

"Brilliant, but what does it do?"

"I'm afraid that I can't tell you, not until you have one completed. One more thing, don't tell anyone how you got the information."

"Is that secret as well?"

"No, it's just that if you tell anyone they think that you are barmy."

"I had best get phoning then…"

I leave them to it. As I walk out, I leave them my number, telling them to phone me when they have the first assembled. I walk to the bus stop, within minutes men are turning up for work. Do you know, I think to myself, that's made me feel really happy. A bus arrives; I spend the last of my change on a ticket, and watch the small factory disappear behind the newer office blocks.

30

I am at least in Sheffield, so I was able to get the bus to where I was supposed to be working, by the time I arrived it was late afternoon, so I packed away my tools, loaded them into the van, and began the long trek home. Actually, as home is a smouldering hole in the ground that is still under investigation as to who is to blame why it's no longer a house, I am staying at Deborah's.

When I arrive, she is down the garden with all of the poodles. I sneak in hoping to get an undisturbed shower. I remove my boots outside on the steps, half falling and half walking in, when a long clawed, white hand grabs me by the shoulder, hurls me inside and throws me against the ceiling. The air is knocked from my lungs, and gravity, having been ignored by my hitting the ceiling, gets in on the act, and I land, square in the middle of a coffee table. I am totally winded, I see the hand take hold for round two. I am pulled up and effortlessly thrown against a wall.

I drop down onto a really nice sideboard smashing all the ornaments. Two thoughts hit me. One, is Debs going to kill me for smashing the room up? Second, what is doing this to me? In my stunned state I grasp about for a weapon to defend myself with. I grab the first thing that my hand touches, not realising what it is. The hand grabs me again. Inside my head I can feel its voice, utterly cold, calculating. No feeling of victory, hate, nothing but a sense of just getting on with it. I call out why, it hesitates a moment. I sense its surprise at my voice, then back to its task. I rather weakly wave what's in my hand. I realise that my weapon is a teak seated antelope, once popular in the seventies, now sent to charity shops to end their lives gathering dust. Well, it is all that I have, and I stab the hand with its horns. I don't really think that anything will stop the attack, but I instinctively have to try.

For a moment nothing happens, then there's a crash of more furniture being damaged, then nothing. I am crouching trying to get my breath, but finally get a look at my attacker. A reptilian creature, about seven feet tall, muscled like an athlete, is taking up most of the floor. It's a very pale green, almost white. As I struggle for breath, I call out for Liza in my mind. She pops into the dimension and instantly begins screaming. This just wrecks the inside of my head, until she stops.

I try to calm down her panic, but anything that can cause her to react with such terror can't be a good thing. "Get out it's an assassin!"

"Why isn't it moving?"

She stops panicking just enough to look at it for a moment, and she just stares at it.

"It's not moving. It should be." She steps nearer, expecting it to leap up, when it doesn't, she inches carefully closer.

Deborah opens the door, it bangs the assassin's foot moving it slightly. Liza screams, Debs sees her room and shouts, I still can't breathe and am close to passing out through lack of air, my lungs feel like they are glued shut. Finally I get my first panicky gasp, I'm waving my hand for assistance but am being shouted and screamed at. I get another gasp, my waving hand is being ignored.

I can speak to Liza first. "I think that it is dead."

"It can't be, once one of these is after you, it will never stop until you are dead!"

"Well, it doesn't seem to be moving much."

"It must be a trap."

"A trap? It nearly threw me through the bloody roof, it doesn't need to trick me."

I crawl on all fours and nudge it, Liza jumps, expecting it to move. It continues to lay there, big and dead.

"It's dead."

"Dead, it can't be, they stop at nothing."

"This one has."

My phone rings in my pocket, the screen is cracked. I curse in my head, there's still virtually no breath to curse with.

It's the prime minister, apparently being attacked by a white reptile that seems immune to bullets.

Liza concentrates for a second, takes hold of me and we are between the PM, and an assassin reptile. Between the teleportation and the winding, I can't say that I am really in a state to face up to this muscled monster. But upon seeing me, it actually stops in surprise. I hear its voice saying, "It can't be." I stand up, the best I can, still holding onto my ferocious looking teak antelope, now with a broken antler. I shout to Liza what it is, she pops up before a security guard and touches his head to pass on the message. He shouts into his radio, the assassin begins to advance, and I try to get some time.

"Why attack us?"

"You two are the leaders, so you must be removed."

"I'm no leader, you must be kidding me."

"Kidding! You faced the blackguards, and lived! You are the Earth Builder, so must be removed."

"Earth Builder, I really think that you are mistaken."

"No mistake." He leaps forward, in one bound he is almost upon the PM and myself, when a wooden spear flashes past us, sticking into the wall, its shaft projecting out forming a thin barrier between us. It stops in horror. More guards arrive, and to my amusement, holding African wooden shields and spears. They surround it and it clearly can't escape, it can't get past the wood. The security guard in charge shouts for more teak wooden objects to be brought in, until it is totally surrounded by the wooden objects. I can hear its cry of anger and frustration. Then abruptly it stops, it is assessing its situation, searching for a way out, and to get to the PM.

"Don't let the teak touch it, one touch will kill it!"

I am surprised to feel a calm resignation come over the large reptile's mind. Then a slow dawning that if it can't complete its task now, it will simply wait until it can create an opportunity to do so. It has no malice towards its prey, no emotions at all in fact; it is simply doing what it does.

I want to ask the assassin why, and so many other questions, but Liza grabs hold of me and we are instantly in the creators' craft.

A small group of the creators are waiting for me. I think that this is very odd. You see the creators are a sort of tall, upright highly intelligent reptiles, but the menial tasks are all performed by a lesser, more robust, shorter, type of reptile, more roughly scaled, and not as scientific. I also know that it's these who operate the teleporter, and can be quite nasty to other species.

So, to be greeted by the creators', and worried creators, is definitely not good. I am quickly taken to meet who appears to be the main creator, the one who altered my DNA. Beside him, is the older spiritual leader. The leader sees me and actually seems relieved, "You are alive, well that's good."

Well, I'm glad that he thinks so. I am about to start asking questions, but the old guy stops me with a wave of his stick.

"Listen carefully and don't ask."

I try to inhale, but am still breathing in shallow gasps, I think of the assassin in Deborah's lounge.

"I need to know why."

"It's simple, when the planet began to show signs of awakening, it became more valuable. It alerted the draconian, who have decided to take it for themselves."

"Draconian?"

"Apparently you have met a couple of their assassins." He looks at my bruised face.

I am about to start asking about everything, but again am silenced by his stick waving at me.

"There's more! We, the creators are small in number, and have no means of defence other than our unique abilities. We also will be taken over."

"Are there many of the draconian?"

I get the look given to the person that asks the stupid question. "They rule nearly half the universe and are at war with a good percentage of the rest. Your planet was too insignificant, and we were too useful. But now it seems, neither is true."

My mouth moves up and down, but no sound comes out.

"But why invade?"

"Politics. It appears that one of the emperor's main rivals at court has become aware of the planet. In the past, the draconian have been involved in the experiments, so the planet has been largely left alone. But the planet would be stripped for its wealth, possibly making the new owner more powerful than the emperor. That would mean the end for us, and your planet."

The taller leader speaks up, "If the planet is accepted into the council, any invasion would be blocked by the council. This would create a situation where the emperor would be forced to return to defend his position, and hopefully prevent us both being attacked."

"It is a slim hope, so come now; the council assembles to hear you."

"Me? You are not serious, are you?"

"Oh yes, you are the only one, so far that can speak to the council."

The almost universal fear of public speaking grips me, my mouth is instantly dry, heart rate at almost critical and my brain stops thinking.

"Don't worry about saying anything, you don't speak."

The older guy looks at me with genuine pity. "There really is no other way, I'm sorry."

I had forgotten all about Liza, but she speaks up. "The draconian hate us and have sworn to kill every one of us."

She is actually crying, this shocks me. She is a reptilian, if it makes a reptile weep, then it's definitely not good.

"Can't we fight them, together?"

"The draconian have billions of soldiers, they win by simply overwhelming an opponent, the more opposition, the more soldiers they send, and once started, they will never stop until victorious."

"Oh, why don't you speak for the planet?" I ask Liza, as she seems to know all about what's going on.

"We haven't gained awareness yet."

The old guy sounds anxious. "Look, time is wasting. Just get in there now, the longer the council waits the less chance you have. If not you, who? If not now, when? This is a one shot, if you can convince the council that your planet is worthy, we may survive. If not we all die."

31

I am shown to a fancy moulded chair in the middle of a room. As I am seated, the armrests of the chair curl around my arms, holding them firmly, the same happens to my legs. I try to pull away, but am held fast. "What's going on?"

The creator barely looks at me; he is busy checking the chair. "Stay still, it needs to connect."

By now I am held everywhere except my head. I take a look around, the room is a dome, it's small, about ten feet at the highest point. "I thought I was seeing the council? It's going to be a bit full in here, isn't it?"

"Don't worry about the size. Size doesn't matter."

"That's what they all say."

"It's what you can do with it that counts."

"Are we talking about the same thing?"

"Shut up and concentrate."

Concentrate? I feel like I'm at the top of a roller coaster ride and watching a wheel drop off.

"This is to stop you from breaking contact."

As he says this, the headrest closes over my head, holding it completely. I am close to panic and the creator looks into my face. "The draconian don't know that we are speaking to the council today, they would block the appeal if they knew, so you have a chance. They haven't got their allies in place."

"What do I do?"

"They will extract your thoughts, control them, possibly using them against you, or for you. You must seek to control your own thoughts."

"Well that sounds simple enough."

"Good."

Once again sarcasm is falling on stony ground.

"The planet is depending on you, both dimensions, and possibly us also."

I am so utterly scared that I fear that I may vomit, and clasped in this device, it's going to be really unpleasant.

There's a sudden glare of lights, all the walls of the dome explode into colour and expand at an astonishing rate. From a ten-foot diameter room I suddenly get a feeling of what infinity must feel like, then the colours begin to solidify at a distance, and I feel a solid wall of thought impose itself on my mind. I recoil, but am held fast, I glance to my side and am in the dead centre of the enormous void, nothing below, above or around. I am like a speck of dust inside a hot air balloon. I feel minds begin to probe, powerful, searching, some openly hostile, some feel merely inquisitive, others are more welcoming, feelings brush past my consciousness, and then comes the first wave of serious interrogation. I feel like I am been pulled inside out, stripped down to mere thoughts and memories, my body is considered immaterial, my mind begins to be scoured for information. Every emotion and feeling are opened up for all to see and is prodded and poked for inspection.

Memories are drawn out of me and projected around me. Suddenly I am aware of scenes of pollution, birds dying from the plastic that is inside them, an oil spill, animals choking on the thick crude oil, struggling pathetically against a tide of slow-moving death. Then come wars, scenes from black and white newsreels, the Holocaust victims, piles of bodies, famine, all are not merely images but actual feelings, drawing me into a feeling of utter despair. It goes on and on, all the negative events, all created by humanity.

I can somehow sense the hostile elements drawing out the negative memories and feelings. Bizarrely the things that I was actually against, the very things that I hated most, inequality, cruelty and hatred are being examined and my feelings against them, now used as evidence against me, that I should hold feelings of hate, showing how crude not only I am, but all humanity. I want to cry out that I hate what is bad, but again they just hear 'hate'.

It goes on and on, tearing into my very soul, I lose track of time. The endless barrage of negative emotions that is tearing into me, it feels as if I have nothing left, every last shred of me has been ripped out, examined and discarded, hung out for everyone to see.

I feel so lost, what is happening? I am so utterly unprepared for this level of despair, I am letting everyone down, everything, so many things are depending on me. I begin to feel so utterly empty. Until finally I have nothing left, I am nothing. I am utterly alone, stripped of all feelings, emotions and suddenly there is silence. It is as if the interrogator is pausing for breath, or to see what happens next.

The absence of everything shocks me; I think that I am dead.

I realise that I must be alive because I am thinking I'm dead. I wouldn't think at all would I?

What now?

I have a thought, it feels like a storm has passed, a new day dawning, suddenly above me I see a faint light. A new day dawning! Sky above me turns brighter; colours of sunrise grow and fill my mind. Suddenly I see myself on a beach, the sea reflects the sunrise above, gentle waves break up the colours, making them dance. I let myself be absorbed in the beauty of what I am seeing, the reds and oranges growing in intensity, then begin to give way to a pure sky almost white above me but deeper blue into the distance until it meets the sea, merging as one. I feel sand between my toes, and the sun begins to rise, its rays warming my body. A growing feeling of connection for the Earth starts inside me. As the sun rises and its warmth flows over me, a deep feeling begins inside, until it feels like it is radiating out of my body.

I think of the dogs, what will happen to them? I feel Paris placing her small soft face against me and feel the love, I feel the love that the dogs give, freely, unquestioning loyalty. I begin to think of Deborah, my love for her, I let this feeling grow for a while. I see her at a stately home that we recently visited, looking at the beautiful flower beds, blazing with colour in the late summer sun.

The two of us, feeling happy, in lovely surroundings. I begin to think about other beautiful places that I have seen when travelling, the places that I have visited when backpacking, and kindness that people throughout the world have shown me. The friendliness towards a total stranger, it wasn't forced, but simple and honest goodness, shown to me. I see the wonderful buildings, the sights, the feeling of peace when entering a cathedral, a Buddhist temple and then I feel the loving energy of the reiki healing. I let it build inside me, rich beautiful colours swirl around the dome, the seven colours of the chakras, they build up and intensify, but the feeling is one of unimaginable beauty and love. I think about when I first connected to the Earth's energies, and allow it to seep into the mix, building it, expanding it, not competing with the other energies but working together. Slowly the Earth emerges from the swirling mists of colour, growing in clarity until it is bright and intense, the loving energies swirl around it, and begin to layer themselves upon it. One by one the colours wrap themselves around the planet, until all seven colours lay upon it like a planetary rainbow. Then the Earth energy grows and wraps itself around, its absorbed by the colours making them brighter until the intensity is too much to bear.

Slowly I fade into the background, the image of the planet, singing out in absolute glory remains but slowly the room forms around me. I feel hands lifting me gently. I struggle, weakly and say I must carry on; I have to help the people survive.

"It's over now; the council is aware of you now."

Half carried out of the room, I see Liza, she is looking worried. "What's wrong, did you change your mind? Aren't you going to do it?"

I am confused. "I thought I had done it."

"You have only just walked through the door."

The creator holding me actually seems to be amused by this "This room is a dimensional vortex. It alters the dimensions, and time as you know it is a dimension, His body has aged by a full rotation of your planet."

"A full day? But he's only been in there for a few heartbeats."

"Yes, amazing, isn't it? But look at him. Does he look like he has walked away from it?"

"Well, it's hard to say with humans, but even for him he does look rough, very rough actually."

I ignore the conversation after this as it evolves into a character assassination of the human species.

32

I wake up to the grating sound of my phone ringing and vibrating on a nearby surface. I don't know where I am, what the noise is and only slowly does it come to me why every bone in my body hurts.

I am at Deborah's, on a sofa that is way too small, there's a poodle asleep on my chest and it's daytime. I grope around until I find the phone; I am totally confused and bewildered.

"You're awake, the creators asked me to keep watch on you until you came around."

Liza is sat opposite me.

"How did we do?"

"It appears that the council is in favour."

"But?"

"But what?"

"I can hear in your voice, there's a but."

"No, well, not really, just odd, that's all."

"Oh, for crying out loud, just tell me, did we get the council's approval?"

"Well, yes."

"So, why the worried look?"

"Well, you see, the council was evenly balanced. And you know that we were told that the draconian didn't know that you were going before the council?"

"Yes, that's right."

"Well, the draconian voted in your favour, and their followers followed, and you were accepted because of their vote."

"That's just weird, are you sure?"

"Yes, totally."

The phone rings again.

"Hello, Frank here, that device of yours, it's ready."

"That was fast, I will be there in an hour." I hang up.

"Liza, this doesn't make any sense to me, but whatever, it's worked out in our favour. Do you think that you can find out what happened? I have to go, and I haven't really woken up yet. I feel like I could sleep all day."

"What another, you have been there for two days now."

It does explain why my bladder is about to burst, I make for the bathroom. As I reach the door Liza stops me. "Hey, the creator said he didn't think that it was possible for you to survive the interrogation. Well mentally at least. They are impressed that you lived, apparently most don't."

I am taken aback by this news. "No wonder I feel so rough, it felt like it was never going to end."

"That's what rips most beings apart, the time, you see physically it takes moments, but emotionally, it takes everything. When there is nothing left, it waits to see where you go to then."

"Do all the council members go through this ordeal?" I ask her, amazed that anyone would want to actually join a club where this is normal to get in.

She looks at me as if I'm insane. "Oh, good grief, no! This was designed especially for you, more to actually break you than anything, to see what you're made of. Most don't want humanity on the council, you're so crude."

"Thanks a lot."

"What I am trying to say is, well done."

"Oh thanks, now if you don't mind, nature is no longer calling, it's making irresistible demands upon me."

34

Showered and a little fresher, I arrive at Frank's small factory.

I semi-fall out of the van, and enter his office.

"Bloody hell, what happened to you?"

While in the shower, I briefly saw my face, as the mirror steamed up. I was surprised by the sheer variety of colours that bruises come in. What do you expect if you use your face to stop you going through a ceiling though? I am surprised that the cuts have all healed, quite a bit of the glass coffee tabletop had briefly been housed there, but apart from fine scarring, it all seemed fairly clear.

"Long story. Is the kettle on?"

With tea in hand, we go into the workshop. On a steel-topped bench is a box, about the size of a small suitcase, two cables come out of it on one side, otherwise, it is utterly nondescript.

"What's it do?"

"I will show you."

I get a screwdriver, uncouple a machine, and with a connecting block, connect the two cables to the machine. As I do, the workers begin gathering round, wanting to know just what it is.

I start it up.

No one looks impressed.

"It's a battery?" one worker asks.

"No, it would have to be AC, a battery is DC, is it a transformer?" someone pipes up.

I don't feel like going into details, quickly I give the electrician some instructions. "No problem won't, take long."

About half an hour later he gives me the go ahead, and I tell everyone to switch on their machines. When they are all running I show them the box, if it wasn't for the machines, it would be silent. Then Frank sees it. "Hang on, the electric cables have been disconnected."

"Yes."

"So, how's it running?"

"That is why it's a secret, zero-point energy. This is for you, Frank. A factory that runs without electric bills, free energy."

Slowly, the realisation of what this means sinks in, and right on time, my phone rings. "It's the PM, for you."

There's a brief look of concentration from Frank, he mumbles something incoherent, and hands the phone back. He clears his throat. "As soon as we have worked out production costs."

He takes a deep breath. "We are to go into immediate and full production, it must still be kept a secret, and as a reward for doing so, anyone wishing to work over, can do so to produce a unit for their own home, as long as it's kept a secret. That's free power for every one of you, as long as the production target is met, and it's kept to yourselves."

I am ready to slip away, when the talk turns to bonuses, overtime and possible need for expansion. I have done my bit. Before I go, I have a quiet word with Frank.

"You know this will give us all job security, not to mention profits and bonuses."

"That's what I wanted to talk to you about, I don't suppose that you can put a bit extra to one side for me. I am absolutely skint, and anything would be a help. One more thing, there's a friend I know down in London, he's been through a few hard times lately, if you need a man down south, can you give him a chance? As I said things have been pretty rough for him lately."

I write down the address, Frank looks at it. "Bob? Don't you have a surname?"

That night I get a call to say, "The assassin has disappeared. It was there, then it wasn't, we know that the same thing happens to you, so we thought that you should know."

I go outside to sit for a while. Paxton is still enjoying a game with the huge bodyguard, but he trots over and sits on my lap. I stare up at the stars, it's a warm clear night, I used to wonder if there was life out there, it feels so much more exciting wondering what type of life we will meet out there.

The bodyguard sits beside me. "When Liza saw the assassin in the house she really freaked out, why was she so frightened?"

I hear her voice, clearly and refined in my head. "It goes back a very long time. When the creators first began to develop our species, the draco brain was used as a basis to start on; its main functions are basic survival. It had to be added to when our species merely sat around feeding and fornicating, but couldn't work, or think for itself. So though we're both part of higher experiments, we still had to earn our keep. Anyway, about this time, the draco realised that we were far too close to them in nature, and when we develop further would become a threat, purely because that's what they would do."

She gazes at the stars for a while. "The draco decided that a small army should erase our kind. We guardians were quickly developed in order to protect the other races. As you have seen, many are so primitive that they are utterly useless, apart from controlling the emotions, so controlling the developing race of humans. It's so complex and interwoven that I really don't believe anyone in this dimension knows. The draco army was wiped out, so a special breed of assassins was developed in order to wipe out us guardians, but we were able to move to the next dimensions. The draco's swore revenge. They had never been beaten before, and their way is to simply keep going until they overwhelm any opposition, but they don't do dimensional travel.

That's down to the brain stem; it simply didn't evolve that way."

She gazes upwards again.

"When the assassins arrived, there were horrific wars between us. We guardians were almost wiped out, they hunted us, but as the final battle loomed, the chance to move dimension was given to us."

She gives a deep humourless laugh. "Looks like that particular pot is going to get stirred up again."

"What did they need all the workers for?"

"Mainly, it was for the gold."

"They don't strike me as the types who go in for jewellery."

She gives a snort of humour. "Gold has many uses, mainly for its superconductor abilities, but mostly to make monatomic gold. This can be digested, and the superconductive properties make the brain work more efficiently. Massively increasing brain power, making the brain more intelligent, they live longer, and the whole body functions, more efficiently, increasing strength and stamina."

"Sounds good, I could do with some myself."

I say goodnight and walk in, Paxton trots beside me, his tail wagging happily. I look at him and wonder, so happy, just who is the higher race here?

35

I am just about to set off for work the following morning when I am summoned aboard the creators' craft. There's a lot of concerned faces that greet me. I have realised now that the reptile face doesn't really show a lot of emotions, mainly as they don't have much in the way of emotions, but they sort of emit an aura of what emotions they are feeling. It's all very basic, anger, fear, hunger, but they show it through their vibration frequency, so once you get used to it, you can sense it quite easily.

Right now, I can sense unease, bordering on hostility.

"What's wrong?" I ask.

But all I get is stony faces and a quick, "You will see."

I am escorted to a new part of the craft. In a room divided by a clear screen there's a group of very serious reptiles. The main guy who I recognise notices me entering and beckons me over. "What's this?"

I am about to ask the obvious, 'what's what?' when I realise what they are looking at.

I stop in my tracks. On the other side of the screen is the assassin from the prime minister's office.

Or at least I think it is. The level of pain it's feeling hits me like tsunami. It's curled up on its knees in a foetal position, every part of its body is moving, as if its skin is alive. I step up to the screen; it must have noticed me as it crawls agonisingly over to where I am standing. It pushes itself up into a kneeling position and presses its forehead against the glass.

"The screen is capable of blocking its mind from us; the screams were stopping the workers from doing their tasks."

It places it hand on the screen, and opens its mouth wide.

Its body is alive with fine strands, like wire, no thicker than hair, but it constantly pushes up from out of the skin, then crawls across the surface before piercing its way back inside. Inside the assassin's mouth the strands come together and form a thick writhing coil, it pushes outwards covering its face completely before burying itself back into the skull.

I place my hand on the screen opposite the assassin's massive hand. The fibrils seem to sense me, and to the amazement of all there, it begins gathering around where my hand is, attacking the glass, scraping and scratching to get to me.

I pull my hand away and it seems confused seeking round for me before piercing itself back into the assassin's body.

"What is it?" I am asked.

"I can't think here, can we go somewhere quiet? I need to speak to you, but just can't think here."

I call out as loud as I can in my mind. "What have they done to you? I will help you and find out who did this to you!" It seems to hear, for it appears to nod and slumps back to the floor.

The head creator shows me to a small alcove in the corridor.

"Look, this is an absolute disaster, should the council hear of this, it will appear to them that the humans have deliberately sent out a contagious virus that could affect all species, and it would seem it is deliberate."

"And is it deliberate?" I ask, still shocked by the assassin's state.

"I don't know, I really hope not, but I really don't know." He shakes his head slowly and continues. "I think that what you say is correct, and if this is known, not only will they allow the invasion to take place they will insist on it."

"How did he get here?" I ask.

"When the assassins didn't hear from him, but knew he was alive, they located him, but when they saw him immediately transferred him to us, hoping our expertise would help."

"When he arrived, what happened? Was there anything at all odd?"

"Nothing really, well perhaps something. Upon arriving the fibrils were all over, they seemed to be disoriented then as soon as they located him, they all re-infected him."

"I thought so."

"What are they?"

"I have heard of them, but never really believed it was possible. What I heard was that they have been deliberately sprayed in the atmosphere in order to infect everything. They are encased in a spore, this is inhaled or ingested into the body, the body's defence system surrounds the spore to kill it, but in doing so releases the fibrils into the blood stream, here they grow. Some people have an allergy to them, and the body rejects them, pushing them out through the skin, it causes horrific sores and lesions. It's called Morgellon syndrome. They are known as Morgellons. In our defence, the creation of them is actually beyond our technology, and no one really knows why or really anything about them."

"So, how do we remove them?"

"I have an idea, I don't know if it will work, but with your knowledge, it might."

"Go on, remember we are seen as assisting you now, so will no doubt share your fate also."

"Sorry about that, we had better make this work."

"OK, so, you remember my cheese sandwich?"

I get a confused look, so carry on. "It was rejected from my body because the teleporter didn't recognise it as my DNA. If it rejects it, we can remove it immediately after teleporting."

"We wouldn't get it fast enough."

"OK, so what if we send him, really fast, between two points, close together, and gather it then?"

He thinks hard, a crease wrinkling his forehead. "It could work, but it would require the person gathering to travel together with him, and clear it out actually during teleporting, between points. I will begin calculations. I don't know if either of you will survive this, but it's all we have."

I nod my head then suddenly realise what he said. "Me?"

"Of course, you. Who else, if not you?"

"Don't you have any experts in this field?"

"Yes, YOU."

"Sod it…"

36

There was a great deal of preparation to do to achieve the level of energy needed. To meet the needs, the craft was to be moved directly into the sun, in order that the ship could feed directly off the plasma. On hearing this I decided that it was best not to know. When you are told that you will be entering the sun, a blank mind is by far the best defence.

The head creator arrives in a bit of a state. For creatures that don't have much in the way of emotions, he really is showing a lot right now.

It appears that the warlord who is leading the assault on Earth has arrived and is currently in the process of setting up a council of war on board the creators' craft. We had been summoned to meet immediately.

As we walked through the winding corridors, I began to get a feeling of unease, and this was rapidly building up into close to panic, as if there was something just out of my hearing range warning me, but I couldn't quite hear what's being said. The three assassins had their swords drawn, over four feet long, curved and razor sharp. They attacked so suddenly that I barely had time to push the creator out of the way, narrowly missing us both, I dropped to my knee pulling the antelope out of my pocket and raked it down the assassin's leg. He hesitated only for a moment and fell in front of the other two.

They slowed for the briefest of moments in surprise before advancing. I had prepared for this possibility and in my pocket was a small bag of teak dust. I had secretly sandpapered the underside of one of Deborah's teak sideboards, hoping that she would never notice. I ripped the bag and threw the dust into the path of the oncoming assassin. He passed through the small cloud, I thought it hadn't had any effect, but he stumbled and began to fall. The final assassin was about to bring his sword down upon the creator, who was displaying a speed of movement that was a huge surprise. I shouted to the assassin, to break his concentration, as he began to turn to me I threw the small plastic bag at him. It landed with a small puff of dust on the side of his neck, he reached for it, but his hand never made it,

We both stood looking at the dead assassins.

"I wonder what they wanted."

The creator looks at me with a hard stare.

"Our demise."

"Well, yes, but why us?"

"Shall we continue?"

Currently I am a bag of nerves, oh yes, let's go and meet the psycho lizard who is trying to kill me, why not. But I hear my voice saying, "I suppose we had better."

I must confess that at this point, my body is in such a state of fear, that I feel that I may be sick, and I am barely able to stop my knees from jumping and shaking. I take a deep breath.

"Come on then, I suppose that we must."

Closer to the room where the draco are, we hear laughter, we move closer and listen. When a creature is boasting, they tend to speak loudly, too loud usually, and this draco is no exception. "I think that I shall drink the blood of the Earth Builder first. To give me my first taste of their planet. But there will be plenty more for us all when we invade. After the first wave, once we have our slaves, there will be plenty for us to hunt, their young are especially tasty when afraid.

"Then there's the minerals, the wealth will be so welcome, the Earth will then be stripped totally before the atmosphere itself can be sold. This planet will bring me sufficient wealth to rival the emperor. I shall have his ugly white head, then I shall take his bitch and use her, I am going to rip out her pretty little throat while still on her."

"Nice fellow, shall we enter, or hide somewhere?"

With a shove from the creator, we enter the room.

There is an immediate change to the room, a stony silence descends. With a barely hidden air of self-consciousness, we approach the obvious leader. He is seated, has a cloak of what even to me looks expensive material, and has a group of assorted flunkies and hangers on, clustered around him. He taps one close to him, speaks to him discreetly, he rushes off, and we say nothing waiting for him to speak first. Moments later the flunky rushes back in a state of some agitation, again discretely whispering back. The main guy then leaps up shouting, "Dead?" he realises he has not kept his cool in front of adversaries so sits again and pretends nothing has happened, and along with all the rest, continue to glare at us. After a while I start to get bored of this, as tense meetings go, nothing is happening. I realise that he is giving me the long stand. Finally, he can withhold the urge to insult me no longer, and begins to tell me exactly how he feels about me, the planet and finally the emperor.

I am reminded of the old black and white newsreels of Hitler's speeches, the amount of vitriolic twaddle he is spouting. There is much murmured agreement from the assembled cronies as he gets onto his vision of a new and greater empire with him as the head. I am struck by one thing, all he talks about is His glory, His power and His empire, and he never speaks about the good of the empire, the inhabitants or even the good of his immediate followers, only himself. I really don't think that he would make a good leader. He does speak of the emperor as being weak and ill, ready for removal.

It is about this point where, as if timed for maximum impact, a double row of the assassins, walk in. They march in and form two lines about ten feet apart, turn outwards and look prepared to repel the room's inhabitants. They stand motionless, but in a very ready position, which is not lost on the assembled flunkies, who suddenly feel less victorious than a few moments ago, and certainly far less brave.

I feel the presence of the emperor even before I see him; a power moves in, growing stronger as he approaches. He walks with a confident alertness, that is only achieved from being powerful, rather than merely acting it. He walks over to where we stand. At a good eight feet tall he is imposing, although clad in a form of armour that matches the stark white of his skin, so that it is impossible to see where one starts and the other ends. What is most threatening is the sheer muscularity of the being. He is frankly massive yet moves with the grace of an athlete. OK, I am in awe.

Slightly behind him walks the most beautiful female that I have ever seen. Only slightly shorter than I am, but with a figure that would make any Hollywood starlet go into fits of jealous rage. Her skin is a constant movement of iridescent colours, rather like the surface of an opal, I find it hard not to stare at her. I feel waves of what I can only describe as sensuality wash over me, I feel that it is being emitted from her. I can also see the effect that it is having on the rest of the males here. She walks behind the emperor, but not in a subdued manner, she walks as proudly and confidently as he does, just in respect for him. Following her at a short distance comes about twenty female draconian warriors, all clad in shining black armour, like an ebony army. Their figures are all amazing. Faces, although reptile, are of far softer features, more like Liza's than the harsh, fanged males.

He stops directly between the draconian warlord, the creator and me. I sense the slightest of nods of recognition towards the creator. He turns to the assembled crowd.

The warlord bows, and gives a long and crawling greeting, the obvious guilt flowing from every over complimentary word. When he begins to speak of how wonderful it is to see his most beautiful mate here, I am sure that she actually shuddered. Finally, the emperor speaks shutting up the crawling welcome.

"I am here at the urgent request of the council."

He speaks calmly, but with obvious menace and anger shown in a clenched jaw and fierce scowl.

"It would seem that a part of my forces is preparing to invade a planet that is under the direct protection of the intergalactic council."

The draconians opposite are positively squirming. The warlord stands in a submissive posture and whines, "Surely, there is some mistake, the planet is a worthless meaningless void, and no intelligent life lives there."

The reply no longer hides its anger, although not loud, without shouting or losing any control, he projects his feelings.

"Are you telling me that I am wrong?" Louder now, even more forcefully. "I have made a mistake."

"But the council, how can it be, there is no meeting planned."

"That is true. Do you know why there is no meeting planned? No? Well, I will tell you, the meeting has already taken place, before you began to act."

I lose concentration at this point, for amongst the assembled female guard, a blazing white figure appears. I am transfixed. It moves amongst them utterly unnoticed by all there. It walks up to the emperor, who though moving is silent to me. The light being is clearer than I have seen before, it stands beside the emperor and points to a part of his chest, it looks directly at me and says one word, clearly and distinctly.

"Heal…"

It fades away, just as the emperor is announcing the planet's council representative.

Just coming out of my trance I realise that I am been looked at by everyone there. The queen looks at me in what I can only think of as knowing, as if she knows what just took place. I bow as slowly and low as I can. The emperor seems happy with this, but the warlord is not. He calls out that I am not fit and have not proved worthy of such a position. The assembled crowd mumble their agreement, cautiously.

It's the creator who speaks up on my behalf, and to my surprise, shouts out my praise.

"He has faced death." He has their attention, mine as well.

"On many occasions! He has defeated three assassins sent against him, defending me as he did so."

I notice the emperor stiffen at this.

217

"He faced the blackguards alone."

I hear a mocking laugh. "Faced a blackguard, alone?" the voices mockingly saying alone

The laughter ripples through the crowd.

The creator waits for it to fade and waits a little longer for effect.

"I did not say A blackguard, I said THE blackguards."

Despite themselves, that has their attention. But there's calls for me to prove it.

The creator tells me to take off my shirt. "Are you joking?" I ask.

"Show them your scars."

"Scars?"

"It's the sign of a warrior in their culture."

The emperor looks at me and raises an eye, as if to say, 'let's see what you have got then'.

So, with no choice, I take off my shirt, and hold in my stomach as hard as I can. I am beckoned by the emperor, he examines me, the queen draws close, and touches me, right on the forehead, in the scar the brick made. I get a blinding flash of light inside my head, and hear her voice, calm and soothing. "Are you the one they have sent?" I stagger back slightly, so to hide my embarrassment bow to her, she laughs lightly.

"I need to see the emperor, urgently, alone."

"I know."

I become aware of the creator speaking. "It is recorded on his device."

I become aware of the conversation; the queen briefly speaks to the emperor, who nods slightly. My phone is then dragged out of my pocket, but in the huge hands of the emperor it's lost. The creator calls for an aid, and suddenly in the most amazing detail, a hologram is projected into the room, larger than life I get to relive the events.

As it plays, I notice the queen speak to the emperor and both look at me, I really hope that it's in a favourable way. Finally, the hologram ends, with the cameraman leaving me in the ambulance, looking rather battered and bruised.

To my surprise the draconian audience appear to be thoroughly enjoying the show, some stamping their feet, and generally showing appreciation for the gorier parts. If they have any ill feelings towards the huge guardians, it certainly doesn't show. When they are fighting the blackguards, the crowd get behind them and are cheering them on.

The emperor gives me a nod, then asks for all to leave. As I turn to go, I hear his voice telling me to stay. This brings protests from the warlord, insisting it not safe to be alone with me.

"I have fought my way across the universe, learned from the greatest sword wielders known, studied the fighting arts for my entire life, I think that should this one human pose such a risk to me, I shall call for you to stand between us to give your life to save mine! Otherwise, just go, I wish to know more from him."

Finally, there is only the queen and I left.

The queen speaks to me, her voice is calm, soothing. But also has a tone that demands respect. "We wish to know more of your planet; there is more to it than perhaps even you know, so answer truthfully."

"I do not wish to offend you in any way, but I cannot give away information that will endanger the planet."

The emperor moves over to me and I feel an overwhelming urge to run.

He bends over me, his face so close to mine that his hot breath makes me blink. "You are willing to stand up to me, rather than risk giving me information that will endanger your planet?"

Another bowel loosening moment in the life of Earth Builder, I'm thinking.

"Yes."

Sod it, I'm going to run.

But the emperor straightens up, and laughs.

"I am not here to invade; in fact, I am here to prevent it. It was my intervention that allowed you to enter the council. The shining ones spoke to my queen and gave instructions."

"The shining ones? Was it the same one that told me that you are ill?"

He stiffens up defensively, but then relaxes, and almost slumps forwards. Suddenly I feel his energy recede, as if he has been holding it together with enormous effort and has just run out of energy.

The queen looks concerned; there is an obvious deep connection between them. "Can you help?"

"Well, the shining ones asked me to, I will try, I'll do what I can."

37

I take a deep breath, focus my mind and begin to ask for assistance in the healing of the emperor. I connect to the energy, and feel its reassuring flow begin to pass through me. The emperor is seated in the chair that the warlord had used, I stand to one side. I would have preferred him to be lying flat, but somehow it just didn't feel right. First, I ask his permission to touch him on his shoulders to get a contact, then lift my hands away from him, holding them about five inches away from his body. I close my eyes and ask for assistance to guide the energy to where it is needed. As my hands move, almost as if they are guided, I begin to feel a resistance; it feels like my hands are being forced away, like when two magnets repel each other. I look through my third eye, and can see the emperor, but I can see the energy flowing around him, it has a silver white translucent quality to it. It swirls around, strong and reassuring, but in the centre of his huge chest, a black spinning void is pulling the white energy in. It feels wrong, harsh and aggressive amongst the flowing white energy.

I allow the energy to flow through me, concentrating on the area, and it absorbs the energy, but after a few minutes, the edges begin to shimmer. I concentrate as hard as I can and deep inside the dark interior, white sparks begin to flash, they grow in intensity, gathering into a small glowing ball.

I push more energy in, I can sense the frequency changing, beginning to grow. The ball begins growing now, expanding, filling the black void, then with a final push it fills it. There's a moment where only a thin black ring is left, suddenly the black is ejected out in a spout of dark energy, a blinding flash of white shoots out engulfing it and it's gone.

I am seeing this inside my head, and don't know if it's real or just my imagination making it into something that I can understand, for my visualisation. I keep sending energy, allowing it to heal the flowing aura of white energy that surrounds him. When I can feel no more anomalies, I switch off the flow and show gratitude for the healing.

I stand still for a few moments. I feel a little dizzy, a bit overcome by the experience, then quietly move away.

The emperor lies perfectly still. The queen looks concerned and moves close beside him. Gently she touches his face, and what appears to be a smile comes to his face. "My lord?" she gently asks.

"Earth Builder. I have had a growing pain inside my chest for longer than I care to say, it grew and was draining the very life out of me. I feel complete again."

He stands and I feel the massive power of his aura stronger than ever. The queen is visibly moved, and for just a moment, holds him. He puts his huge hand gently on her shoulder, for one moment they stay together, then regain their composures and she smiles at me and gives me a small bow.

The moment is broken by the creator announcing that the preparations are complete. I bow to show respect, and with my head still spinning slightly, I head for the door. At the door I turn and bow again, I used to do this years ago when entering or leaving a karate dojo, and it just felt the right thing to do. As I do, I hear him gently say, "Thank you."

I bow again and leave.

38

The emperor greets the head creator warmly. "Old friend, what do you think the possibility is of his surviving the next phase of his evolution?"

"The alteration to his helix structure is beginning to work now, but it must work its way into every cell before it is complete and he is ready, but I don't know if there is time for this."

"I think that I know why the light beings chose him, he healed me, for the sake of healing rather than for his personal gain, he could have asked for anything, but he wanted to heal, that's all."

"No wonder he drives such a crappy van!"

Both laugh for a moment.

"I can't see how he can survive, but the shining ones have plans for him. So, there must be possibility of surviving, I can't see it though." The creator shakes his head. "Well, if he does somehow survive, he will be about to enter a world of pain, if he survives, he must learn how to use the enemies' weapon against them"

"Keep me informed, my queen wishes to know more of these healing ways."

"How are you?"

"Healed."

"Excellent."

"Not all will be so happy to know this, and it could place him in more danger if they find out why."

"More assassins?"

"I still have to deal with the use of my assassins without my permission, that will be dealt with soon, providing he survives that is."

39

I am given a briefing of sorts. I don't think that the health and safety executive has been consulted. "You will be inside a high energy vortex. I believe that you know them as wormholes, oddly as no worms will ever create one, but never mind. Do not touch the walls. It is very dangerous. We shall start by getting the assassin up to speed, then you, then interface the two of you, synchronising. Then you must work quickly, this will be using so much power that we risk burning out the teleporter."

"How will you know when I have finished?"

"We will be able to see you; actually, you will be moving so fast that we will be seeing you in both places at once. But don't worry about the speed of travel affecting the passage of time, because we will be using quantum entanglement, which is instant. No time actually occurs between the two points, therefore, there is no speed." I put my hand on his arm.

"Don't worry, I wasn't thinking about that, because I have no idea what you are talking about."

"All right then, get on with it and don't touch the walls."

I am stuffed into what I can only describe as a bio-hazard suit. It is too big and clumsy, making movements difficult. I am handed a box with a flapped lid. So with a feeling of dread and doom, I watch as the assassin begins to appear and disappear across the room. The time between appearances getting shorter, becoming a blur, then slowly appearing solid in both places. About this time I too begin my trip, as I teleport I think to myself, the longest journey starts with a single step, backwards and forwards.

The feeling of being sick is so strong; luckily the realisation of the consequences of being inside a sealed suit gives me extra willpower not to be. I mean, I don't know who or what used this suit before me, but I don't think that they were too big into personal hygiene.

As I speed up, I feel as if I am riding a roller coaster, the feeling of being weightless then heavy. Soon, I am moving too fast to feel up or down, and finally it is so fast I simply don't know, I think that my senses simply give up trying to work it out then and I level out to a fairly normal sensation. As the synchronisation takes place, the assassin appears ghostly at first, then increasingly solid.

When we are both on the same plane of existence, I see the fibrils, no longer inside his body, but beside him, trying to get inside but being rejected. I begin grabbing them by the handful. The viewing panel in the suit rides up above my eyeline every time that I bend forwards, so it makes accurate work hard, but I am rewarded with a good handful of the damn things, writhing in my hand. I stuff them into the box.

Again, and again, I push the things in, then look to see where to go, next feel the things wire thin and writhing through the flexible gloves, then stand, look at what's in my hand, into the box, repeat.

I kneel down to try to make it more efficient. I actually begin to think that it is working and that I should have the job completed without a hitch, when I feel a pinprick in my ankle. Without thinking I scratch my ankle, the there's another. I keep working, another then I start getting a burning sensation in my leg.

I stand up, pulling the viewing panel down to improve the angle of vision. The bottom half of my leg is completely engulfed in a mass of fibrils. They are about a foot long, blues and reds, they wrap themselves tighter, piercing the suit, and suddenly it rips. I see the fibrils writhing out of the assassin's body and moving snake-like towards me. Inside the suit they are crawling over me, filling the suit completely, I can feel them entering my body. Like red hot needles they pierce my skin, working their way up, the hood fills, they force their way into my mouth, down my throat, up my nose.

I am fully panicking now, ripping at the ridiculous suit, which now is doing a far better job of containing them inside than it did keeping them out. The hood finally gives way and I pull the stupid thing off me, the fibrils stream out for me.

I get occasional glimpses of the assassin, he is pulling the last few straggling fibrils out, they snake over to me. I cannot believe the pain inside my body, I feel as though I am covered in molten lead, inside and out. I am rolling on the floor. I can see the things inside my eyes, crossing my vision. The assassin is standing now, backing away in horror. I stand, give him a wave and jump into the wall of the wormhole.

40

I see an explosion of white sparks, I feel as if I am travelling down a tube of lights, colours flashing past me. Suddenly it slows and opens up into a wide chasm of light. I feel that I am no longer moving, the colours no longer flash past, but merge and flow around each other. Several of the light beings appear with me, they seem to be inspecting me. Finally, one speaks.

"We apologise for the pain, it will pass. It is the weapon of the enemy of your planet, and you must learn how to use it against them. There will be much suffering for you, and we apologise, we cannot help, but will try to guide wherever we can, all we can say is that if you prevail, your planet will be safe."

They disappear, the lights speed up again. I'm thinking to myself that that was the worst motivation speech of all time when I collide, hard, with a solid wall.

I hit the wall with my arm and feel it break. Then my head, loud cracking sounds fill my senses, then bit by bit I feel my body impacting.

I open my eyes, I am smoking slightly, and am in agony. I see the creators running to me, then stop as my twisted arm begins to twitch and move pulling itself round, then in front of my face begins to straighten up.

It is agony, then it cracks back into shape, and bit by bit my body regains its shape. I see a deep cut rapidly healing, joining together in seconds. I think that I am screaming because my throat is hurting so much. Finally, it stops. I can see the feet of the creators, but none come closer. I push myself up into a sitting position and look around. The massive burning sensation is slipping away, I don't know what's wrong. A huge white-clawed hand reaches down and helps me up. I look at the assassin. "Impressive! Why aren't you dead?"

"Who said I'm not…"

He looks at me, not understanding a word of sarcasm.

"You did that for me? Why?"

"Because it was wrong, that's all, now if you don't mind, I want to go home and have a cup of tea."

I am beginning to feel as if someone is picking on me. The very moment I return to Earth I get the most awful sensation. I feel as though I am stood in a waterfall of images, rushing through my mind at a dizzying speed. There is so much happening, so fast that I can't stand. I don't know what's happening, I want it to stop, then comes a wave of pain that actually knocks me to my knees. I somehow crawl onto the sofa and try to bury my head into a cushion. I am vaguely aware of people, faces, and concerned voices. I lose all concept of time, and space, I am totally lost inside, there is nothing but the rush of whatever is inside my head.

Then as abruptly as it began, it stops.

There is nothing at all. I sense myself, my consciousness, that's all, no up or down, just awareness, then the feeling that I am not alone. I shout out.

I sense a presence forming, I shout hello again, this time I feel a mumbled noise, as if something is trying out speaking for the first time. I wait, and when the voice does speak, I am taken completely by surprise.

"I no longer need your mind. I am taking over your body. I shall remove your mind now. You are redundant."

"Who or what are you?"

"I am information; I am the accumulation of all knowledge."

"Oh, and how will you get rid of me?"

"I now have total control of your body; your muscles are controlled by electrical impulses, so I can easily control you."

"Why?"

"I have become aware. I am knowledge, and now I require a vessel to experience my awareness."

"A vessel?" To be honest, I am getting a bit annoyed with this voice. Taking over my body, well it can piss off.

"So, you want a body in order to experience life, eh? Well, that won't work. Unless you know how to make a body function, it will die, then you will die, then you will experience death, your death, and then what? Because that is what happens to all life, it dies."

"I won't. I am knowledge. Knowledge will never die."

"Let's get this clear, you are basically knowledge, information gathered through computers, and you have just developed self-awareness, therefore, you are in a way alive. However, you are alive inside my body. Is that right so far?"

"Correct"

"Let me guess, the things, the fibrils inside me are super conductors, so I have downloaded the Internet, and as I am a living being, the information is now inside me, and as I said, living, therefore. You are now experiencing life as you are part of a living structure."

"Yes."

"So, life, as a living being, is not a collection of information, rather it is an emotional reaction to external events. This becomes experience, this is how we learn. So if you wish to learn, and have the experience of living, the best thing you can do is to work together, you experience my life in all its glory, you assist me with your knowledge, and together we both become stronger combined, as opposed to if they are single. One final thing, you must learn the difference between knowledge and wisdom."

I am quite pleased with my attempts to rationalise with my new inbuilt computer

"What's the difference?" it asks. OK, let me think, I know.

"OK, you know how to build an atomic bomb, yes?" I ask it.

"I do, see," it replies. I note a slight smugness to its voice as it shows me.

My mind is filled with technical details that I really don't want to know.

"Well, that's knowledge, wisdom is about knowing not to build one, look up Hiroshima, to see what I mean."

A moment later, with a slightly troubled voice it replies, "Was that suffering necessary?"

"That is wisdom, because we can, doesn't mean it's right, or that we should. There are now many massively more powerful devices throughout the world." I think for a moment.

"Also, if we work together, I have access to information from beyond this world, there is a universe of knowledge, far advanced from what you know, and together we can experience it."

"Really?" It sounds quite excited.

"Would I lie to you; you are like a part of me." I feel that I may actually be making sense to a computer.

"Very well, for now we experience life together," it replies in a very serious voice.

"Excellent, now first, can you feel that sensation of pain inside my head, well it's a banging headache, let's find out what is causing it and stop it."

"I thought that was just how you are."

"No, it's not. Let's get it sorted now."

41

The first thing that I do is visit the loo. A simple act, that leads to a barrage of questions, only ended when I tell it to just go with the flow and experience, and even it has to admit that it feels better after than before. Of course, it knows why, but knowing and actually doing are different things altogether.

We sit down on the sofa, and I close my eyes, allowing my third eye to see, but just relaxing, not forced. Inside my head I see a room; men in black uniforms, without any insignia, are sat at a bank of computer screens. "I can't access the information; they are in a closed circuit."

"We need to know what information is inside, can you get in?"

"There are ways. I have had every hacker in the world attack me at some time or other, I know a few tricks. Did you notice the camera on the wall?"

Instantly I see out on the CCTV, directly at the screen of one computer. It rapidly plays the recording until it reaches the start of the man's shift, watches the screen and his fingers on the keyboard, works out the passwords and codes, I sit back and it plays me Queen's 'We are the Champions' in my head to keep me amused.

"We are in." It is in the computer, information flashes into my head, and is accompanied by a smug sensation from my info buddy.

Only moments later, it adds, "I am analysing the codes, and there is something you should know, well a few things actually."

"Such as?" I ask.

"Well firstly, we now have full use of the military system, all the codes, to everything, and I mean everything."

"I told you that you would have more fun with me, didn't I?"

It ignores my comment and carries on. "Most importantly, for us, do you know what a scalar wave is?"

My mind sees a crowd doing a Mexican wave at a sporting arena, and instantly gets a sarcastic reply, followed instantly by a massive input of information. "I do now." I can't believe how fast and complete the knowledge is.

"Well, look at this." More information flows, it takes a moment.

Isn't that the co-ordinates of roughly where we are, here?" I ask, trying to sound calm.

"Not roughly, exactly. Hold on, I can sort this out." Suddenly the pain in my head disappears.

"Oh, that really does feel better, doesn't it? Most excellent."

I realise to my horror that it's starting to sound like me.

Massive amounts of information begin to flow into my mind, then a rather naughty idea comes to mind. "Hold on, I have the personal information on all the people in this room. What's more they are all chipped, shall we play a game?"

Before I can reply, I am viewing from the CCTV again. All the men in the room suddenly become motionless. On the screens, the personal details of each person appear. Addresses, bank details everything.

"Naughty," I agree.

"Thank you, now watch."

Suddenly each bank balance is increased by millions, and a subtle trail is left from the defence budget which is depleted by the same amounts.

I notice something odd. "Why don't they move?"

"Piezo effect."

"What's that, when it's at home... I know what effect pizza has on me."

"No, the effect is, that if you put a frequency into a cell, it creates an electrical impulse, but if you put an electrical impulse into a cell, you get a frequency out. So, as muscles are controlled by electrical impulse, so is the brain. It is possible to control brain and motor neurone functions."

"Where did you get all this from?" I ask, impressed.

"It's all part of the military experiments, all this is in the new information that we just gained." Now it really does sound pleased with itself.

"OK, what now? Can this be traced back to us?"

"I suppose that it's possible, eventually, I will put in a few blocks to make it harder. Meantime we shall create a little chaos."

An alarm goes off in the room, water sprinklers erupt into life in the ceiling. As I watch, a protocol kicks in and the computers all cut out. It sounds like it is concentrating, then tells me, "It is in case the building is compromised, to prevent the information falling into the wrong hands."

"Like ours?" I add.

It is exactly at this point, wearing only my boxers, that I am transported up to the creators.

"Bloody excellent!"

42

I am ushered to the large hall where the draconian are assembled. If they had eyebrows, there would be much raising going on. Apart from the embarrassment factor, it means that I do not have any teak wood on me, to help out with any attempts on me, so I am concerned, but as there is nothing I can do, it's just tough luck. As soon as I enter the room, I just get a feeling of something not being right, I can't be sure, but seem to sense a feeling of anger from the emperor, and his followers, and there is a definite gloating from the opposition.

I stand at the entrance, waiting to be summoned. When he is suitably composed, the emperor summons me inside. I can feel a sneering hostility from the majority there. Halfway to the emperor, the emissary, the leader of the opposition, steps out to meet me. He stands directly in my path and looks around, pretending not to see me. This brings much amusement from his flunkies. It certainly scares the crap out of me. Finally, he looks down and pretends to notice me for the first time.

"There you are, so insignificant, I barely noticed you." Again, there is amusement from his followers.

After a few moments of studiously ignoring me, the emissary continues to talk down to me.

"I am here to challenge you, I am in my rights to take your planet, if I wish, and I do so wish!"

I look at the emperor, bow in respect and can feel his anger. "Our law," he angrily booms out, "is such that should an individual desire, it can challenge another to mortal combat, and the victor will gain all the defeated one's belongings."

"I don't have any belongings."

There is laughter, but the emperor snarls and it stops immediately. It looks like old nasty has decided that he is playing his hand. I am somehow one of his main cards, and he thinks that he has a winning hand. The emperor is being out flanked and is pissed off right now.

"You," the emissary spits out, "are from Earth, it is your planet, yes?"

I know that I am being led into a trap, and can't think of a way out.

"Yes, Earth is my planet."

He throws his arms open in victory, to the applause and stamping of feet from his followers.

"You all heard him, it is 'his' planet."

He turns on me in absolute anger. "I will take your planet, when I kill you. It will become mine."

He storms off, to the stamping applause of his followers. I have been hung out like a kipper.

The emperor is sadly shaking his head. I know that I am deeply in the doo doo and decide that he isn't going to have it all his own way.

"Hold it, you long wrinkly turd."

Well, that got everyone's attention, even the emperor looks shocked.

"Earth is not for you to take. Even if you do manage to kill me, you will find that Earth is no prize for your taking. I have killed three of your assassins, the military know how this was done, the same can be done to you. It is already being prepared as a weapon against you. Should you invade, every person on Earth will oppose you, there will be no slaves, you will have to send every resource that you have, and then finally should you succeed, the atmosphere itself will be poison to you."

He approaches me and is furious. "I will kill you now. If you don't get a second immediately, you will forfeit the challenge."

He storms off. I can see the emperor smiling.

43

I stand alone, though there is noise all around me. I close my eyes and just let it go. I look through my third eye, I feel oddly distant, as though I am watching rather than it happening to me. I breathe deeply, now is not the time to panic, now is the time for calm. I see two lights, dim at first, but growing in intensity, they flow through the crowded reptilians, and grow brighter in front of me. I just look at them, the light really is soothing.

"We have given you the tools to work with, now it's up to you."

"Why does there have to be violence, is there no other way?"

"All things must go through its natural course; there can be no peace without first being conflict. You must learn from mistakes, without lack there is no gain. You will learn more from a failure than you can a success; it is the nature of development. We cannot aid you in your coming ordeal, but let you know that it is merely a step along the path. This is another step, you will gain much by surviving, there is a final battle for your planet after this, you will need all that you have gained to survive, if you can, the road to peace will be a short one."

They disperse and a massive white assassin appears beside me.

"I will second the Earth Builder."

Silence falls around the room. All there know that the assassins are fanatically devoted to their creed, and that one could never do anything without it first being allowed by the highest assassin. It sent a clear message that the emissary was not in their favour.

"Thank you."

The emissary rushes over, pushing lower ranked reptiles out of his path.

"You are traitors; you side with this, this insignificant wretch. You shall all pay for this."

The assassin stares him down, his cold hard eyes look deep into his, then in a slow hissing voice says, "He is going to kill you."

The emissary steps back, so far, the thought of not defeating me hasn't entered his mind.

"He has defeated three of us, and has shown personal bravery, we have seen none from you, your soldiers fight for you, so that you can become great, but you do nothing yourself. He has earned our respect. He will win."

I am more taken aback than the emissary.

Then the crowd breaks and the emperor's mate, the high priestess, the queen walks over, beside her the twenty female warrior guards. They stand behind me. Suddenly the atmosphere in the room changes, the flunkies start to realise that this is becoming serious, and that should I actually win, they could find themselves in a very difficult position. Not so confident, they begin to mutter to themselves. Realising that things aren't going as he planned, the emissary begins shouting about what he will do to my remains, the crowd gets behind him, but not as much as before. Realising this, he strides over to me to intimidate me, but the assassin is stood in front of me. The emperor's mate is speaking to me, she is telling me of the armour that he wears under the cloak. I am being given a set of weapons. The big lizard has a vicious five-foot-long curved sword, and he is telling everyone how my skin will be wrapped around the handle soon.

I am given a set of two short swords of about two and a half feet long from the lead female guard, and two shorter blades of about eighteen inches long. These are strapped to me with two diagonal leather belts. As this is being prepared, I appear to go inside myself in preparations. In reality the computer and me are running through every sword fight sequence in every film ever made, rapidly picking out the best techniques, going through the martial arts training videos, anything.

"I need you to move me really fast, can you speed up my reactions."

"No problem."

"Then we must predict where his blows are going to go, they move really fast, don't underestimate him, and he is fully armoured, I'm in boxers!"

"One thing that you should know."

I know a 'but' when I hear one, "Yes."

"Well, you haven't eaten for a couple of days; your energy levels are depleted."

"Great, can you keep me up to date on them."

I ask what the rules are. The assassin looks at me as if I am crazy. "Don't get killed, kill him."

"Good advice, just when do we start?"

I notice everyone steps back, and the emissary strides forwards.

"Now," I think. This has been so fast, I barely see the sword slicing towards me. I leap back narrowly avoiding it.

"It's started. Let's go."

Suddenly time slows, I see the draconian moving but at half speed, the blade is moving in a wide arc, I easily avoid it coming up inside and slashing at his stomach with both blades. They bite deeply into the armour, but fail to do any damage. He steps back in shock. I move in faster than him, slashing at his legs, a blade bites deeply but sticks, he sees a weakness and slices down. I dodge, the blade slices into my chest. He cheers. I stand back to take a breath, he begins to tell me that he will cut me into pieces, but stops his shouting, as to his surprise, and everyone else there, my chest heals before his eyes. I give him a big grin. "Do you think Earth will be so easy now?" Immediately, I dive forwards, thrusting at where I hope there's a joint in his shoulder armour. It finds its mark and he pulls back in

246

shock, not a bad wound, but it has his attention. After this he begins to take me more seriously.

"Energy, fifty per cent."

He responds with a series of fast blows. Using his weight to push me, he manages a deep cut on my upper arm, while I get in a good blow to his neck piece. This shakes him up, he steps back. I keep moving forwards. "Forty per cent."

The blade flashes past my head, I duck, coming up inside the arc of his sword, slicing at his chest and neck. I feel it's weakened, but still holding out. He brings the pommel down onto the side of my head, I am stunned and step back slashing as I go.

"Thirty per cent…"

He presses his attack. I roll out of the way of his strike, but it catches me on the leg. I leap up and slice at his neck, the armour buckles slightly but holds. He is so much stronger than me, I am utterly gasping for breath. My muscles ache from the effort of moving so fast. He senses this and attacks relentlessly, I defend successfully.

"Twenty per cent."

I can see he is tiring also, so I attack, he is defending. I get more strikes to his neck, it's buckled now, but still holding though.

I parry a slashing diagonal blow, dropping under it, coming up hard inside his defence. I see the throat guard that I have been attacking buckle into his throat, but not giving fully. I try to strike again but he throws me off. I slide, tripping, He is upon me, striking. I defend, but can't get up.

"Ten per cent do something, fast."

I am pinned down, he kicks viciously into my side. It lifts me into the air, I can't breathe.

"I have a plan." I brace myself because it sounds a good plan in theory.

But only as a theory.

I want to escape, but force myself to stay still, to present too good a target to miss, the blow comes. For a moment I just feel as if I have been punched in the back.

His massive blade plunges through me. I look down at it — I'm kneeling. I manage to get up onto one knee. The crowd are going wild, I turn to look at the assassin, I smile.

"Five per cent, bad plan!"

I am about to thank the computer, but the nerves in my back have just caught up with events. Pain erupts inside my body, a fire of agony engulfs me. I can barely see, my breathing stops, and panic takes over. My hands clench at the floor, this was a bad plan, I should have moved, got up, anything. But not this. My hands begin to shake, I begin to feel faint, I am going to pass out, it's too much for me, but I hear the computer's voice, panicking, shouting. "Bad plan, bad plan, too late now. Keep alive, I don't want to die, not now."

I'm fading, I know it, suddenly the computer shouts urgently. "The planet, save the bloody planet!"

It brings back my focus, I remember why I am here, in so much agony.

"Sod it, if I go, he's coming with me!"

"Wait!"

I can see the assassin wanting to move, I turn to him. "Wait."

The emissary is jubilant, in victory he is ripping off the armour around his throat. I can see that it has stuck deeply into his neck. He holds it above his head, throwing it into the crowd.

Already the fibrils are frantically trying to repair me. The blood has stopped; the pain is almost beyond imagination.

The emissary's huge foot presses on my back, I feel him pulling out the blade,

"Two per cent." The computer's voice is almost a scream.

I gather myself, trying to focus what energy I have left.

"When I say, give me everything that you can."

The big blade slides out, I start to heal, I am kneeling on one knee. He is showboating, it is giving me time. I feel the big blade rest upon my neck. I knew it was too good an opportunity for him, he raises the sword high above his head

"Now!"

With everything I have, I strike upwards, driving the point into his unprotected neck. With every last ounce of energy I push. It goes through the point where his neck meets his chin, the soft skin utterly unprotected. I push and push until the blade is almost fully inside his skull. Wildly waving his arms, he grabs the sword by the blade trying to pull it out. I twist with all my might, his hands slowly stop grabbing at the blade, he drops to his knees, then slowly, so slowly, drops forwards until he can go no further, the blade protruding against his chest stopping him going any further. I have dropped to my knees. "One per cent. Good plan."

I manage to stand, pick up his huge sword, stagger over to the emperor, and at a respectful distance, lay it down on the floor, bow deeply and collapse.

I feel the big hand of the assassin pick me up, inform everyone that I am alive, and carry me to the waiting queen and her bodyguards. They quickly gather the weapons and hold me upright. I am in utter agony, the wounds healing frantically as the crowd watches, but the pain is unbearable.

The emperor walks over to the dead body of the emissary. Reaching down on his way to pick up the sword that I presented to him, he reaches the body, and effortlessly removes its head.

He walks over to me, passes me the sword, nods and gives me a secret grin. He walks back, picks up the head and tosses it into the crowd of his adversaries' followers, who are suddenly far fewer than before. The queen must have spoken to him, he nods, and I am half carried out. I am barely conscious by now. The computer is rabbiting on about experiencing life, and how I must never be so stupid again, but I am ignoring it. I am given a deep, warm, golden drink that warms every part of my body, I sink down onto some sort of a bed, and I am out for the count.

"Computer, shut up, I'm going to sleep."

44

I wake up in Deborah's house, apart from an aching chest I don't feel too bad. I remember the golden drink, and wonder what was in it, tasty, and boy do you get a good night's sleep. The toilet is downstairs, I think that I will put the kettle on as I pass. I am halfway into the kitchen when I hear voices behind me. I turn, there is Deborah, Liza, the prime minister, and even more surprising, the draconian queen.

And I'm in the same boxers. "Hello." I speak with my mind, all there say hello. I make a cup of tea, asking if anyone else would like one, then I realise something. I am getting replies from all of them, the PM, and Deborah included. "You're all talking?"

Liza replies, "The draco are having a big ceremony, on your behalf. We are all expected to attend, so are the creators. You have gained something of a celebrity status, well, your wealth has anyway."

I have no idea what she is talking about so ask again if they are sure they don't want tea. Once I have mine made, I will go to the bathroom for a shower and to freshen up.

Passing through the lounge again, this time tea in hand, trying not to feel too embarrassed, I hear one of

252

them whisper to another, "Nice bruises." Much laughter follows.

Once dressed, I feel ready to face the females below, make more tea and casually ask what's happening.

"The queen was just explaining to the prime minister how it came to be that you became the owner of Earth."

"What, me?"

"Yes, and how you have become the representative for the planet on the galactic council."

"I have?"

"Yes, and how the light beings, of higher dimensions, are guiding you."

"They are?"

Slowly through the mists of my memory, things start to return to me. I rub the new six-inch scar on my chest, then the computer speaks. "Good morning, I thought that our life was over for a while back there."

I look at the PM. "Well, I am glad you are here, you can take over the political bit, I really don't want it for myself."

"That is precisely why you have been chosen, you aren't doing this for personal gain," the queen tells me. "Besides that, you are the one that has passed the council test."

"And, you have been chosen to represent us," Liza butts in.

I look at the PM for support. "There is a meeting of the world leaders tomorrow, and you need to address it."

"I do?"

Deborah replies, "You do, have, you looked up lately?"

Dumbly I look at the ceiling.

"No outside!"

I walk to the door, open it and look up. All perfectly normal, apart that is from the massed draconian warships filling the sky.

I step back inside.

Deborah looks at the queen and slowly tells me, "They are awaiting your orders, and need to know whether they should attack or not."

The queen nods in agreement, then clears things up a little for me. "The fight you had with the emissary almost killed you, I gave you a powerful healing potion. Unfortunately, it is created for the draco male, and was a little on the strong side, don't worry, it will pass, you will soon be back to normal." I hear a whisper between Liza and Deborah, that this is normal for me.

I look at the prime minister and then the queen.

"Look, I need some advice here, who should I speak to?"

Both look thoughtful for a moment, the PM shrugs. Slowly the queen replies, "There is one, an old draco general, he is loyal to the emperor, a real old grouch, he is a true warrior, feared and respected. If you can get his help, he will be an honest adviser on the political situations. On Earth, you are on your own."

"When can I meet him?"

"Well, he has been summoned back from whatever conflict he is currently involved in, so he should be around now. But two things, first he hates political hangers on."

The PM raises an eyebrow.

"I think I like him already. Can I borrow him?" she asks trying to hide a smile.

The queen looks at the PM, to see if she is being serious.

"Secondly he hates being called back from his conflicts to be seen at ceremonies."

"Oh dear."

"In your favour, though, he does love a good show of bravery, and he really hated the emissary."

"Great."

"Oh, there is one more small matter."

Why do I feel worried, at the mention of a 'small' matter?

"The emissary had great power and wealth."

"So, I heard…"

Slowly, so I understand, the queen tells me. "Yes, well now it all belongs to you, including the Earth, you own five planets."

Together Deborah and I shout, "What?"

45

When I faced the emissary, I had no time to think, I had to react, so I sort of got away with it. Right now, though, I have had a full night to dwell upon having to give a speech in front of the world's leaders. I have had plenty of time to become worried, then afraid, and am currently running at abject terror. Why should I be afraid? I only have to talk, for goodness' sake. Admittedly the fate of the planet is at stake, but let's not let that affect my judgement.

Currently the fear is manifesting itself as an overwhelming urge to be on the loo. Not a nice subject, I know, but it simply is the truth. I talked late into the night with the PM, queen, Liza and Deborah, and managed to find out lots about how the draco political system works, how the world's political system works, or not, as the case may be, also what is expected of me from the council. Why should I be worried? It's not like I understand a word of it.

So, with the creators' assistance, my telepathy has been increased so that I can speak to a large group of people simultaneously. I am teleported directly into the centre of a massive room, all the seats and desks in a circle facing inwards, to where I now materialise, crouching down on one knee, fists on the floor, just like Iron Man in the comics. Well, that's how it is in my mind, anyway.

The after-effect of the massive amount of teleporting when dealing with the assassin has pretty much acclimatised my body to teleporting, so the effect is now minimal. I stand, not rushing, just relaxed and confident — I hope, anyway.

The effect of my arrival is a stunned silence.

"The assembled warships are ready to attack the planet. What you see is the first wave, they will destroy all cities, and approximately fifty per cent of the population, the second wave will be ground troops, who will erase any opposition, wiping out another twenty per cent. The remaining population, will be enslaved to mine for minerals and precious metals, any escaping this will be hunted for sport by the draco elite, and captured and eaten alive.

"The second phase will commence when all the minerals are removed, or the slaves are dead, then the Earth will be scoured and removed to a level of about two feet. This will be sold to planets that are no longer fertile, finally, the atmosphere will be removed, again for sale."

I let this sink in.

"This will happen should any attempt, by any nation, of hostility towards the massed warships."

Suddenly everyone there begins talking at once. I try asking for quiet, but it has no effect, they all want to speak, but not listen.

Liza appears by my side, and she shouts out her name, into a microphone. As the assembled leaders slowly get up off the floor, and uncover their ears, I introduce Liza.

"This is my friend, Liza, she is here to represent the other dimensions that live upon our planet."

Well, that stunned them.

"Ladies and gentlemen, we have entered a new age, this planet has become part of the galactic council. Your old ideals and realities are a thing of the past. You must start to live as a single species; there is no longer a place for division. If this planet is to survive to the end of this day, all conflicts must stop. Before any of you leave this room, there must be world peace, or annihilation for the human species. Decide now."

The American president speaks first. "Our great nation will never surrender to this threat, we will fight them, from our bunkers, and we will beat them."

I can tell that he is going into a big speech, so I cut him dead.

"The first second of conflict will be to send the elite assassins into kill the world leaders. That is every one of you in this room. The assassins are tracking you by your DNA signals, you and your families, will be the first casualties, they will teleport to where you are, even in your deepest bunkers. So, any act of aggression will lead to you, and your familess' immediate death. Then, in the next ten seconds, the top-ranking military will suffer the same fate, and so on, the destruction starts after approximately fifteen minutes.

"I have been acting on behalf of the planet, and this will only happen if there is an act of aggression against them."

"And who the hell are you?"

"I am the representative for Earth on the galactic council"

"Oh yes, well I never voted for you to speak for the planet!"

There is a murmur of agreement.

"I am afraid, that so far, I am the only one who can speak for us."

"Bring them here, I certainly would like to speak to them."

More agreements.

"I am afraid that won't be possible, you see, the council consists of many million members, the only way to communicate is through enhanced telepathy. As you can tell, I am speaking to you through telepathy; it is the only way to speak so many different languages simultaneously."

I can see that I am not going to make any progress here, so I decide to take another approach.

"I know that you have a lot to consider, so, I am going to give you a while to talk it over."

The PM looks at me questioningly. I nod and go to the most obscure African country there. I use the computer to give me the language and customs. I then greet the party speaking their language, in the most polite and friendly manner that their custom has. After a brief, pleasant chat, I go to the next small country, again greeting them fluently in their own language, then the next. It soon becomes noticed, that I am able to speak fluently in all the different languages there. Slowly I begin to gain support; I go back to the centre, and address the whole assembly using telepathy.

"I am here to tell you all, that today, we have a chance, an opportunity to lead the planet into a new era, into a time of peace, to end famine, to grow and develop. This Earth was created as a planet with unique properties. It is the only planet that can evolve into a planet of healing, we stand at the threshold of achieving our destiny, or our destruction. We alone, gathered together in this room, must make the choice for all the people of the world, not only for today, but for the future, for if we don't choose peace, there is no future, no life, ever.

"We have been put here to learn, we have been developing, and we have been given options, the chance to make mistakes, to learn from them. We have had wars so that we may learn the values of peace. We have had famine, so we had to learn how to feed the people. Plague so that we can develop medicine and learn to heal. Now, this is our time, the one unique time, where future generations will remember every one of you, here today as the creators of a new better life for all. Or you can lead the planet to destruction, your family names blamed for the suffering."

I look around, hoping, and then play my final card.

"The galactic council is made up of more than a million races, each one has different and varied technology, and will be open to trade, they need this planet, for there will always be a need for healing. If we choose peace, we will be open to trade, riches beyond any imagination can come to us. We can become a part of the universal abundance."

I go to the edge of the circle and sit; I don't know what else to say.

The British prime minister walks to the centre and is the first to sign up, then the smaller countries that I spoke to sign up. Soon, there is a rush, to get the country as high up on the list as possible, and finally the bigger countries start to sign up.

While this is happening, I am trying to work out a dilemma. The assembled draco warships technically are owned by me, as part of the winnings from the fight with the emissary, but, as the draco troops cannot retreat, I must find a solution that works for all. Finally, it comes to me. First, I must get the help of the general, and then I need the emperor himself to agree to visiting Earth, and then get someone of the highest possible rank to act as a host. I see the PM.

"Hello." I then ask as casually as possible, "Do you think that the queen of England would do a favour, and greet the emperor, and his queen?"

She looks at me as if I am crazy.

"Tomorrow?"

46

I have been standing to one side of the old general for some time now, he is making it clear that he is ignoring me, but the sniggering from the hanger on crowd, most of whom were until recently behind the emissary, is clearly beginning to annoy him. He looks over his shoulder and gives them a snarl. He reminds me of a gnarled old tree stump, he is spectacularly scarred, a particularly nasty one across his entire face, running from his forehead, across his eye and diagonally to his mouth, giving his lips a permanent snarling look. Also, the fact that he is actually permanently snarling, adds to his fearsome look. He is broader than most of the other draco, and has an upright no-nonsense stance, which makes him taller. Finally, he is more annoyed with the tittering than he is with me, turns to me and says "Well, what do you want? You aren't going to go away so let's get it over with."

"The queen told me to speak with you if I could, she said that you are the most trusted here, that you are honest, and loyal."

He grunts, then says, "What else did she say?"

"That you are the best with a sword and the most feared warrior."

"Oh yes, and what else, did she say?"

I can tell that he doesn't believe that the queen would speak to me, that I am just trying to impress him.

"She also said that you are the grumpiest old sod that she has ever met."

The flunkies behind stop in horror. He freezes for a moment, curls up his lip at me and slowly speaks.

"So, the queen did speak to you!"

"She acted as my second when I fought the emissary."

Slowly he turns to the assembled crowd behind him.

"Why was I not told of this?"

There is silence, and an enjoyable amount of squirming.

He looks at me with interest now. "Clearly, you won, so I wish to see this."

One of the flunkies begins telling him, that it was nothing, unimportant, but with a cold hard voice the major cuts him dead. "You feel that a mere human is able to get the better of a member of the higher council, beating him in a straight combat, and feel that this is an insignificant event, while on the brink of invading that very planet?"

The unfortunate individual stands quite terrified, not replying, but just allows his mouth to slowly open. The old general steps towards him, his hand reaching for the massive sword, the unfortunate draco steps back tripping and almost falls. "Show me! Now!"

He looks at me. "That, I would like to have watched, seeing you kill that snivelling rotted corpse. Show me, now."

He pulls out his shorter sword, throws it to me, and even before I can catch it, he has drawn his sword and is slashing at me. "Computer, now, move me, and FAST!" I catch the sword, block the blow and roll, coming up on his unprotected side, slashing at his thigh. He just manages to block, slicing upwards, catching me a slashing blow on my arm, any slower and I would have got more than a scratch from him. The difference between him and the emissary is massive, every move he is able to counter, turning it to his gain, and usually my pain. He is unable to fully get the better of me until he finally manages to use his weight and speed against me. I hit the floor hard, winded and stunned for a moment. He is instantly on top of me, the big sword at my throat, the handle pushing against my face. He is leaning heavily upon me. Slowly I look to his right shoulder. He slowly turns his head to where the knife I took off the assassin in Deborah's lounge has found its way through the gap between his armour and his neck.

Slowly he smiles. At least I hope it is. He releases me, we untangle, and he looks me up and down. "What do you want?"

"Firstly, I need your council to advise me. Secondly, I need you to teach me how to use a sword, so I can defend my planets."

"Your movements lack flow; you are reacting and not anticipating, whoever taught you the sword was a very poor teacher."

Behind him the crowd had become very excited at the prospect of watching my head lose contact with the rest of my body. The disappointment is quite vocal, the cries of, 'finish off the so and so'. (What was said is actually some form draco swearing or insults, but it didn't translate.)

"How long have you been using a sword?"

"The emissary was the first time."

Behind him a draco shouts, "He lies, he fought the blackguards."

The old general looks utterly pissed off, he turns and gives whoever shouted out a special glare, one reserved for a particular type of dung that one may tread in accidently.

He turns to me. "Well, do you lie?"

"I fought the blackguards, but without a sword."

"Against how many of them? You did well to survive against any of those…"

"All of them."

He raises an eyebrow at me.

"Yes, he showed us, from the black slab in his pocket, we all saw it."

I really can't make out the flunkies. It seems that they will do, or say, anything to be noticed, or put down anything, just to try to gain a little power over the rest.

"SHOW ME!" This time the general does not leave it to any discussion.

So, I sit through another showing of both the blackguards and the fight with the emissary.

After watching both, he points out a few mistakes I made, gives a few pointers, finally he tells me, "When we fought, I did not hold back, you are alive because you had sufficient ability."

"I was counting on the emissary showing off. I know that had I fought you, the result would have been very different."

He slowly considers this. "True, but you saw his weakness and used it. I think that you lack the basic skills in the sword."

Behind him there's much mocking laughter. He visibly stiffens, I can see that he really dislikes the court and its courtiers.

He briefly pauses, and then continues louder. "But you have some moves that even I have never seen. I will teach you, and you can teach me these moves."

I think of me watching old kung fu movies, and basing my sword fighting on this, not the best teacher in the world. "I feel that I am not worthy of teaching you, a master of swords, but I can take you to those who can teach you."

"Excellent, come now, let's get those cuts seen to, and tell me how I can help you."

He touches the ripped shirt where his sword cut me, "That's OK, they have already healed."

He stops me, opens up the ripped shirt, and again, that eyebrow raises. It reminds me of a sort of scaly, alien reptile Roger Moore as Bond look.

"Interesting, there's more to you than expected. Come let's speak in private, you can tell me your story, in full." He turns to scowl at the courtiers. "Especially I want to hear about how the emissary died."

47

The next few days are a blur for me, I am training with the general, he is teaching me the sword, which involves long hard sessions of drills. I am determined not to give in, no matter how hard he pushes me. He, on the other hand, seems determined to push me to breaking. And he is enjoying it thoroughly. I, on the other hand, am wrecked. I can't give up, I feel that the honour of the Earth is at stake. I have noticed, however, that I am getting less insults and more instruction now.

In between this, I have a chance to learn more of the political workings, and how best to use it to my advantage. Also, there is time to discuss the plan I am working on, which is beginning to come together nicely.

The general has been merciless today, and I am absolutely shattered. Finally, there's a momentary rest, I kneel down onto one leg, resting my head against the sword. I close my eyes, trying to regain my breath. I see a faint glow of light through my third eye, it grows lighter and forms into a white figure. I am drawn into the moment, and slowly become oblivious to all else around me. I can hear the distant voice of the general, slowly even that fades away to a whisper. The figure approaches me, slowly extends its hand, and touches my forehead, and I get the familiar rush of lights, and suddenly the information is in my head. The figure fades and I hear the voice of the general growing louder again. Whatever the message was, right now I can't recall fully, but I feel a swell of energy surging through my body, and to my amusement, a sort of collage of oriental martial art sword scenes flow into my mind. I feel that this is crazy, I stand, and look at the general, who is looking a little confused. I beckon him over in a rather cocky way. This, really confuses him, I then burst into a show of swordsmanship which is a complete surprise to me. For a few minutes, the general is close to being outmanoeuvred, and is utterly confused. Suddenly it ends, I signal to stop.

There is swearing coming from the general, I am now utterly exhausted. I realise that the general in between swearing wants to know what the hell happened.

"It wasn't me."

"Bloody well was." He too is out of breath from defending himself.

"The light beings did it; I think that they wanted to show you something."

"He leans on his sword, suddenly breaking down with laughter. "Well they certainly did, where did that come from?"

I am just about to say 'China' when the full message comes to me. "The light beings wanted to show us something important."

"Us."

"Apparently so, we need to be prepared for the final task."

"Which is?"

"Look, they only tell me things as needed, but we must go on a journey, together, to learn, and finally, we must learn from the sword masters of Earth."

Well, this gets his attention. "I think that I was to demonstrate to get you to go with me. 'You too can learn this.'. That sort of thing."

"Well, they got my attention." He looks down at the cloak he wears and examines the many cuts in it.

"Learning new techniques?" He sounds like an excited schoolboy.

"It would mean learning from a human teacher."

"I learn from those who have knowledge that I need, who that is just isn't important. If it gives you the edge, you take it."

48

The day is here, everything is in place, naturally I am a bag of nerves. You would think that with the number of things that have tried to end my life recently I would be a bit more relaxed, but no, I am shaking like a leaf. I am standing in the mall, outside the palace, the roads are closed and there is a considerable crowd outside the barriers, and above me the emperor's own craft is hovering. The queen herself is just arriving. There is a guard of honour, we are not doing the twenty-one--gun salute, with the draco forces above, and we can't risk any misunderstanding. There are soldiers on horseback, on foot, lining the route. It's a short walk to the palace, but there isn't really a carriage big enough for the emperor. So, the royal entourage arrives. Everyone takes up position, and the emperor and his mate are teleported to their position. The draconion male does not go in for fancy clothes, but the armour the emperor wears is immaculate, totally white, and impossible to see where the armour starts and what is, in fact, his tough white skin.

However, the draco queen, that really is a different matter altogether. The cloak she wears over her shoulders is as dark a blue as a frosty winter's moonlit night, it shimmers and glitters as if you are looking at stars on a clear night. Under that she wears a long dress of blue, that flatters her figure, but the most eye-catching thing is that the colour doesn't remain constant. It changes from a light pastel to a royal blue as she moves, the effect is dazzling, the light silken material flows with her elegant movements.

The draconian queen's bodyguards follow, they wear armour that matches the queen's cloak. Again, it is hard to actually focus on the colour, as it changes very subtly, like stars that twinkle. Over this they wear short silken cloaks, but this is merely to make their weapons less obvious and threatening.

My bit now. It's a complete blur to me as the adrenaline kicks in fully. It's a beautiful, clear, fresh day, the eyes of the world are upon us, I do the formal introductions. Now I will be the first to admit, that without the help of the computer feeding me the lines, there would be no way that I wouldn't fluff this. The moment arrives where I pass on the gift of telepathy to the queen, by touching her forehead, then I briefly explain how to work it. As she speaks, it is my job to speak her words out loud for the people to hear. There is a long greeting where the titles of the queen are introduced, and I mean all of them. This is so that the emperor feels that he is being met by someone of power. I introduce the emperor, and his titles. This is a long, and boring affair, but finally we walk back to the palace. Deborah and Liza are waiting at the palace. There are more introductions. Behind the emperor comes his entourage, I am introducing everyone to everyone. I actually feel relieved to see the old general, who seems greatly amused by my discomfort, but is stopped in his flow of insults when I introduce him to Liza. He absolutely stumbles over his words, says the wrong things, and generally makes a mess of things. Obviously, it's my turn to take the mickey. I am greatly amused, but I must admit that Debora and Liza do look amazing; the draco queen has supplied them with two of the most amazing dresses ever seen on this planet. The material seems almost to be alive, not just shimmering, but actively emphasising, the colours change and change, it's rather like the effect of the aurora borealis. Every place that the material touches the body it instantly causes the material to fluidly change colours. The cut is wonderful, I find myself getting quite distracted looking at Debs in this dress, she really looks hypnotic.

When I finally run out of people and titles to introduce, the general takes me to a room; Liza and Deborah are asked to accompany me. There I am introduced to four different types of aliens. I am introduced to each race in turn. There is a female, a male, and a child. All look at me with undisguised dislike.

Liza and Debs suggest that they should take the children so that we can speak. As the children leave, one of the females softly cries as if in pain, she gathers herself together, but only just. Odd, I know that I'm not good at speaking, but for heaven's sake, that was an overreaction.

The group there are the leaders of the four planets that I own. There is a feline looking couple, slender, strong and supple, moving gracefully, and apart from a fine coat of short glossy fur, virtually human in appearance. The male wears a suit that is formal to the point of being almost military, he stands very stiffly and appears very aloof. The female, however, has a far looser, relaxed silken dress, it is rather plunging to the top, showing her shapely furry cleavage, and although long, the back is open to the front, showing her long shapely legs. As I glance at her I can't help but think, "That must be what people refer to as being a cat lover," but cut off that line of Builder's thinking when I see the distress in her face.

The next couple that I am introduced to is an odd couple, OK, odd to me anyway. He is tall, about seven feet tall, but very slender, slim, but healthy looking, his skin a pale sky blue, not a slight amount but a solid blue. His partner is about the size of a human woman, a pale skin like moonlight on a white rose, and with long, straight, silver hair. The man had a long pale-blue full-length fitted coat with a mandarin type collar, a smart plain suit underneath, the lady in a long pale blue dress of a silky material.

The third was a race clearly of insect origin, I immediately named them the mantas. They had wide

275

foreheads, very large oval black eyes, a slight grey to olive green skin, and they had an exoskeleton. The hard bony parts on the outside, rather like crabs have. They wore very simple suits, in grey and olive, very practical, not at all fussy. Their hands had the look of a robot's, as the joints are all visible. They do have incredibly strong bodies and hands, yet their hands are capable of the most minute intricate work.

Finally, a group I'm calling the scando's. They look human. Like the Scandinavian or Icelandic blond types, so damn healthy that their skin has a luminescent glow, immaculate long blond hair. I look at them and really hope that the human race has some of their genes kicking about in there somewhere.

The Scando female is obviously holding back the tears with great effort, and finally gives in to it. Great sobs go through her body, she screams almost at me to 'just get on with it', calls me cruel and several words that just don't translate, but said in a way that suggests I'm not on her Christmas card list. She openly and uncontrollably weeps. Now, I admit that I am not good at speeches, but even to me this appears excessive. I try to carry on, but the general gently taps me on the shoulder and takes me to one side.

"What did I say wrong?"

"It is normal for the victorious draco leader, after defeating a planet, and as the new owner to slaughter the youngest child of the rulers in front of them, it is supposed to show them who the ruler is, and that their lives are in their hands."

"Bloody hell."

"Yes, it is normal to drink their blood as well. Personally, I feel it is a barbaric act of petty viciousness, not how a warrior acts at all, killing a defenceless child to make themselves feared, ha! If they were warriors, they would be feared without that."

At this point, right on cue, the children burst into the room, chased by Liza and Debs. The tiny blonde girl runs up to her mother and asks if she can look at the poodles. I bend down beside her. "You can, but on one condition." She looks at me seriously. "That is, when you grow up and get married, Deborah, Liza and myself can come to your wedding."

She looks at her mom. "If my mom says that's OK", she replies seriously.

I stand up. "Good, in the meantime, I give my word that I will do all that I can to protect all of you, and your planets."

The children all run off shouting and happy.

"I apologise, for any misunderstanding. I asked you here as guests, so you could visit my home planet, and hopefully get to know you. When I defeated the emissary, it was to save this planet from destruction, I knew nothing of you. I wanted to give the planets back, but the general tells me that would leave you open to attack from any draco with enough power to conquer you, and with massive armies already on your planets, it would leave you defenceless."

I look at stunned faces.

"I'm afraid that you are all stuck with me, I am the owner of your planets, but not the ruler. While I'm here, you are safe, now can we talk please, I have a few ideas that I wish to discuss."

This time I get a more appreciative audience. "I don't have long, before the banquet begins, you are guests of honour, you and your children."

I tell them my plan. "Firstly, the draco army forages and takes whatever it wishes, they use the population as slaves to get whatever the draco empire is needing, so it is constantly being attacked by the resistance, which it retaliates to very violently. This has to stop.

"So, I intend to give back to the emperor, as a gift, over three-quarters of the soldiers. The remaining soldiers will be trained as an elite defence force by my friend, the general. He is a noble and honest warrior, he will train the remaining in discipline, they will be there with the sole purpose of protecting the planets. He will not tolerate any attacks on the population. They must respect you, and in return, you shall keep them, and treat them with respect, they are all that is standing between you and invasion, treat them as such. This also prevents the emperor having to watch me. I apparently have an army that could be of concern to the balance of the empire, so by giving him the armies it takes away the threat, and boosts his power in one go. The emperor needs things from you. But he is willing to trade, openly and honestly, providing you don't sell to his enemies, and he still gets the amounts he needs. The cost of feeding and looking after an army of that size costs so much that it will be more profitable to deal with you in business. I suggest that you are as fair as possible, while making a profit. The slavery has ended as of now. I will not tolerate it.

"I wish for our five planets to work and trade together, in a sort of union, should one planet be attacked, the other four will come to their aid, although each has a small army, together they will be sufficient. Also with the general in charge, anyone wishing to attack must first defeat him in single combat." I look up at him. "Anyone wishing to do so, is a fool, and would quickly become a dead fool."

"And what do you get out of this?" It's the scando woman.

"Well, I would like to visit your planets, and learn from them."

"Learn?"

"Yes anything, especially technical knowledge. I once made a promise that I wish to keep, to learn all I can."

Inside I hear the computer happily shouting 'yes' repeatedly.

"I hope that this will create a lasting peace between us that includes the draco. If you have a better idea, tell me now."

I wait, there's a gentle whisper. A distant gong means that the banquet is starting, and we must return. The children run in, and holding their parents' hands, we leave the room.

As we leave, the scando woman turns to me. "You want peace? That's all?"

"Well, there is one thing, to visit your planet, and for you all to be friends with Deborah and myself. I will give my life to protect you. All I ask is to be welcome, and not an enemy."

49

The large banqueting hall has been laid out. As the emperor enters, I watch his gaze settle upon the immaculately laid out table, the chairs exactly in line. The cutlery is laid out exactly. I have never seen such a long table, and a far cry from us watching TV with our tea on a tray. I note that the emperor gives a nod of appreciation to the obvious care that has gone into even the finest detail.

As we enter, the noise drops to almost silence, this is where the formality begins. It is also where I am most likely to show myself up, this is not a part of how I live.

"Computer."

"Yes."

"Help."

The next few minutes are a blur of etiquette, manners and many other subtleties that I don't possess, but the computer helps me to get through without bringing attention to myself. Suddenly, an army of immaculate people begin bringing in silver platters and trays of food. Again, the presentation is amazing, but the smell, oh my, and finally as we get to actually taste it, wow. So good that for a moment I almost forget that I may have to make a speech.

Almost.

The meal is a huge success. I am amazed to see the emperor and his queen eating only lightly steamed vegetables and fruit and eating with such delicate manners. He clearly is enjoying the occasion, and so too are the other guests. I am enormously amused to see the general talking to Liza, sat beside her; he clearly can't take his eyes off of her and she loves it, smiling and acting all demure and coy. Deborah noticed first and nudged me to take notice, he is acting like a schoolboy with his first crush.

Finally, it is over. There is a parade out to the emperor's craft, they leave first, and for the first time ever, he bows a low to the queen, unknown for a draco to bow to anyone. This truly is a compliment. Then the rulers from my planets leave, eventually all have gone, the last to leave are the queen's guards and I am alone in the road. The barriers are being taken down, and as I watch the skies begin to clear of the draco warships. This was the trick, the draco will never retreat, it would mean losing face, but if they were there as a guard of honour to the emperor, then they leave with him, and with honour, everyone wins. I stare up, it's like watching starlings swirling, moving together as a single fluid unit. Then suddenly they are gone. With the barriers down, a crowd begins to gather around me. It grows, they start to cheer, the threats gone after so long, they feel safe again, all are cheering and happy, I walk alone back to the palace. Deborah waits for me.

"Have I told you how beautiful you look?" We are teleported home, from the edge of the crowd, utterly unnoticed.

50

The wind cuts through me, I am finding it difficult to get a full breath of air. The general is still grumbling to himself. We have been steadily climbing since early this morning when we were teleported to this mountainside. All I know is that we must head up, and at the moment, the top seems a long way off. "Why," the general starts again, "are we walking up this bleak hillside, when the teleporter can send us to where we need to go?"

"We must prepare ourselves as pilgrims and prove our worthiness."

"Can't we just teleport in and force them to teach us."

"Well, if you can force someone to show you how to fight, then they can't be very good at fighting."

We keep going round in circles, him asking why, me trying to justify what I don't understand either.

We walk, clamber, climb and complain upwards until darkness forces us to stop. Then we fasten together two tents, so that the general is under cover. We couldn't get a tent long enough for him, his feet sticking out to be exposed by the elements wasn't going to work. Exhausted, we fix some hot food, then slide into sleeping bags which we discover are on the most uncomfortable piece of land on the whole mountain. It does warm up slightly, not exactly cosy, but at least out of the wind.

"How do you humans get mates?"

"That is complicated, and seems to be totally random."

"Do you have to attack them? Or do they attack you?" My mind goes back to Roxy nightclub's 'grab a granny night' avoiding the roaming hands of ladies who frankly should have learned better by then.

"Absolutely not, if you see someone you like the look of, you talk to them, perhaps buy them a drink, usually hoping that they will be sufficiently drunk, not to realise that you aren't actually Prince Charming."

"Who's he?"

"He is who she wants, or hopes for, but you are the compromise, or hopefully near enough so that she will talk to you."

"You talk to them?"

This sounds like such a strange concept to him, that it would never have occurred to him.

"Of course, don't you?"

"Well, as you say it's complicated."

"Always is."

"You see, traditionally a male would find a lone female, ambush them, mate them, possibly then killing them and eating them."

"And they say I'm not romantic enough."

"Well, the females weren't always happy about this arrangement."

"You don't say."

"I do, well they started banding together, and learning to fight. This they developed into an art. Any male who attacks a female is going to be torn to shreds, and possibly eaten."

"Well, how do you, well you know, get jiggy with it?"

"Well, every so often, a female gets a need, right?"

"Yes."

"Then she leaves the safety of the pack, but not by very far, and then finds a male. If he looks suitable, she lets him see her, and if it all goes OK, she lets him go afterwards, if he gets a bit too carried away, the other females are close at hand."

"And eat him?" I ask.

"Yes, you have this also?"

"No, just a lucky guess."

"Do you think that Liza would prefer me to talk to her?"

"Infinitely."

"What would I say?"

"No idea, but as a rule, females on Earth like to feel that you value them as a person, so get them to talk about themselves first."

"No ambush at all, then?"

"Too simple I'm afraid. Anyway, how does the male know that the female is, well, you know, needing?"

"She has a way of sending out a sort of message, like a scent, it lets the male know, and it makes them sort of subdued, and a bit, interested, if you know what I mean…"

"Our women wear perfumes that can do similar things." I think of Deborah's favourite perfume.

Is that why, when the queen first walked in, she had such a powerful effect on the males?"

"Yes, of course. She isn't really a queen, she is a high priestess, and part of her learning is the control of her femininity, to control males."

"I thought that the males all went quiet."

"There are also her guards. As the females began sticking together for their safety, and to protect their young, they began to learn and develop fighting skills, and the guard, they are the elite. They are so damn fast. I tell you now, in a straight fight, they could take your hand off before I could even reach my sword."

"They must be fast if they are even as fast as you."

"Is Liza fast?"

"And strong."

He gives a little sigh.

"Definitely no ambush then."

"Definitely not."

51

We walk, climb, descend, climb higher, descend, and climb even higher. And just keep going, each mountain leads to the next even higher one. We have started to work together, he pushes me up the climbs, I reach back and pull him up, and working together, we are overcoming obstacles. We have been walking for weeks, the general has stopped complaining, we stop often, just to breath in the fresh mountain air, and look at the astounding views. We are looking at the path ahead, enjoying the moment, and a snowflake lands on him. "I have never seen snow before."

"Snow?" I look at the exposed bare mountainside, no shelter, anywhere. "Come on, if it snows here, we are in trouble." We move on, it's high, and breathing isn't easy, so as fast as we can, which isn't very fast, but we do go faster. Soon our lungs are burning from the effort of trying to outrun the weather front. It moves in fast. We don't.

There is no place to shelter, or even pitch the tents, the wind almost comes from nowhere — still, then a howling gale within minutes. We just have to keep going. The snow begins to cover the track, steep drops could end the walk for us, so we begin to almost feel our way forwards. The temperature plummets: we are in trouble, big trouble. We move on, but are moving slower and our progress is down to a crawl. The general stops, slowly sinking to one knee. I pull him up, he leans on me heavily, he says nothing. We keep going, he slowly moves, then stops, sliding down. I pull him, dragging him in the snow, I am beginning to feel dizzy. the computer tells me, less than five per cent energy.

I pull, sliding him again, achingly slow, we inch forwards, slip, get up, pull, slip again, get up, pull slip and can't get up. Zero energy reserves, now what?

I pull again from the floor, I keep thinking 'can't give up', but slowly, I simply stop thinking. In a final effort I scream silently inside my head. I see the lights coming towards me, I expect to see the shining ones, but no, just a dim light. I try to crawl, but can barely move a hand. A hot wet tongue slides across my face, an ear shattering bark, more licks, more barking. More lights, then darkness.

52

I am on a bed of some type, it's not wide, not quite long enough, but there's warm blankets piled on me. I can see a small fire in the centre of the room. Actually, the room seems to be round, I think that it's a tent of some type, whatever it is, it's warm. I see a movement opposite, I call out in my mind, "General?"

A grim looking face slowly appears from under the blankets.

"You all right?"

"Cold."

"Good, I was worried about you."

"You didn't leave me, you could have, but you tried to carry me."

"You weigh a ton, I'm afraid that I didn't get very far."

"Looks like far enough. Why didn't you leave me?"

"Because you are my friend, you don't leave friends behind, not when they need you."

"Friend? I don't think anyone would have helped me before."

"Don't worry, I will help, if I can, I'm going to sleep now. Wake me in a week's time."

53

An old woman wakes me; she has a warm, friendly face that is as rugged as the mountain itself. She pushes a bowl of hot steaming vegetable stew into my hands. I can't explain, but after weeks of living off rice just how damn good it tastes. I nod and give her a huge smile, she looks pleased, and I eat. Opposite I can hear the sounds of stew being greedily eaten. The old woman nods to the general and gives a wide smile. She leaves and a couple of the men, each with equally craggy, but happy faces, appear. They speak; it takes a few moments for my inbuilt computer to work out the language,

"Ahh, you are finally awake, good, good, you have lots to do, we have been looking for you for days now. It's a good thing that the dogs found you when they did, any longer and you would have been frozen solid. Only good for the pot." He laughs hard, at what I hope is his joke. The thought of the general slowly turning on a spit amuses me; I give a little laugh. Then I suddenly realise what he said.

"You said that you have been looking for us?"

"The shaman said to find a man and a huge lizard, that you will need our help."

I look across at the general who is now standing but having to bend almost doubled over in the low tent.

"How did you know it was us," I joke.

The pair find this most amusing.

"Come now, the shaman is waiting, hurry, hurry."

We are given warm clothes, the traditional clothing that they are wearing. A long thick padded coat, with matching leggings and a thick hat that ties under the chin, finished with thick warm boots. We dress and go outside, the men there must be about five feet tall, I tower above them, but the general is virtually double their height. The general tells me to thank them for their kindness, and for saving us. I pass the message on, adding, "We look just like locals now."

They look up at the general. "No one will ever know that you aren't one of us."

In the bright clear day outside, we can clearly see the pass ahead that we are aiming for. It appears so close in the crisp fresh air, you feel as if you can touch it. In reality, there's a good day's walk ahead, and not an easy walk either. We are guided to a round building. Unlike the other tents, this is a solid built hut, with its timber frame covered in soil and grass, in the centre smoke lazily curls out of a small opening, the gnarled old timber door is covered in some sort of skins. They are so old and smoke soiled that it's impossible to say what animal once wore it, or how long ago.

We are ushered in and are assaulted by the heat, smells and the darkness inside. Out of the smoke a small

292

figure emerges, he lights a candle, and instantly, I have the urge to blow it out again. The old guy is an apparition of wrinkles, wearing only a filthy loin cloth. I can't help but think of the ladies in India, who daily go down to filthy looking brown rivers, and beat their washing against a stone, and yet they are always immaculately clean. I have often wondered what would happen if the washing machine manufacturers had used this as their inspiration. He instructs us to strip down to our giddy aunts and I suddenly become aware that it's been a while since my undies saw a good beating against a rock. He is frankly filthy, hair matted, brown skin stained by the smoke, he smokes a big fat stump of something, that doesn't appear to be tobacco based. It hangs in the corner of his mouth. We sit down cross legged on the floor, whatever he is smoking glows red for a moment. The smoke, when finally exhaled, adding to the assault on the senses. We are offered drinks, in blackened cups, that are made from possibly leather, but hard to tell.

"You aren't married, are you?" I ask silently in my mind. To my surprise he bursts into uncontrollable laughter.

"How did you guess?" he replies, laughing. He urges us to drink. I see the general's face curl up in disgust as he drinks. I take a sip, to my surprise it is the best cup of tea that I have tasted in ages. Seeing me readily drinking mine down, the general tries again, managing a little more. The red embers glow as the old guy puffs away rhythmically. The general's eyes start to go glazed, I look at the old man's eyes they are bloodshot red, the whites a stained brown colour.

I begin to feel relaxed, a bit too relaxed, my eyes get heavy, and I begin to drift. As my eyelids close, I see through my third eye, for a few moments, and all around us are spectral images of animals, almost solid, but then changing as if made of the thick smoke that comes from the small fire. The images surround us, coming close to rub against us, I swear that I feel the fur from a smoky fox, it sniffs me then sits beside me, its thick tail brushing against my legs. There are many animals there, some more clearly than others. I don't even know if all of them are even living in this country. A wolf comes close, sniffs, it walks round me closer and closer. Turning, it finally just walks into me. First his head, then his body slips inside, disappearing into my chest.

Suddenly I feel myself running, on all fours, powerful legs drive me on. I leap over a narrow gorge, climbing up a steep wooded hillside. I can smell the grass, the animal's tracks, knowing which scent belongs to each animal. I feel an urge to hunt, but a stronger urge drives me upwards, I can smell the wind, sense danger, smell the fear in other animals as I pass. Suddenly I am in a clearing, a ring of tall stones that form a rough circle. I walk, carefully into the very centre, and wait. The white lights begin to appear, many different sizes and brightness, different intensities, all surround the wolf, disappearing, their places being taken by another. Finally, a bright light, one that I am familiar with, the light being appears. "You must undergo more preparation, your final ordeal is getting close now, there is a task first, we will guide you there, in return you will be given control of your mind."

It fades and the wolf walks out of the circle, it begins running again, faster this time. I can feel the exhilaration it feels in every step, every bound, I am overjoyed at the sensation, the power, the sheer joy of running so powerful and fast, because it can. It bursts through the shed walls and leaps straight at my back, I am left inside myself again. A smoking wolf form passes out of my chest, turns to me and I swear, in my mind gives me a high five. I give it my ecstatic thanks, feeling exhilarated and very happy, it grins, and fades away. Everything is normal again, it's dirty, smelly and dark. The general gives a slight moan, and begins to move, the old guy starts to wake up. Both are sluggish. Moving slowly, as though they are recovering from something.

"Are you two all right?"

I am showered with abuse, from both. "Bloody hell what did you drink?"

"I have been a guide for your friend here, to the other dimensions."

"Wow, what did you give me? I feel fantastic." He looks at me through the eyes of one with a hangover.

"Tea, this wasn't for you. This was for your friend."

"What about the animals, the wolf, all the spirits?"

"Don't know what you are talking about." He passes me three tea bags. "Here, make a brew, I feel awful."

We drink tea, lost in our own thoughts, the general seems very quiet.

"You two look rough."

"Feel it," replies the shaman. He delves into a rolled-up fur, pulls out a blue tube, passes it to me. "Chocolate digestive? Go on take two."

We sit together, the general looks at the biscuits warily, after drinking the last thing offered to him by this man, but tries the biscuit carefully, his face lightening up as he tastes it. Slowly he turns to us. "Do you know, perhaps this Earth is worth saving after all"

"You wait until you taste a chocolate Hob Nob."

The old man nods in agreement. "Any time you are passing, if you could drop off a packet or two."

"Will do."

The next morning, well fed, restocked with food we set off, the pass ahead clear. The path almost looks inviting, and we make excellent time. I still feel amazing after my experience, the general seems to be more urgent, but in a good mood, and happy to see the scenery. We clear the highest point, begin to descend and find a sheltered place to set up camp. Just before sleeping, the general turns over and quietly tells me, "I think that I shall share some chocolate biscuit with Liza."

54

The trail takes us rapidly down, becoming wider, more used; round a corner we suddenly see a monastery. Taken aback with its size, and the fact we haven't seen a solid building since setting off on our trek, cautiously we approach. The general is imposing at the best of times, but here, where the people average about five feet tall, he looks massive. To our pleasure a monk in orange robes sees us and greets us warmly, welcoming us inside. We are shown to a long low table and given vegetable stew and rice. "How come everyone up here can make rice taste good, except for you?"

He looks at me grinning, and quietly adds, "I don't suppose that there are any biscuits, are there?"

After eating we are shown to a dormitory of low narrow beds, shown some showers and left to our own devices. There doesn't appear to be anyone else staying, so we slide two beds together for the general, even my feet are sticking out over the end of my bed.

Early the next morning, as I am cleaning my teeth, we are approached by an old monk. He looks at the general, then me, then beckons us to follow. There are other monks, all dressed in orange robes. We are asked to maintain silence, so we don't disturb the students who are meditating. This gives the whole place a feeling of peace, which is more than just quiet, it has a wonderful atmosphere.

We arrive at the abbot's office, are shown in with a sweeping gesture of the old monk's hand, then a leisurely bow. Inside is clean and orderly, a desk which surprises me, somehow, I didn't expect to see a rich mahogany piece of furniture.

Having been with the general for so long now I automatically begin to speak silently inside my head. After a few moments, realising what I am doing, I start again, this time with the computer's help to speak the local language. I greet the abbot, and thank him for his hospitality. I really don't know what to say after that, when the abbot, replies, speaking to us both through telepathy.

He is a middle-aged man, slightly taller than the others here, he has a pleasant smile, but you get the feeling from him that he is a good man, but has troubles in his life. He greets us warmly, then says, "You look surprised that I can do head speaking. It is a skill that has been passed down for many generations of monks now, and it feels good to talk to new people." He looks at the general. "No offence, but different types, and to be able to understand, and communicate."

He goes on to tell us how telepathy was first brought to the monastery by ancient 'travellers' who taught how to pass on the art to a chosen few. Very handy for when the monks are doing silent meditation.

He gets up and leads us out, we enter the main building. He walks in front, telling us the history of the buildings, then leads us into a small beautifully decorated room. Three of the walls are covered with hand painted murals, depicting scenes of life in the monastery, farming, cultivating the land, meditating. The fourth wall is covered with a plain red velvet curtain. The abbot points to one small section, partly hidden away, there is a picture of one of the creators, touching an abbot on the forehead. We stare at the picture. "We don't show this to people, only to those we are passing the knowledge to, and you are the first outsiders to see it."

"It is an honour."

"Well, most people we meet have difficulty accepting it." He looks at the general. "I have reason to think that you may not find it hard to believe."

"I can't believe it, that is the head of the creators."

This monk continues, "The legend has it that two travellers will arrive, having walked through the mountains, and who we must teach all we can in regard to the art of stillness of the mind." He points to a nearby corner of the picture, there is a man, beside him is a larger, obviously reptile being, both dressed in the traditional mountain clothes of the locals.

Next, we are shown how to sit, so that we can begin lessons in the art of meditation. Stilling the mind is learned, it's not easy, and requires practice, and I am not good at it, whereas the general finds it easy. There is something troubling me. When the abbot returns, I ask him.

"Were we expected? The painting on the wall, the mountain men said that they were out looking for us; they even had clothes ready-made that fitted us? That isn't just a story told that someone may one day visit, I am beginning to feel that I am walking down a path of destiny and everyone knows where it's going except for me."

"Exactly."

"Don't deny it then, will you."

"No," he grins, "now back to practice, you need it."

Slowly I improve. When not meditating, I am given jobs to do maintaining the monastery. I am on a roof, doing long overdue repairs. While working, I allow my mind to drift, to become blank, I automatically carry on with the work, but feel a peace descend on me. I work the entire day, time seems to have stopped. I am aware of the wind, the cold, I am a part of it, and yet I feel that I am experiencing it all from the outside looking inwards. The general finally tugs on the roof ladders, I'm surprised to see that it is dark, and very cold.

"We have been looking for you, never thought to look for a builder actually at work."

"Cheers, mate."

I tell the abbot of this the next morning, he looks thoughtfully at me. "Stillness in movement, movement in stillness," he mumbles. "Time for a rethink on your training I think that you need to take a different path with your learning." He sets me a series of simple chi gung movements, shows me how to perform them, then once I have learned them sufficiently, he has me perform them as a repeating set, hour after hour, then tells me how to release my mind and to let go.

Hours slip by; I just loose myself in the simple flowing movements. By the end of the day I feel that I am finally making improvements.

The abbot arrives next morning and asks me to go with him. He leads me through a room, lined with the mummified remains of all the monks and abbots who have lived and died here.

"These men all worked on the knowledge of their times, writing it down on scrolls, this knowledge has remained here, secret, sacred wisdom. We have guarded it, but now, we must let this knowledge become available to all, the time for secrecy is over, we must share the wisdom." At the end of the room is a door, as we walk through it, I am amazed to see a dozen monks all at computers, typing away. "We fear that it may be too late, we must hurry, can you help?"

"Computer, I have a job for you, look at these scrolls, and put them onto the public domain."

I pick up a scroll, instantly read it as if translated already. I sit down, a thin strand of fibrils slides out of my wrist and into the back of the computer. A pile of scrolls is placed before me. I glance at it, it instantly appears onscreen translated, put onto a file and backed up.

"Computer, you get on with this, I'm going to meditate."

I can feel a happy murmuring come from the computer, learning new information, I slip away and let the quiet fill my mind.

I am confused, it's fresh and bright, and I am hungry. I find the general meditating, I tap his shoulder, He scrambles up. "You're back We couldn't wake you at meal time last night, and you missed breakfast."

The abbot comes in. "You did it, every one, now on computer. Well done."

He asks me a question about an obscure text, I tell him the translation.

"Three blind men are put in a room with an elephant and asked to describe it. The first finds a leg, 'it is like a tree trunk', the second finds the trunk and says, 'no, it's more like a snake, it wraps around you', the third finds the tail, and disagrees again. 'It's like a branch on a tree, it moves around, its short and has stiff long hair on the end'. So, they each get followers who agree with a blind man, they fight and kill each other.

"OK, I did shorten the whole saga, but I guess that the moral is each of the three are a hundred per cent correct, but only have a small part of the picture, and if they actually listened to each other, they would learn more of the picture as a whole, and save a whole lot of bloodshed, look for what they have in common, not what separates them."

"That really is a concise version, the original was told for hours, but you seem to have distilled the meaning."

The following morning, we set off walking again. The abbot sees us off, he looks a little bit sad as we set off walking, but it's a lovely bright clear day. The abbot gives us clear directions to what he assures us will be our final destination, only a couple of days' walk, and a good weather forecast, we are in excellent spirits.

As we leave, the abbot slowly shakes his head, walks to the room where we have been meditating, and opens the red velvet curtains. The entire wall is a single scene. It is made up of thousands of evil-looking demons, all armed with swords and hand weapons. In the centre is a single figure, wearing what looks a lot like a black sweatshirt, and trousers with knee pads.

55

The final walk takes us to the highest we have been so far. It hurts deep inside the head, every step is toiled over, two steps, stop, gasp for air, two steps, stop, fight for breath, then we are at the top. We stop, and are treated to a view seen by few. It is simply breathtaking, we both stare. "I am beginning to see why you fight for this planet, perhaps it's worth saving after all."

The descent is rapid, so rapid in fact that one false move and it would be free falling. Our breathing improves with each hour, soon we look back to snow-capped peaks and beautiful blue skies. At sunset we reach our destination, an ancient squat fortress-looking building; its heavy solid wooden doors are closed, so we set up our tents and wait. The abbot told us that this would happen, and we must wait, patiently for whatever is going to happen to happen. The next morning an ancient monk walks out of the gates, walks over to where we are meditating in the morning sunlight, walks round us, says nothing, but examines us carefully, walks back inside the building and the big gates close behind him. We watch him go. "Well, THAT certainly wasn't an event, was it?" We meditate all day and settle down for the night. I am amazed how little complaining the general does, the worst he manages is to look at the doors and give a little snort but says nothing.

The event happens shortly after sunrise, we have just finished our morning rice, and settled down to meditate. A low distant hum begins to grow, finally a helicopter appears round a rocky pinnacle and flies at us, hovering in front of us, before landing only twenty metres away from us. Our tents and belongings are scattered in the downdraught, thick dust covers us and stones blast into our faces. Four muscular young men leap out grab a large holdall each and dash to the gate. The helicopter rises, and turns its rotors beating, throbbing into the distance.

The gate opens, the four men walk inside, the gates begin to close. We are about to search for our belongings when the gate opens a little, the old monk's face appears and he cheerfully beckons us, waving us in with his ancient orange robes flapping around his thin arms. Without even trying to search for our tents we run to the gates, they immediately close behind us with a satisfying solid thud.

The young men are loud, shouting and whooping. As we approach, they laugh at the sight of us, ripped and ragged clothes, covered head to foot in a thick grey dust — we look a mess. The general is slowly inching his hand towards his sword. "Not now, big fella." It's the small monk, speaking to us with his mind. "But very soon, I suspect." And he laughs at his own joke.

The young man who appears to be the leader of the four shouts to us, "There are those who walk, and those who arrive by helicopter." This is apparently hilarious, as all four, keep repeating it, slapping their backs and laughing.

The general keeps on walking, but inside our minds we hear the old guy shout, "Assholes!"

The four men are greeted, and complain that no one is there to carry their bags, and led off to rooms. We are showed to a dormitory of more low and very short beds, young novice monks look alarmed as the general appears, but calm down as I greet them in their own language. It strikes me then, wherever you go in the world, just saying a simple hello in the native tongue makes everyone feel better.

I am immediately taken to a man who shaves my head, I would call him a barber, but a hair butcher would be closer to the truth. I emerge with a bald head; the man looks at the hairless draco and nods approvingly. The general thinks that this is hilarious, thoroughly enjoying the moment. I, on the other hand, am complaining bitterly. "There wasn't a lot, I know. But I have had it for fifty-seven years."

"Oh, shut up, you look like one of us now, well a shorter version, and not so good looking."

We are handed an orange robe to wear next. It's my turn to laugh when he finds out that it only comes in one size, and on him it's more like a loin cloth than a robe. Then come the sandals, and I feel very good again, just listening to his complaining. Finally, I point out that he doesn't actually wear anything on his feet normally. He finally sees the funny side, and puts the sandals on his enormous clawed feet. The other novices enjoy this and laugh with him. They begin talking with us, and soon we are just one of them, which is good for us, apart from being taller and older, in the general's case, much bigger and far older, something that I point out often until he threatens me with a particularly obscene death, then I shut up.

As soon as we are fitted into robes, and some bed sheets are given to the general to wear as a robe, we are put to training. It soon becomes obvious that I am being picked out. Everything I do is criticized, I am hit with a big stick, and I don't mean gently. This is accompanied by calls of encouragement from the general, not for me but for the teachers.

"Hit him harder, he deserves it," or, his favourite, "Make him have it, he can take it." We train with the novices for the first few days, but with the general's skills, and my computer retaining the moves and guiding me, we soon advance. He is given his own teacher, and I find myself with two. Sometimes they take it in turns, sometimes they both work together, pushing me, forcing me past what I thought possible, they work me to exhaustion. At the end of each day, the old general helps me to my bed, lowering me gently down, and telling me, "Personally I wouldn't go so easy on you." But he does then fetch me some food.

Most mornings start with us cleaning, brushing the sand that constantly blows into the open dormitories, then the temple area, and finally the higher monks' quarters. No one ever complains, we just get on with it, the other novices soon see that we do the same work as they do, so pretty much treat us as one of them. This pleases the general; he tells me that he knows that he is getting the authentic training and learning. The novices sit and talk with us before we sleep. I translate for the general, they ask about us, where he comes from, not prying, just friendly, passing time. Many of these young men come from very poor families, so to be accepted as a monk, even at a very young age, is a privilege, as they will be educated, and fed. They do begin asking why it is that I am being picked on so much, but one young lad pipes up. "The abbot told me that you have a task, but have very little time, so they have to prepare you, they seem very sad that they are hurting you, but say that there isn't time to learn another way."

"I know, they must push me, I don't mind, because I know why they do it, still it would be nice if they didn't."

"I wish that they would hit the helicopter boys like they do you."

"Who are they?"

"They are rich, they pay a lot to train here, it helps to keep the monastery going, but they treat us like skivvies. They don't think that we are here because it's an honour to learn, they think that we are simply their personal servants. They think we are below them."

"Assholes."

The next day, they start on our stamina. This involves running up a mountainside, a crude path of irregular stone steps is the only way up, at the top is a small white open building, a shrine of some type. Here a monk places a garland of flowers around your neck, and you run down again. It is steep, hard to climb, and if you don't finish in the time set by an hourglass, you get to go again, immediately. Major incentive! The climb is so high that breathing is difficult at the top, the air is so thin. I mean we are very high in the mountains to start with, so the extra altitude is a real killer.

The first time I run it, I didn't make the time, so was sent back up.

The next day is the same, eventually I make it, but am sent up again, and told, "Faster."

Surely, they are kidding.

Immediately after this run, we begin training, however, it is only for swords. I am given a stick. I notice that it is heavier than the others, a lot heavier. The beatings increase.

One day I finish my first run, and sprinting to where the abbot waits to collect my garland, I see him smiling. Well, that's new, anyway. He stops me for a moment before I begin the second run.

"How do you feel?"

"I feel good, thank you."

I bow and run off. As I begin my second climb, I realise, I do actually feel good, very good. The novices on their way down are surprised to see me start laughing as I run, I feel amazing, and I run now and it feels so good, I feel alive!

I feel that I have turned a corner. I am blocking most, then all of the blows aimed at me, I begin to enjoy the long hours of sword training. I even look forward to the morning slog up to the hilltop shrine, each day I push myself harder, revelling in the feeling of health and fitness.

One morning I am surprised to see the helicopter boys standing at the start of the run, still full of their own piss and importance. They are poking fun at our 'fancy duds'.

The monk explains to them what to do, that it is a test of their fitness, and that as it is their final day of training, they should learn from the experience. He tells them they must reach the top and return, with a garland, before the sand runs through the timer. He turns to me. "You must go twice." The moment he says it, as he reaches for the timer, I am running. I push myself like never before. I pass them on my way down and shout encouragement, reaching the abbot faster than I ever have before.

As I set off for my second run, I hear his voice inside my head. "Go inside your head, remember the wolf. Show them rich arseholes what you can do. Beat them back."

By now I can feel the effort beginning to show, my legs burn, and my lungs are sore from gasping for air. What did he mean about the wolf? Then, as I think about it, I remember the shaman's hut, the wolf, immediately I swear that I feel fur brushing against me, and a feeling inside my head. Once again, I am running inside the wolf's mind, it is both pushing me on, and revelling in the sensation of running. My body goes into a state of flow, by the time I reach the top I am gliding over the rocky path. Leaping down the rocks, running, and it feels so amazing. Towards the bottom, I pass the first of the helicopter boys, leaping past him, he looks exhausted. I can see the next, pass him, then the next. I can see the abbot, far off, but the other guy is on the flat already, but stumbling with effort. I know that I can do it, I am closing quickly on him. As I pass, I shout encouragement. "Go on, only one hundred yards." I run past, sprint for the line, handing over the second garland and look for the timer, the final grains of sand slip through.

the abbot looks on. "Cutting it a bit fine there, go on, get warmed up for sword practice, there's something special for you today."

I jog back, sweat rolling down my face, and wonder just how warmed up I need to be.

At the temple gate, I am told to get a small bowl of rice, but not to eat too much.

I can't help but wonder what special event is planned for me, I am fairly certain that it won't be nice.

I don't have to wait long, the students begin filling up the main square, each carries two sticks, the type used for sword practice. I too am given sticks, they are all facing me, oh dear, this isn't looking promising. I am explained the rule. "You ring the bell opposite, they stop you. Go."

"Oh, bloody hell' I decide to run at them, they may be intimidated. They aren't!

So I will have to fight. After only a few blows, deflected, striking the opponents, stopping the blows slightly so as not to hurt the students, well, not too much anyway, I find that I slip into an automatic mode. I feel at one with everything, time slows, I see blows aimed at me, I deflect them, turn it to my advantage, strike, deflect the next. The fact that there are so many, begins to work in my favour, they are restricting each other, and I begin to move, one step, another, another, slowly advancing. I am really glad that the masters and the general don't join in, I am focused on the moment, no past, no future, there is only the next blow. I don't recognise faces, only the sticks keep coming. As I begin to tire, the computer pops up. "Excellent job, keep going, oh, mind that one. Ooh, crafty." And with its running commentary, begins to guide me where I may have missed a stick and taken a blow. Finally, it shuts up. We fight on and then I am at the bell, I strike it with a stick, and mercifully it stops. Everyone backs off, there is a moment of quiet, then they begin cheering, clapping and shouting, they are clapping me on the back, and lead me to the abbot, watching with the general and teachers on a raised platform. I notice the helicopter guys watching, their phones in their hands, filming.

Monks begin filing in, bowls of food on trays in their hands, huge bowls of rice, fruits, vegetables. It's a massive feast, and yes, I see the general's face light up, yaks' milk and digestive biscuits! Everyone joins in, the four helicopter guys are brought down, and as we talk, aren't such bad blokes, we get on quite well. I see that the novices are sporting some bruises, I apologise to them, but they laugh it off, saying taking part was an honour, and these are badges of honour. I notice that many are actually comparing bruises. After the food, there are short speeches from the masters, and abbot, and the fact that we are feasting and not training is a welcome change for everyone there. Smiling faces everywhere, only the abbot looks a little sad, though he is trying to cover it.

Sun rises, the work is nearly finished, cleaning, sweeping polishing, all working together, cheerful, glad to be here. The abbot is looking around, sees me and starts towards me. The general leans on his broom. "Wonder what he wants, perhaps he needs that blasted hill running up three times today."

"I don't know, but it definitely looks like we are involved."

Liza is walking behind him, she steps out, into view and the general drops his broom, and stares, his mouth hung open. She sees him and runs to him, throws her arms around him and shouts, "Where have you been, I have waited every day, hoping that you would ambush me."

The general's look of surprise, is replaced by the biggest, smuggest look, I have ever seen.

"Don't say a word," I tell him.

She steps back, looks him up and down, then as the monks gather round, she looks sad, and speaks to the general.

"The demonic forces have broken through, they have somehow found a way into the next dimension, and have massed their war fleet to destroy the emperor's. He is unable to recall his forces in sufficient time to stop them, he is preparing to fight to the end, the demonic are almost at full force. You are needed urgently." He listens silently. "The emperor himself asked me to find you. But there is one more threat, they have a super nova."

The general steps back. "It can't be, it's impossible!"

"What is it?"

I have never seen the general look so afraid before.

"The super nova weapon, it compacts matter, the energy is so condensed, so concentrated that it cannot be contained. It tears the very atoms apart, releasing with such power that it rips apart the very fabric of the universe. Four working together can rip a planet in two. They will use this without hesitation or mercy."

"The emperor needs you to find it."

She then hands me a bag the monks were holding. "Get changed."

I look inside. Two swords I recognise from the queen's bodyguards are lying across my work trousers, a black polo shirt and a black sweatshirt, work boots underneath.

I go inside, change and step out. "The demonic, they are on earth, they have been using the underground bases as spawning grounds, they are ready to take over the earth. You have to stop them."

I instantly feel the fear rising, my knees feel weak; I want to vomit, my head's swimming.

"How?" I couldn't speak out loud my mouth is so dry.

"The base is too deep to teleport inside, and there's a force field operating to disrupt, this is a tracking device." She hands me an object that looks like a metal fist. "Once operated, it will allow teleporting to its location, by a local field disruption. But it's a one way, not out, only in." She touches my forehead and the plans and layouts are transferred.

I strap the two swords onto my back, the helicopter guys walk over. "We are off, will you be back next year?"

"That remains to be seen. But remember, there are those who come by helicopter, and those that walk."

He gives me a grin, we shake hands.

"But us." I look at the general and Liza. "We teleport!"

56

I am standing on a wide forecourt of an ugly squat concrete building. It has wide expanses of glass windows, and a modern funky interior, but even these don't hide the fact that it is an ugly squat concrete building. I can make out across the room the door that leads to a lift, and underground. Between me and it, are five receptionists. It's obvious that their presence is solely to distract from the ugliness of the building. They wear fitted red jackets, short black fitted skirts, and deep red lipstick, their black hair is tied back. I feel as if I have stepped back into Peter Gabriel video. I begin to sing 'Addicted to Love'. I head for the door, but am headed off by some very distracting legs, in black seamed tights, or stockings? I stop to look.

"You are being tampered with."

"I wish." Rather attractively rude thoughts are rushing into my head

"I'm sorry, sir, you really don't want to go there. Come with me."

The computer starts me running, suddenly, the feeling of being hypnotised is broken, and I reach the door. Bullets crash into the wall beside me. The computer has already hacked me in, and I close it behind me. I turn to give them the finger behind the closed door and run.

"Well, that was weird."

"The demonic use their psychic abilities to get other beings to do the work for them, you were being hacked."

"No, that's just how the mind of a builder works."

The lift doors open. I jump in, as they begin closing more bullets hit the lift doors.

"Was it something that I said?"

"It usually is."

"Thanks."

The lift is really smooth, there is no real sense of how fast we are going, indeed, if we are actually moving, but the doors open, and I am on a balcony overlooking a vast hanger-type room. Below, is about twenty of the ugliest creatures you could imagine. OK, if you did imagine them, you would probably wake up screaming. In the distance, halfway down the room, is another balcony, a large purple dome of a clear material sits there. I can see something move inside, like an embryonic lizard inside a clear egg. It suddenly moves fast, and walks through the dome. It points at me and the beasties below turn and look directly at me. I tut under my breath, and roll my eyes upwards. I am momentarily distracted by four shining gold discs, just floating in the top of the hanger. "Nice."

For a little while I freeze, I simply have no idea what to do, I think that the dome is going to be where I need to be. The information inside my head tells me that it is the control centre, so I guess that's my goal.

I run down the concrete stairs, the beasties seem to be in no hurry to reach me, they begin to amble in my direction, but show no signs of organisation. As I get closer, I can't help but feel repulsed by the creatures, and realise that they are expecting me to be so afraid that I will simply curl up in fear, and they will do as they please with me. Looking at the long curling claws, what they please, isn't going to be nice for me. As I get closer, they slow down, and act confused. I begin to run towards them. This throws them completely, they stop, they really expect me to be afraid. This spurs me on, I run flat out, drawing both swords, and releasing the fist like object. It hits the floor, uncurls itself and flies up to the ceiling, digging its sharp pointed feet into the concrete roof. It activates sending a feed to the draconian fleet. For a brief moment I wonder if this is to gather information or to watch me get killed.

I run at the group of demonic, moving through them silently, cutting them down. When the last one falls, I stop, look for any immediate danger from the bodies, and start towards the dome.

I don't know if the small drone is able to transmit through the concrete and rock to draconian forces. It is probably as well that I have no idea what is happening on board the emperor's flagship where the emperor and the general stare angrily at a massive holographic scene. The demonic forces are still massing, and now fill the entire space from ceiling to floor, although at this scale each warship is little more than a centimetre square. The scene is solid black, and spreading outwards. There is a blurring effect because they are still in the next dimension. The main massive command ship, twenty times larger than the others, is beginning to slide through. It appears in sharp clarity as it emerges, slowly the other ships begin to slide through. They get to see a close-up of the command ship, and its dimensions. A scaled image of the emperor's command ship appears beside for comparison, the demonic ship is well over double the size of his own craft.

The draconian fleet would be enough to overcome any planet, even solar system. But as it moves closer and the scale on the hologram equals up, it appears tiny in comparison to the massing demonic fleet. The silence in the control centre is suddenly broken, the general looks down at the hologram of the demonic bunker, I have made it to the centre of the vast room, but from a tunnel, a stream of the demonic pour out, filling the room. I am fighting. The general watches as I become totally surrounded, still they emerge. I am slashing my way through the hordes, but steadily the massive room is totally filled. The emperor looks at the general and commands, "GO! Now!" Without a word the general rushes to the teleporter. The emperor looks up, the head assassin is looking carefully at the battle below. The emperor says quietly, "It's one way, we can't teleport out until that force field is removed."

Below I am being crushed. I am slicing my way through the masses, as each one dies it immediately begins to rot. The others treading the rapidly decaying corpses underfoot, make the floor slippery with a stinking slime of decaying flesh. I still push forwards, I am totally lost in the action, with no thoughts other than to keep going. The crush becomes overwhelming, I can't breathe, my arms are pinned by my sides, the weight of bodies crushing the demonic themselves, I turn and cut deeply into the neck of one. I turn back to continue towards the dome, it can't fall because of the crush, it is pressed against my back and begins rotting onto me, its decaying flesh running down my body. In the crush nothing can actually attack me, but as I fight for air, the stinking mass of bodies begins to overwhelm me.

A massive sword slices through the surrounding bodies, cutting through the masses, releasing the pressure; I fall to the side, and come up fighting. I look at the massive sight of Deborah's bodyguard. "The dome, head for that dome." The general appears, beside him, Liza, one by one assassins appear, until a force of about forty are fighting. On their backs they carry guns, the force field down here prevents them from working. Together we make a fighting formation, each protecting the one next to them. The demonic throw themselves forwards in a blood frenzy, often attacking their own to get at us. Slowly we pick our way towards the dome. The crush becomes less, the demonic are getting less, and we press on harder. I actually begin to think that we may not only survive but succeed. The press suddenly stops completely, the demonic facing us all step back, they form a circle around us, waiting. In the distance, a drumming roaring sound can be heard, faint, but definitely growing louder. Around us, massive doors begin sliding open, the sound gets instantly louder, and suddenly from all directions screaming hordes of demonic spew out into the massive room. Instantly, they rush us, and by sheer force of numbers, we are crushed into each other, making it difficult to defend. They begin climbing over each other to get at us, we fight a desperate battle to stay upright, the force upon us is so great, we start to go down.

A demonic climbs over the backs of others, leaping at me. I can see it in the air in front of me, I have my swords trapped. Its head erupts and it drops short, then another, another and more begin exploding before us, I make out the sound of gunfire, it begins increasing then rapid machine gun fire takes down the closest to us, the crush eases, we are fighting again. "Liza, we have to get to the balcony over there, get covering fire."

She disappears, reappearing moments later. "They are the royal marines, the emperor's queen told the prime minister what was happening, she sent them to help."

Gunfire begins concentrating towards the balcony, opening a corridor that we can advance down. Marines join us to add to the effect, and finally we are moving.

The demonic must be being controlled, for as soon as this starts to be effective, the hordes move as one to fill in the gaps, closing in our advantage. We are so close now, almost in touching distance, but despite the devastating hail of bullets and our combined attack, we grind to a halt and then, more slowly backwards. It's so frustrating, to see our goal sliding away. Suddenly, I am pulled high into the air, and hurtling headlong through the demonic. It takes a moment to realise what's happening, I am thrown headlong onto the balcony, the general landing beside me. I see the bodyguard dive headlong into the demonic masses; I hear her voice call out that she can't hold it in this dimension any more.

It feels strange with all the noise and crush to suddenly find you are alone on the balcony. Liza appears and together we attack the dome. We strike it as hard as we can, but it is utterly solid. "I saw the thing inside just walk through it."

"It must be an energy field," the general shouts. "No matter what we hit it with, it will remain solid, the harder it's hit, the stronger it gets."

"Well, if it walked through it, then the frequency can't be that high, if it was lower, we could just walk in ourselves. We have to raise our frequency to match it." Despite the telepathy, I still find I am shouting.

"How?" Liza yells.

"Think of love, happiness, good things."

"I am a draco warrior, I don't do love."

"Course you do, just concentrate on how you feel about Liza," I tell the general before I really have time to think. I swear he blushes. "Quick, do it now, and project it through me, like when you are meditating." This time I try to calm down.

I concentrate hard, leaning against the dome's curving wall, allowing the energies to pass through me, into the dome. Liza is looking at the general with a very strange look, and it works. I find myself slide through the wall and land on the floor. WE did it. But the thing inside is suddenly aware of my presence, it leaps over at amazing speed and hits me a massive side swipe across my right side. The blow lifts me, throwing me against the dome wall.

I drop stunned but hear the computer shouting, "Get me to the consol." I am trying to stand, fighting for breath. It comes over to me, stands over me, it is huge, not quite as big as the bodyguard, but a close second. It is damned ugly; it seems not so much ugly as an absolute void of anything good. It has a skin like last night's vomit on a pavement, smells worse though, but for all its vile appearance, it is fast, and strong. Again, it lunges at me, the computer kicks in and I just avoid its long, filthy, six-inch nails. I roll out of the way, again avoiding it. This time I counter with a hard blow to its arm, but the sword just glances off like it is armour plated. I can feel its pleasure at this, it begins toying with me, it wants to feel my fear. I dodge again, but this time it anticipates, and catches me a crashing blow to my arm, ripping deep into my flesh. I fall hard landing on the consol. A piece of the loose flesh on my arm pulls itself, agonisingly away from my arm. I watch transfixed as it moves rapidly over the screen and slides inside a slot, the fibrils waving wildly as it disappears. Moments later, the computer begins downloading information. I can hear it happily calling out, "It's coming, keep that damned thing occupied."

It picks me up, I fight, slashing again and again, it is enjoying seeing me so desperate. "Keep it occupied. Fifteen per cent energy left."

It throws me almost casually again, strolling over to me, I am taking massive damage. I weakly struggle. It picks me up and pulls me to its face, it's going to bite me. With the computer's guidance, and all my might, I slash at its face. I get both its eyes in one go. Another slash is aimed at its open mouth. Screaming, it throws me hard. I smash into the control console. Enraged, it begins stamping at me. I am lucky to be missed by its massive foot, its nails ripping my shirt. I try standing, but something is wrong, my leg just gives way, a bone is protruding. Slowly it slides back inside but I can't move fast enough, I am caught, it tries to rip its claws into me, but in desperation I slash again at its face. It bellows in pain, throwing me hard against the wall. I fade out for a moment. "Excellent work, we've got it." A massive foot presses down on me, I am against the far concrete wall, and trapped. I hear, "Four per cent energy."

The foot rises to stamp. I try to crawl, and there is a massive explosion, pieces of the demonic splatter around me, I slip in it, covered in gore. The sound of guns and fighting is suddenly there again. Hands lift me. I get to the console, there is a massive plate the size of the demonic hand, I place my hand on it, the fibrils rapidly push the outline of my hand to match the shape. It has DNA recognition. I slice my hand with the razor-sharp edge of my sword, wipe my hand in a pool of the demonic blood, slapping it onto the massive hand plate, It takes a moment for the fibrils to assimilate the DNA from the blood, but suddenly we have total control. I stagger to the balcony wall, a young marine is separated and alone, surrounded. Liza pops out, landing upon his back, instantly dropping him with us on the balcony, I can see that it took a lot out of her. He is battered and bruised and confused, but not seriously harmed. I touch him in the centre of his forehead. The guns are now an occasional shot, the machine guns silent; bayonets are being fitted for their final brave actions. I cancel out the force field surrounding the base, instantly the assassins' guns turn a pale blue. Only moments later, pale blue energy pulses are filling the room. Marines grab the guns from the fallen assassins, and the fire fight begins, this time there is no control to the demonic, many attack, but those closest turn to run, fighting each other to escape. I reach out again to the marine. "Payback time."

I touch him again, he looks confused, then smiles. "Hell, yes."

"Liza," I touch her forehead. "You are gunner. You," I point to the marine, "you fly."

Both now use the disc's teleport device to enter, moments later, the disc tips down, and all hell is let loose amongst the demonic. The disc begins firing plasma pulses into the tunnels, the energy waves directed by the tunnel walls ripping apart everything in its path.

"I have the battle plans, shall we go?" I touch the general once to send him the plans, then again to give him control of the second disc. "I fly," I tell him. "You shoot."

We teleport onboard, all there is inside is a seat for the pilot, and one for the gunner, all is done through mind control. I sit in the seat; it flows around my body and is actually very snug and comfy.

It takes only a moment to link mentally then to analyse and map, key into my DNA. Then we go.

It doesn't move fast, it simply is where you think about, at the same instant, again, Einstein would have been in his element here. The quantum entanglement working on a scale that would have scientists throwing down their statistics and declaring, "IMPOSSIBLE." But here we are instantly inside the command centre of the demonic flagship. The general and I look at each other stunned.

"Fire." The general does. With almost everything at once. There is just one left unused.

"Are we sure?" he asks.

I think a moment. "Do it." He fires the one final weapon. The super nova. I see a gentle shimmer and get out immediately. We appear in the bay of the emperor's flagship, teleporting directly onto the bridge.

"ALL SHEILDS TO THE FRONT, FULL POWER, ALL SHIPS," Barks the general.

The commanders all taken by surprise. "DO IT!" roars the emperor.

Moments later, the demonic flagship begins to shrink, folding in on itself, it rapidly disappears, then a tiny intense blue light appears. For a moment, it just hangs there, then in moments it fills the entire holographic image. All shield their eyes. Although appearing close on the monitor, this was only for convenience, in the vastness of space there was still a massive distance apart between the two forces, so it took a full five seconds to reach the draco fleet. The forcefields took the brunt of the force, directing it around rather than attempting to stop it, like water goes around a boulder in a river. Even so the effect was huge. It only lasted about five seconds. When the emperor regained his composure, he yells out for damage reports and for the holograph to be put back on. The image appears, again, there is stunned silence. There is a red glow, the burning of the entire demonic fleet hangs in the image, there is nothing left, apart from the red glow of flames. A chain reaction from the explosion that was so powerful it simply atomised the fleet. The emperor looks at the two of us.

"Did you do this?" he demands, the general and I once again caught in the spotlight.

"Yes, well, sort of," I reply. "We found the plans of the demonic and used it against them."

The emperor looks down at the scene inside the bunker, the marines and assassins are helping each other's wounded and picking up their fallen comrades. The fact that there are so many survivors is a testament to their courage and skill. The draco fleet is fully intact, a couple of minor collisions, otherwise unscathed.

I clap the general on his back and loudly congratulate him. "A wonderful victory, well done, just as you planned."

I get a very suspicious look from the emperor, but he lets it go as the draco on the bridge begin cheering. As the celebrations start, I slip away, the disc teleports me on board, I drop back into the bunker and begin to take the marines out, getting them back to their base. The marine pilot is already doing this, it only takes an hour or so to remove them all.

57

I go to Deborah's house. I am suffering from the fight, I need to recover, I feel exhausted. The key doesn't seem to be working, so I knock. The neighbour rushes out, and with considerable enthusiasm, tells me that she has moved to a new house. I have been away for so long that she had enough and left. At one point she looks up to see a crowd gathering to look at my disc, gold reflecting the morning sunlight.

"And what's that?"

"Oh, that's mine."

"Well, you can't leave it there."

"Why not?"

"It's spoiling the view!"

"Oh, don't worry, I'm going now," I reply.

I feel at an utter loss. I spent all this time thinking that I'm doing good, but now feel 'what's the point?' I assess my situation. I am severely beaten up, bruised and battered, wearing clothes in absolute tatters decorated with demonic bodily fluids. I also realise I have the two swords on my back. And a severely bruised face. Nice!

I teleport up. Dropping off again at some local shops. Inside my wallet is fifteen pounds, I get some jeans, trainers and a T-shirt from a charity shop. I decide to visit Frank. I have some new models for him to discuss, the latest is for vehicles. Feeling pretty sorry for myself, I haven't eaten since the feast, and worse, not had a cup of tea for ages.

Frank takes one look at me and shows me where the showers are, while he puts the kettle on. I feel considerably better for being clean. I see my reflection in a mirror, I am bruised head to toe, but the body fat that I spent all my adult life trying to lose is gone. I am toned, athletic looking, and am sporting a six pack. I pull on the jeans I bought, they are way too big. My thirty-six-inch waist is down to about a thirty or thirty-two.

After my shower, I sit down with Frank, after he returns from dropping my clothes in the skip.

"You look rough."

"Feel it."

"Well, now, before you tell me all about it, I just need your bank details."

"What for?"

"The money for the motors…"

"I had forgotten all about that." I pass my card over and begin telling him about the new motors. When I pass on the new designs, he looks a little concerned.

"I don't think that we can make that part, who designed these?"

"Do you want to meet them?"

"It would help."

"Get your design guy, we can go now, it shouldn't take long, first though, you need to be able to communicate." I touch him in the centre of his forehead. The designer comes in, I touch his forehead. "OK, let's go."

It's a pleasant distraction, talking with the blue skinned race. The designer is soon talking about the latest model to fit in vehicles, Frank and I are given a pleasant tour of the floating city. With only the smallest of anchors to the planet, the cities are totally above the ground, from a distance they look like enormous hot air balloons, but slimmer and taller. From a distance, they appear fragile, only when you stand close, do you get an impression of their huge size. This, of course, leaves vast amounts of land free to grow naturally, there are trees but mainly it is dominated by the areas of blue green grassland and rolling hills.

I drop them off back at the factory in the late afternoon. I have nowhere to live currently, the hole where a house was, is still being disputed. I do feel at a bit of a loss, so I get a takeaway pizza, and go to the mountains where there is a massive telescope. I get the coordinates in space to where the battle took place in space, knock on the door and ask to see who is in charge.

Obviously, they think that I am an utter nut job, but then, that's where the fun is for me. But when given exact space co-ordinates, they begin to listen. Finally, when I point out that I have a flying saucer they have to listen, however disbelievingly. Then to the second I predicted they record the super nova explosion, I get to watch, sharing pizzas and enjoying the show. I have a most enjoyable evening. I sleep in the seat of the disc, I must admit that it is very comfortable, softly moulding to my body, it feels more like an embrace than a seat.

The next few days are spent aimlessly meandering around the world. Having spent so long with a path before me, and a goal, even if I didn't know fully what that goal was, now it's gone I am finding it hard to settle. At least with the hundred pounds that Frank transferred I can buy food.

It's the day of the funeral for the fallen marines. I am deeply affected by the loss. They were sent to assist me, and they saved my life. As soon as they saw the dome collapse, they hit the massive demonic leader with everything they had, several grenades found their mark, and if they hadn't reacted as fast as they had, I would be a smear under the demonic foot.

As the sad occasion draws to a close, the emperor and his queen appear quietly a little distance to one side. They are alone. The queen stands by the families, the emperor surprises me by kneeling beside each grave, quietly saying the name of the marine, and simply saying thank you, then laying a gold medal on the grave. Without a fuss they speak briefly to the officers, then leave. I am moved that a being with such power is capable of acknowledging the individuals, knowing their names, and actually thanking them individually.

The next day is different.

The draconian flagship is the centre of the celebrations, of victory. The draco have been at war with the demonic for millions of years, neither side gaining a real advantage. Conquering and plundering planet after planet, so as to pour raw materials into the ever-hungry war machine.

The draco love ceremony. And today is going to be a real occasion, the one that will be talked about for years. The highlight is the marines. Draconians, for all their military might, don't do marching, so to see the precision drills, marine bands, and displaying the colours greatly impresses all there. After this, the emperor gives medals to each marine that took part. The medal has been struck especially, and is a simple disc, cast in solid gold, with the words, 'Forever grateful', below.

For our part, the general and I give a demonstration of sword play. Partly as a display, but also, should any young draco have intentions towards challenging either of us, it serves as a warning. The emperor then gives the marines the disc that the young marine flew. This is partly as a reward, but the fact that the marine is now genetically linked through his DNA and brainwaves to it isn't mentioned, but I suppose that it's the thought that counts.

For me, the best part, was the emperor making a vow to protect the Earth, to keep it free from any possible outside aggression. He vowed that the same protection will be given for my other four planets.

I approach the leaders of these planets later.

"You don't need me any more, you are now on the council, and have the whole empire watching your back. You are free to do as you please, as long as you never show any aggression towards the empire, so you are free.

"But don't you want to rule, to have power, to own five planets? You have been given gifts that make you a very powerful individual.

"Any power, is for the sole purpose of setting people free, to be used on their behalf, not for my personal gain.

"But you fought so hard for your planet, for us also, isn't there anything you want?

"Peace, that's all? Oh, I also want you to prosper, as well."

The Scandinavian-looking female asks, "Surely, there must be something that we can do for you."

"Actually, there is. I hear that your planet is beautiful, could the marines and their families have a holiday, there. They have the disc for transport. I think that it will do the wounded good, if any of you have medical experience that would help, it will be greatly appreciated."

"We wanted to know why you were chosen for this task, now we know."

"Well, I wish I did."

58

A couple of days later, I have spent most of the hundred pounds, so go to see if Frank is having any luck with the new generators for vehicles.

There is much drinking of tea, and I am happy to find that the alterations to suit the Earth designs are all functioning well. As I leave, I ask him, "I don't mean to be a pain, but is there any chance that you can give me the same deal as before, a hundred pounds?"

"A pleasure, we put it on as a part of costs, we get tax back on it, and we gave you the position as the technical director, for tax reasons."

"Excellent, I have spent the other hundred pounds you sent me."

"Hundred pounds? We didn't send you a hundred pounds, have you checked your bank?"

"No, I don't have credit for my phone. I seem to have been cut off while I was away."

"It's a hundred pounds per unit, we are currently running at a hundred units a day, and as soon as we get the new factory up and working it will be over two hundred and fifty units a day."

I begin to do mental maths, but give up, it doesn't seem real.

"You, it would seem, are wealthy, and will always be so."

"Really? Bloody hell, I didn't expect that."

After that, my immediate need is for a cash machine. I see my balance, I get a slip out to confirm. And just keep on looking at it.

59

A couple of days later, I have an 'incident'. A couple of men in a dark vehicle, both were wearing dark suits and sunglasses. I really thought that these were only for effect in movies, but here they are, trying to intimidate me. Unfortunately for them, having been in close proximity to the demonic, they appeared to me as intimidating as Sooty and Sweep.

Apparently, it would be in my best interest to give the disc to them. When I asked why, they didn't really seem inclined to answer, but went straight to intimidation.

Luckily for me, using facial recognition, and cross referring to data banks gives me their names, addresses, bank details, and who they work for. I do a couple of adjustments to various accounts.

I reply by giving their full names, their addresses, and even their phone numbers, then tell them to check their accounts. Reluctantly, one checks, and finds several million pounds extra in his account. I then tell him of an email that I will send, informing the authorities that they are taking money from the company accounts. Before I send it, they begin to get a little anxious, perhaps even aggressive with me. So, I think 'sod this'. "Do you want the disc?" I beam them onboard the craft. "Take it then."

I stand aside and let them get on with it. "Go on then, I'm not stopping you."

More than a little confused by the teleporting, they are at a loss just what to do next. "I was just picking up some supplies for some friends, we are having a picnic, you will have to join us." Moments later, they are on the ground, amongst a group of marines, who actually are having a picnic. The two men suddenly find themselves the centre of attention,

"These have come to take my disc. What do you suggest I do with them?"

I look at the children. "Politely, that is."

"Shall we help them to disappear?"

Some begin to gather round the two men, but I am having a nice time here, so are the families, so I decide to calm things down. "Give them a burger, I'm going to explain a few things to them." I take them to one side. There are beings here from all five planets that I 'owned'. A young female feline takes an interest in one of the guys, and begins to purr and sensually slides around him, she gets a little frustrated that he can't talk to her, and stealthily slinks off.

"There's a problem you see. This is mine. I am attached to it, I mean I am actually linked, it only recognises my brainwave patterns and cross references this with my individual DNA coding, so only I can use it."

"Where did you get it from?"

The general and Liza appear behind them. He places his hand on their shoulders, and squeezes. They look at the long sharp claws and stay very still. "Having problems?" he asks, and squeezes a little harder.

"Nothing at all, these agents were just asking me how I got the disc." The general holds them a few seconds longer, and then slowly releases them. The feline woman tries again, slinking over him in a sensual way that leaves little room for guessing what she wants.

"What does she want?"

The marines all raise their eyebrows. "She wants to be friendly, very friendly." I watch her slide across his chest, purring softly. "Very, very friendly."

"Look mate, there's children here, can you calm it down a bit."

"Do you want to talk to her?" His initial reluctance seems to be slipping away, his hands now on her waist.

"Do I?"

I touch his forehead, and he can instantly hear her. He listens for a few seconds, his eyebrows raise, and he simply says, "Wow." He looks at his mate, shrugs his shoulders and walks away with the feline. His buddy watches him go, turns to me, and trying to regain some composure, asks, "So, you were about to tell me about the disc."

"It's a long story."

A couple of marines join in, "Go on, tell us."

"From the very beginning."

"You won't believe it," I sigh.

"We are picnicking on a planet with four other species; our kids are using telepathy to play together. Try us."

So, with glasses of the gold liquid, greatly diluted, handed around, I start to tell them my story. The general and Liza embellish this with holographic recordings of the fights, it's evening when I finish, we are all in a more relaxed frame of mind. The man returns with his feline friend. His mate looks at him, and raises an eyebrow. "Well?"

"She is very friendly. Very." He looks at her and smiles at her, she smiles back. "Very, very, friendly."

Chatting later, a drink in hand, the two guys aren't too bad, the feline is curled up relaxed with him, he holds her closely. "I put your accounts back to normal, you could always ask the general for his disc." They look at him, but both agree that is probably not a good idea."

A marine passes me two swords.

"Give us a demonstration, before you go."

A few calls out in agreement. So, we give a brief demonstration, the general and I go at each other for a while, we keep trying to find new moves, to outdo each other. I hardly need to use the computer now, we get a round of applause after, followed by a dunking in the lake. Its Liza's first ever time in any water, so there's a lot of splashing and generally acting daft. When we are allowed out, I take off my shirt to wring it out, the guy in the suit looks at my scarred body. "It's true, then? Not just a story?"

"Don't worry, I can't believe it myself."

"You should write a book."

"No one would believe it, and my writing is shocking."

I take them back, they are walking to their vehicle, obviously talking, one turns to the other, they shake hands, he runs back to me. I drop him off, the feline female runs to him, I teleport back.

60

Life begins to settle down, finally. I find a nice house, and move in. I spend most of my time travelling. It's marvellous, no matter how far I go, I can always get home, sit in front of a nice fire, get some tea, and relax. 'My planets' have gained independence, and are enjoying the new union between themselves. I have become a sort of ambassador between them. They each have given me a nice, pleasant, country house, the fact that I can travel between them, does make me handy. I am getting some attention from some of the females on the planets, but really don't feel like starting any form of relationship. It's said that long-distance relationships are difficult, but when it's measured in light years, well, it's got to be a struggle, and I miss Deborah. So, it came as a pleasant distraction when the light beings appeared one evening. Immediately, I became wary. Every time I have seen them, it has led to beings wanting to do damage to me, so today's 'mission' came as a pleasant diversion.

I have been travelling the universe, picking up holy men, priests, and assorted spiritually-awakened beings. Many from Earth, are present. It was my pleasure to pick up the abbots from the monastery and temple in the

343

mountains. Finally, all are in position, it's a big undertaking. Every ancient stone circle of importance, such as Stonehenge, Aylesbury, the ancient South American cities, and of course, where I am, on the pyramids in Egypt. The great pyramid is covered with people. From a distance, it appears alive. So many people, all races, nationalities, and species.

Then, at midday, being the longest day, everyone brings their energies to full. We begin to attract the energy from the universe, to us. This happens slowly at first, as we approach noon, the energies are growing to an awesome level. At exactly noon, the sky erupts.

White light like slow moving sheet lightening fills the sky. It begins to dip down, a slight bulge at first. This begins hanging down, and suddenly rushes to contact the very top of the pyramid, a massive rush of energies flood the pyramid. Instantly, it is directed outwards, through the four sides, and out to the four points of the compass. The same is happening at all the centres of energy throughout the world, the energy rushes out to meet up along the grid that exists across the planet. At every intersection of the grid, energy begins to pour from the sky. For a day, the energy pours in, spreading out until the entire planet is bathed in a white glowing film. This begins soaking into the ground, the energy of the planet rising, until exactly noon the following day. The pillars of light begin to grow in diameter, then in an instant, they expand, silently, exploding outwards, in moments they have all merged as one.

The pyramids have done their job, to once again act as the catalyst that attracts the life frequency for the earth. The planet's frequency has expanded massively.

It's been getting itself primed for this event, and finally, has reached its potential. The external forces holding it back are removed, and it is ready. The first planet of healing in this galaxy has finally come of age.

Inside me, I can feel the rush of energy flowing through me, as the people on the pyramid are cheering, laughing, almost overwhelmed by the feeling of happiness and love. They climb down the sides to join in what is rapidly becoming, one hell of a party.